MURDER TAKES A BOUGH

A BETTY SNICKERDOODLE MYSTERY

PEPPER FROST

WORKING STRATEGY

THIS IS A WORK OF FICTION. Names, characters, businesses, places, events, locales, and incidents are either the products of the author's imagination or used in a fictitious manner. Any resemblance to actual persons, living or dead, or actual events is purely coincidental.

MURDER TAKES A BOUGH

Hardcover Large Print ISBN: 978-1-970044-09-6

Paperback Large Print ISBN: 978-1-970044-18-8

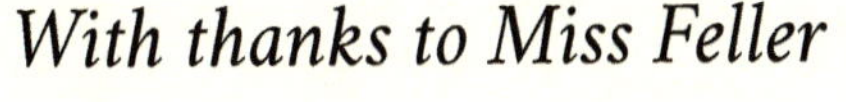

With thanks to Miss Feller

CHAPTER 1

"So lifelike! Especially if your inspiration was a giant electrified carrot," cackled wise-cracking near-octogenarian author Bea Sickles. She was standing in front of a bushy, bright-orange Christmas tree near the front desk of her Christmas-themed inn, wearing her typical outfit of a velour track suit and beige, velcro-fastened sneakers. "Just kidding, Angie. These artificial trees are perfect for the occasion. Orange you glad you gave in and went fake? Get it? *Orange* you glad?"

Despite her crusty, irreverent personality, Bea had found bestselling success writing sweeter-than-sweet Christmas romance stories under her Betty Snickerdoodle pen name for nearly thirty years. Those fabulously successful books had inspired—and paid for—Betty Snickerdoodle's Christmas Inn & Ranch, the charming, yule-themed property she was standing in. Before that, she'd eked out a living in a milieu that was easier to match to her personality: the rowdy poker halls of the San Francisco Bay Area.

The clever young marketer who turned Betty's popular books into a publishing powerhouse, Angela Garcia, was fussing over the citrus-tinted tree. Other orange trees, in different sizes, had been set up in the ballroom and in other spots throughout the inn.

Angela was prepping the decorations for a Halloween party for local kids. She'd come up with the idea for the party after noticing how far apart properties were in their section of the wine country—too far apart for little legs to manage much trick-or-treating. Naturally, once Angela got her mind set on the idea, she went all out. She set up a hay-bale maze in the wide-open pasture beside the inn, turned the barn into a pleasantly scary haunted house, and even lined up a team of costumed volunteers to hand out candy from the inn's guest rooms, so that the kids would have plenty of doors to knock on in pursuit of sweets.

"Droll, Bea. Droll," Angela said. Strings of

lights in the shape of skulls were draped on the tree. Angela was adjusting them to make sure they didn't obscure the ceramic ornaments shaped like black cats, bats, and spiders that were also dangling from the branches. She bent down to pull more ornaments from the box by her feet, her chestnut ponytail swinging over her shoulder. She grinned as she found a pair of knitted ornaments that looked like little white ghosts and held them up for a closer inspection.

"*Droll,* Angie?" Bea said in a theatrically pompous, nasal tone. "Have you been watching black-and-white whodunit films again? Drolly moley, I hope you're not too bothered by my tree jokes. I can't resist needling you, girlie. Get it? Needling?" Bea guffawed and emphasized her enjoyment with a hearty slap of her knee, as she almost always did. Bea was one of those lucky people whose ability to put themselves in stitches meant they were rarely bored or down in the dumps.

"I know you like real trees better, Angie, but these are great for Halloween. The color's perfect. Sort of like a cantaloupe-uranium smoothie. Or Metamucil."

Angela rolled her eyes and shook her head. "I admit these work for Halloween. But artificial trees still bother me. The inn should have real trees year-round. Aren't visitors expecting the ultimate Christmas experience? Cal Banks promised as many as we need for November through Christmas, but he doesn't know if he'll have any at all left after the first of the year. With BettyCon set for the end of January, the month after Christmas is our peak season here at the inn —and I can't be sure we'll have fresh trees. Last year, we had to substitute artificial ones in some spots, and it just didn't seem right. And I'm not even close to figuring out how we'll get any trees for spring and summer."

When they first opened the inn, Angela imagined they'd focus mainly on the winter holidays, but she quickly realized that many of Betty's readers wanted to visit at other times. She wanted every fan who came to the inn to feel immersed in Christmas, regardless of the season.

"Truth be told, Halloween's a better inspiration for my current work-in-progress," Bea said.

Bea's Christmas stories were still selling like hotcakes. Her latest passion, though, was her new murder mystery series. "I look at those strings of skulls and feel a teensy tickle from my muse, but what I'm really hoping for is a party guest showing up with a bloody knife in their brain or some other weeping wound—real or fake, I'm not picky. That'll get the ol' creativity flowing. Speaking of guests, when do we expect the little gremlins and their parents to arrive? I'd like to know how long I have to be on good behavior."

"They'll be here soon. Time to get into costume," Angela said. "And don't forget, you promised to channel your sweetest Betty. For the—"

"I know, I know," Bea grumbled melodramatically. "For the *children.*"

An hour later, Bea returned to the front desk in her trusty elf costume—an odd garment made of squares of red and green felt, accessorized with an elvish hat, striped stockings, and curly-toed booties that were straight out of a Christmas cartoon. Angela was already there, waiting for guests to arrive and chatting with Jackson, the front desk manager. Jackson was dressed up as a lion, complete with a fluffy mane.

Bea looked at Angela, then at Jackson, then back at Angela. "I'm sensing a theme, and it ain't Christmas."

Angela wore shiny red shoes, a blue and white checked pinafore, and a white blouse. She'd tied her thick hair into two pigtails with pale blue bows and carried a sort of picnic basket. "But shouldn't you be carrying your little dog, too?" Bea croaked, crouching over the basket and wriggling her gnarled fingers.

"I'll get the pups once the party's going," Angela laughed. "Maybe dachshunds don't match my costume, but I'm betting the kids will love playing with them."

Connie Hollander, Angela's friend and owner of the property next door, swished in carefully in a pale pink ball gown. Its layers of skirts and crinoline were so wide that the dress barely fit through the door. Connie had to duck to avoid dislodging the tall, conical, silver crown she wore on top of her stylish blonde bob.

"Now I'm definitely feeling left out," Bea snickered.

"We didn't coordinate, I swear," Connie said, her voice tinged with a Kentucky drawl. "Think about it. I'm from the South, and so is Glinda the Good Witch."

"Ha! That tears it," Bea snorted, pointing at Aseem, Angela's tall, dark, and handsome boyfriend, who walked in wearing a convincing scarecrow costume and a big grin on his face. "You really shouldn't try to bluff me, people. Don't you think people will wonder why I don't fit in?"

"Don't be silly, Bea," Angela said, tilting her

head to accept a kiss from Aseem. "You always fit in. Do I need to remind you you *own* the place? Let's go greet the kids. Look," she said, pointing out the door. "Cars are arriving."

"I know that family," Connie said. "One member, at least. That's Andy Mathers. He works for that chain of home and garden stores. He brought deliveries to my place for months while it was under construction."

Eager to say hello to Andy and his family, Connie led the way in her ginormous confection of a dress. Andy, a trim young man, looked neat in his work outfit of a branded shirt and chinos. Most of his short haircut was covered by a cap bearing the store's logo.

Andy was accompanied by a man, a woman, and their three costumed children—a serious-looking girl of about nine with thick, round glasses and her two brothers, who looked to be about four and fourteen. The girl was dressed as a green worm tucked inside a book fashioned out of several large pieces of cardboard. The little boy's cowboy costume appeared to be a hand-me-down from his brother. The cowboy boots were loose, and the child shuffled in them as he walked. His brother, who was already towering over his parents, wore jeans and a t-shirt that read, "This is my human costume. I'm really a giraffe."

"Nice to see you, Connie," Andy said. "This is my sister Helen, her husband, Hal, and my nephews and my niece."

"I hope it's OK that we came along," Helen said. "When Andy told me about it, I thought it sounded so fun." The youngest boy grinned from ear to ear and looked around at everything with sheer delight. The teenager, on the other hand, practically glowered—an expression shared by his father.

Connie raised her wand and welcomed the new arrivals in a sweet, high voice, leaning down to greet the little ones. "We're thrilled that you all came. The more the merrier at Betty Snickerdoodle's Christmas Inn—especially on Halloween! Your costumes are adorable."

As Connie floated down the walkway from the inn entrance, Aseem and Angela walked behind her, holding hands, Bea trailing behind them. Aseem leaned toward Angela and whispered, "Honestly, Angel, I love the tangerine trees. They're so bold, it's like they're not even ashamed of being artificial. But guess what? Remember that tree scientist I told you about? I met him at the office today."

Angela had been watching the children and their parents arriving, hearing only part of what Aseem was saying. But the mention of the tree scientist got her full attention.

"He's a character," Aseem continued. "I didn't even get his real name—get this, he wants everyone to call him 'the professor.' If you want to hear about the rapid-growth formula he says he's invented, I'm sure he'd meet with you. He's hoping for an investment, actually. You and Bea could get in on the ground floor."

For the past few months, Aseem had been working part-time leading a start-up incubator for one of Silicon Valley's most famous technology CEOs. It was a dream opportunity— especially since he could do it part time and continue helping Angela at the inn.

"I'd love to meet the scientist!" Angela whispered back. "Bea should be there, too, though, if we're going to be talking about an investment. How would it work? Would we just be investing money?"

"I think he needs a full partner—not just money investment, but a place to experiment, too. Doesn't that sound like it could be a perfect fit for Betty Snickerdoodle, Inc.?" Aseem was still trying to whisper, though he was clearly getting excited by the idea. "I'll arrange the meeting. In the meantime, we should probably keep this to ourselves—just in case. You know how entrepreneurs get about secrecy."

Angela's expression turned contemplative. "Imagine... we could help the scientist with his groundbreaking work. We'd be saving trees and always have as many as we need for the inn."

"And we'd turn Bea into a venture capitalist in the process."

"That's perfect. She's already an experienced professional gambler."

"This is the kind of wager that could make her a whole lot richer. She could go from millions to billions!"

"And just think of all the good we could do in the process," Angela said dreamily.

Behind Andy Mathers and his guests, several more groups of adults and children were walking from the parking lot. Angela recognized Cal Banks, a lanky man in his forties with a weathered face and hair that was almost the color of Angela's orange trees, heading over from his car with his slender wife and two strawberry-blonde daughters. Cal sold fresh Christmas trees to wineries, inns, and families all over Napa Valley, and was Angela's main tree supplier.

Angela waved at Cal and the others from behind Connie's billowy skirts, then bent down to speak to the smaller children standing in front of them.

"We've got loads of fun planned—games and plenty of candy and more." The children grinned and one little boy hopped up and down. "But first," Angela said, nodding toward the barn, "we've got our very special haunted house. Are you ready to be scared?"

The kids nodded and cheered and Bea jumped out from behind Connie, yelling, "Goody! Happy Halloween! Boo!"

Andy Mathers' little nephew screamed and burst into tears. He ran behind his mother's leg and gripped it. "A witch!"

"That's right, little boy. I hope your name's not Hansel. If you see an oven, don't stand too close to it!" Bea cackled and extended her gnarled hand toward him, and the kid cried louder. "Just kidding!" Bea laughed as the boy's mother leaned down to console him.

"Don't cry, Finn," she said. "That's Miss Sickles. She owns this place. Go ahead, shake her hand." But the little boy shook his head and clung harder to her leg. The wife turned to her husband and hissed, "This is why I told you not to read those scary old fairy tales to the kids!"

"That's OK," Bea said, with another ear-splitting laugh. "I'm allergic to kids, anyway. Particularly the uncooked ones! No medium rare when it comes to children. Gotta be well-done to kill all the germs!"

"Bea!" said Angela. "She's just kidding, of course—"

"Maybe I am, maybe I'm not—"

"Bea!"

"Well, girlie, isn't my costume obvious? Look at my striped stockings and my curly shoes. How could anyone think I'm a witch? You can't get more elfin—"

"He's color blind," Finn's sister said. "Your outfit looks like a witch outfit to him. The stripes and the shoes look black and white. You could be the Wicked Witch of the—"

"So you say, Bookworm," said Bea, rolling her eyes. But after a beat she turned to the little boy and said, "Sorry to scare you, kiddo."

"He probably even thinks those orange trees look real," the little girl chirped.

"Artificial trees are terrible for the environment," her teenage brother said.

"We're working on it," Angela said, winking at

Aseem. "Hopefully, it won't be long before we have nothing but fresh, real Christmas trees here all year round."

The sullen teen snorted. "That's probably even worse for the planet."

Angela frowned and Aseem jumped to her defense. "Not the way we're going to do it. We've got a plan. It's science!"

"Whatev. It would be nice if you tried not to ruin everything for our generation," the teen said. He sighed loudly and looked around with a sour expression. "I guess I'll check out this 'maze.'" His little brother wiped his tears and ran to tag along, keeping a wide berth around Bea. Their sister trailed behind, a cultivated look of disinterest on her face.

"Sounds like that teenage wiseacre is calling you old, Angie," Bea laughed. "Happens to all of us eventually, but I thought you had a few more decades at least."

"We're millennials! We're all about protecting the environment," Aseem shouted after the boy. "The whole point of our plan is to save trees by growing them faster!"

"Didn't you say we're supposed to keep the tree venture secret?" Angela whispered to Aseem. "I mean… assuming we even get to do it?"

"You're right," Aseem said. "I don't think he was paying attention, though. And since the party's just starting, there's almost no one else around who could have heard. We'll have to get used to keeping the big secret from now on. I had to say something. I didn't like him upsetting you."

"My hero," she replied, squeezing his arm.

CHAPTER 2

"I've never been to Emeryville," Angela said as she, Bea, and Aseem walked along the sidewalk of a busy street a few days later. She and Aseem were dressed in thick sweaters and business casual attire. Bea was wearing one of her favorite velour track suits and a colorful scarf. "One minute it feels like a small town, the next a modern city."

Angela had parked near several newer retail complexes, but the avenue they were walking on had a mix of older buildings, mostly commercial ones housing small businesses and restaurants. Long-established trees, with remnants of yellow and orange foliage, dotted their path as they looked for the professor's address.

"Emeryville's got a little of everything," Bea said. "If I remember right, one of the oldest cardrooms in California is on this street. It's been decades since I've been there. That place had hella action back in the day. Could have done with fewer criminals, though. It got scary in the wee hours. Oh—and look at this place!"

Bea stopped in front of the window of an old shop that appeared to be frozen in the 1950s. Her mouth was agape, an uncharacteristic look of melancholy on her face.

"You spend your whole life denying feelings and this is what you get choked up about?" Angela giggled. "A typewriter repair shop?" Her mirth picked up steam, turning into a belly laugh.

"It is kind of fascinating," Aseem said, staring at the antique typewriters in the window. "These machines were marvels in their day. They were a big step in the timeline of technology. Plus, consider the knowledge the people in this shop must have to be able to repair all these relics."

"I remember how you loved that old typewriter of yours," Angela said, getting her laughter under control. "You never wanted to switch to a computer. But you're glad you did, right?"

"Typing is typing. Rebecca is the only

computer I love," Bea said. "Rebecca" was the disembodied voice in the tubular internet speaker installed in every suite of the inn. Bea used hers to do all kinds of research in a fraction of the time it used to take—and engage in occasional Angela-vexing shenanigans.

"Let's keep walking," Angela said. "We're on the verge of being late."

Moments later, they arrived at a run-down, industrial-looking building. There was a grimy pad of buttons with unit numbers and a plastic speaker to the right of the door.

Aseem pressed the button marked "201" and they heard a crackle through the speaker. "Professor—it's Aseem. I'm here with Bea Sickles and Angela Garcia." Before he'd finished the sentence, they heard an ugly buzz and a loud click from the door. Aseem grabbed the handle, and they all stepped inside.

The hall was gloomy and dusty and smelled of stale air. The covering was torn from one of the light fixtures, exposing a fluorescent tube. "Looks like the kind of place that attracts squatters," Bea said. "And not the picky kind, either."

They found their destination at the top of the building's wonky staircase. The door looked like it had numerous uneven coats of glossy black paint.

A gaunt man in his sixties opened it before they could knock. He had a pale, bald pate and wispy strands of dark gray hair hanging halfway down his ears. His outfit included suspenders, round glasses, and a bow tie. He was quite short—only slightly taller than Bea.

"Come in, Aseem," the professor said. "I assume you're Miss Sickles? I'm Dr. Gregory Woodward." He extended a hand to Bea. "And you must be Angela. You can call me—"

"Professor?" Angela said.

The professor nodded. "Though I do not work at the university anymore, scholarship is my vocation."

The three of them walked into the dingy space —an old factory floor reconfigured as a huge single room. A kitchenette had been carved into one corner and a bathroom in another. The ceiling was unusually high, with big windows looking out onto the street. Along with a large skylight, they flooded the space with sunlight. A lumpy futon sofa of uncertain vintage stood by the windows. A lab-style table stretched across the longest wall, loaded with various beakers and gardening pots. More pots and supplies were tucked underneath.

Above the lab table, open shelves held dusty

books and a collection of eight old typewriters—manual ones branded "Royal" and "Remington" that appeared to be from the early 1900s. Near the kitchenette, there was a small table with four banged-up chairs and big stacks of paper piled high beside it. On top of the table were three cups with various amounts of curdled coffee and an electric typewriter that immediately caught Bea's eye.

"I'm surprised that one attracted you. Most people who appreciate typewriters like the old manuals," the professor said, pointing to the antique machines. "Those are the ones that have resale value, though often not as much as people think. Certain imbecilic relations ogle them whenever they visit me. I think they imagine they'll grab the machines and sell them for a hundred times their actual value once I shuffle off this mortal coil."

"I had an old Selectric called Betsy," Bea said. "She was this exact model. Guess it's convenient that you live so close to the typewriter infirmary."

"Yes. That's one reason I chose to live here. No internet. No prying eyes—human or electronic. And easy access to typewriter parts and repairs."

Bea smiled and her eyes seemed to twinkle. Aseem and Angela looked at each other. Bea's conspiracy thinking about technology was the main reason it had been so hard to persuade her to switch to a computer. In the end, Bea only embraced word processing because a burglar destroyed Betsy while ransacking Bea's old Napa Valley cottage.

"I'm not planning on going any time soon," the professor said, "but if anything happens to me, consider this typewriter yours. My personal committee of vultures won't care what happens to it."

"You do all your work on this typewriter? No computer at all?" Angela said.

"Nope, no cell phone, either. If you wish to reach me, I have a telephone." He tilted his head toward a scuffed push-button model on a side table. "The university never liked it, but they fired me, so they don't get to say anything about it anymore."

Angela looked at Aseem with a raised eyebrow. He nodded reassuringly and mouthed, "It's OK."

"Shall we hear about the big tree idea?" Bea said.

"Let's get down to the nitty gritty," the professor said, inviting them to sit down at his rickety table. "I'll keep it simple. I understand you have an interest in fast-growing trees. A commercial interest."

"Christmas trees, to be precise," Angela said enthusiastically. "Our business is a Christmas-themed inn. Bea is a bestselling author of Christmas romance stories, and we built the inn to host her devoted fans."

"Well, I don't really need to hear *every* vapid detail, now do I?"

"Excuse me?" Angela said, mouth agape.

But Bea let loose a cackle of approval. "At least he says what he thinks, Angie. Bet that's the kind of thing that got you fired, though, professor, am I right?"

"I did not intend to offend. Please understand, if I hear too much about your profit-making intentions, I might decide not to proceed with any sort of arrangement. None of us wants that, right? So—I'm simply being frank—if we work together, I will regard it as a necessary evil."

"With that attitude, Greg, it's hard to imagine why you haven't found a backer yet," Bea said.

"I have a grand vision for my invention. Important goals. A legacy. What I don't have is money," the professor said tartly.

"Professor, as I mentioned when we met before, I'm quite sure our interests are aligned,"

Aseem said. "We need a regular supply of Christmas trees, but can't find them year-round. And we share your concerns about trees being a scarce resource—"

"Let me be clearer." The professor sighed with poorly feigned patience. "My rapid-growth solution—my brainchild—was envisioned to provide needed lumber to construct homes and schools and hospitals, with no net destruction of the earth's trees. Providing for essentials of human existence, in other words—essentials that, thanks to modern practices, sometimes run counter to the needs of the environment. I want to protect forests and save the planet. Christmas trees—" the professor winced and drew in a breath. "Honestly, the more I hear that term, the more hesitant I become to engage with a business dedicated purely to frivolity—"

"Christmas isn't frivolity. It's about family and togetherness. Tradition. Generosity, too," Angela said, a slight frog in her throat. "Besides, don't people need fun? Don't all creatures? If you don't think so, I've got some videos of dachshund puppies you ought to see."

Bea looked at Angela with a raised eyebrow and a smile.

The professor leaned back in his chair and

stared at Angela. After an awkward silence and a labored sigh, he spoke again.

"As it happens, I've so far only been able to replicate my results with one or two conifer seedlings—like the one in that corner." Bea, Angela, and Aseem turned to see a small fir tree, about two or three feet tall, in a thick ceramic pot in the corner. "My personal resources are, also, shall we say… running low. Hence my willingness to talk with prospective backers. Technically, you are correct that I'm not in a position to be picky. I need backing to do a full-scale experiment. Once the concept is conclusively proven, then refining it for more important crops begins."

"What type of deal structure do you envision, professor?" Aseem said. Angela smiled at him admiringly.

"Quite simple, really. You fund the trial—including all the necessary supplies. I will need several lines of credit to order certain things personally, to ensure confidentiality is maintained. And Aseem, you already said you can provide a patch of land for our test farm, correct?"

"The land is not a problem. You haven't mentioned anything about an ownership stake in the investment, however."

The professor sniffed. "I suppose that's another

necessary evil. I propose that you shall receive the trees that result from the experiment. After I've documented that it works, of course."

"That's a starting point, but we'll need a stake in the venture to justify the risk and the financial investment. Why don't you let me work on that? I'm sure we can propose something agreeable," Aseem continued. "But regarding confidentiality, won't that cease to be an issue once your patent is granted?"

The professor scoffed. "I haven't applied for a patent, and I don't intend to. That's nonnegotiable. Frankly, I would think you'd know better."

"How will you protect the invention, then?" Aseem said. "And our investment as well?"

"Aseem, have you heard of Robert Kearns? He invented intermittent wipers in 1964. Brilliant man whose invention continues to make cars safer today. He thought he protected himself when he patented his invention—which only helped the automakers steal it from him. Bullies and lawyers enjoy using the very legal system that's supposed to protect the little guy to crush him. And the thieves I'm worried about won't just be robbing me, they'll rob the planet. This is simply far too important to take that sort of chance."

"I think the three of us have some discussing to do," Aseem said. "Can we get back to you in a few days?"

"Of course. In the meantime, why don't you take that potted tree with you? I'm already concerned it will soon be too big to move. Without further intervention, it should grow another two feet or so in the next two weeks and then resume the growth pattern of an untreated tree."

"But it's still tiny," Angela laughed.

"I've told you, I've proven my method works on conifers."

"Salesmanship, Greg—I like it!" Bea said, guffawing.

"You think I'm puffing?" the professor said. "Take it home and see what happens. Just don't put it under anything less than five feet tall."

"I GUESS EVEN IF WE DON'T WORK OUT A DEAL WITH the professor, we get to keep this potted tree. It looks like it might have grown a little since we brought it home yesterday—don't you think?" Angela said.

"Maybe an inch or three? Or maybe it's my imagination," Bea said, moving to stand next to the tree, noting the top of it just passed her shoulders. "When we left the professor's loft, I would have said odds were fifty-fifty he's a quack. Now I'm not so sure."

"It's worth a try, isn't it? I just can't let go of the idea that people come here to experience the old New England Christmas tradition—"

"You mean the one honoring the harmonious, joyous, and bountiful Christmases that never actually existed?" Bea snarked. "I'm aware."

"Perfection can't be achieved, but it doesn't mean people don't love trying, or that it's not worth it. Besides, don't you remember what a wonderful, unconventional Christmas we had here at the inn last year? Even Christmases that aren't perfect can become perfect memories."

"Leave it to you to put the *perfect* spin on it, girlie. Don't worry, I'm happy to take a flier on the tree experiment. Not because of your Christmas conifer conundrum, though. I like the idea of becoming a venture capital investor. It's like a whole new world of gambling! Plus, I want to get into the tree scientist guy's will and get his

Selectric," Bea said, holding the door open for Angela, who wheeled the little potted tree onto the deck. "He's a lot younger than I am, but he doesn't look too healthy."

"Conifer conundrum?" Cal Banks said, knocking on the main ballroom door. "Tree scientist guy? I hope you're not unhappy with my trees. I've got a dozen of my best in my truck outside. I hand-picked them for you."

Angela's face reddened as she pushed the pot into the corner closest to the French doors and hurried back into the ballroom.

"I'm sorry, Cal—it's not what it sounds like. We love your trees. We only wish we could have more of them. Shall we look at the ones you've brought us?"

CHAPTER 3

With the help of Gary Wheaton's team of investment eggheads, Aseem managed to quickly and miraculously pull together a contract that Bea, Angela, and the professor could all agree on. Everyone was pleased, but none more than Angela, who, afraid of disappointment, had been working hard to convince herself that no deal would happen.

It was decided that Betty Snickerdoodle, Inc., would invest the funds needed for a trial crop of fast-growing Christmas trees, and would get to keep any trees that flourished. Reluctantly, the professor also agreed that if the experiment succeeded, Bea and Angela would have an option to buy shares in a new business based on the tree-growing technique.

The professor wouldn't budge on the patent. But Gary surprised Aseem by saying that even though he'd prefer a patent as an investor, he understood the professor's concern, having endured costly legal fights defending his own intellectual property. Gary's legal team even reviewed the professor's university contracts to be sure the school had no claim on the invention. The professor hadn't been hired to work on tree-growth experiments, so they concluded this risk was low.

With no patent for Betty Snickerdoodle, Inc. to co-own, Aseem proposed that the professor agree to transfer the secrets to Bea in the event of his death, assuming they proved the technique worked—and give Bea the right to transfer them to Angela in the same fashion. This way, Bea and Angela could be sure they'd be able to keep the venture going.

And now Bea, Angela, and Aseem were tending to their own tree experiment in the ballroom, which they'd converted into a makeshift nursery.

The professor had tasked them with looking after forty stout ceramic pots. In just a couple of days, the genetically modified seeds they contained had sprouted into evergreen seedlings. Each pot had a tiny port—a drip tube of sorts—stuck in the soil and fastened to its side.

"Regrettably, I can't be here to tend these plants personally—at least not right now," the professor said. "Too much documenting to do. Therefore, against all my instincts, I'm forced to trust you. But only for a week at a time. Please listen carefully to these instructions."

The professor left them with a week's worth of pre-mixed "supersprout serum SUA37-1," as he called it. The combination of the modifications to the seeds and the professor's secret-formula tree food, which he said must be customized for each stage of growth, was what would deliver accelerated maturation. With condescending repetition, the professor explained that the "feedings" had to happen on a precise schedule. Though the pots needed to be kept safe indoors, the team also had to do whatever they could to replicate an outdoor winter environment. He provided a checklist of instructions written at the fourth-grade level, complete with full-page drawings of the pots. He demanded that Angela initial a logbook ten times a day, confirming she'd done each step as required. He insisted she call him at least twice each day as well.

Despite the professor's attitude, Angela's enthusiasm for the tree project was not dampened in the least. If anything, she grew more excited every day, especially as the experiment reached new milestones. It thrilled her that the tree project might not simply solve her "conifer conundrum," but also do good for the environment.

"The professor says the seedlings will be ready to plant outside by a week before Thanksgiving," Angela said, clapping her hands. "Can you believe it? Perfect timing, since that's when the inn's busy season starts. And it's only two weeks from now! We'll have no problem with trees for BettyCon. I bet we'll have enough trees for the entire spring if we want!"

Bea nodded but maintained a neutral expression, concealing her predictable skepticism about the professor and his potential for quackery. It seemed like the professor grew pickier and added more oddball rules every day. The more wacky the requirements he came up with, the more Bea began to doubt that the effort —and her investment—would amount to anything. She would never have denied Angela the funding to try, though. After all, Angela's marketing genius was the reason they had so much money sloshing around. Bea did imagine, however, that between herself, Aseem, and Angela, it was up to her to maintain a sense of rationality about the odds of this fantastical experiment hitting a home run.

"And if it doesn't work, we'll have fun trying," Bea said. "And we know Cal will still provide us with his best specimens."

It had only been a couple of days since Cal dropped off his first delivery of beautiful, bushy Christmas trees. The biggest, most impressive one was with them in the ballroom, but had been shunted unceremoniously into a corner to make room for the prized experimental pots. Another of Cal's premium trees in the reception area had imparted its beautiful pine fragrance, but Angela still hadn't gotten around to decorating it because she was so focused on the professor's experiment.

"Oh—Cal," Angela said, looking wistful. "Thank you for reminding me of him, Bea. What would you think about offering him some of our trees for sale? If the experiment works out, I mean."

"Don't we have to wait? The deal requires us to keep the experiment secret, right?"

"True. I just wish we could tell him we'll give

him some for free. I don't want him to worry that we're competing with his business. If the experiment works, it should be a win for the inn, for the environment, and for anyone who cares about trees!"

"I suppose we could get several miracles," Bea said. "The first being that the experiment works. Then maybe the second will be that it won't turn out like poker, where for every winner, there's at least one loser. But I don't have to tell you, Angie, many things do turn out that way."

As Angela paused for a beat to consider what Bea was saying, Aseem interrupted.

"Angel, can we get started on the shopping list for the next phase?" The list included all sorts of unfamiliar items, like support structures for young trees, fertilizers, hand tools, and custom-designed injectors, but those things weren't what had painted the irrepressible grin on Aseem's face. He'd been researching farm utility vehicles, which were like the souped-up children of ATVs, golf carts, and monster trucks. "I know just the models of UTVs we'll need to run back and forth from the inn to our new tree farm."

AFTER THE TWO WEEKS OF ATTENTION IN THE ballroom, there was no doubt the seedlings were growing at a rapid clip.

"They already have branches and needles!" Angela said, gently examining one of the precious babies. "The professor told us we can't be late in getting them into the ground. They mustn't be allowed to outgrow the pots."

"He called me this morning and told me again that he's still worried about security, especially now that the seedlings look like young trees," Aseem said. "Is it just me, or is he becoming more paranoid all of a sudden? He's more antsy than any of the tech entrepreneurs in our incubator. Trust me, that's saying something."

Angela and Aseem both wore thick hoodies. Warm clothes were now essential in the ballroom, because they were keeping the temperature similar to the weather outside.

"I've already contacted Pat," Angela said. "She'll sleep with the trees for the rest of their time in the ballroom. What a trouper she is—she's willing to stay in here all night, with the French doors open and everything. She said she liked camping as a child and that she's used to cold nights outdoors from her stakeouts.

"It's funny, I can tell they're growing fast, but

what do I know about trees? What's normal? That's the professor's point, I think, and why he's so anxious about secrecy. He says this growth rate is so fast, no one with experience in tree farming would even believe it. Anyone who knows about trees would almost surely be lured to snoop. But still, who's gonna find us out here in the middle of nowhere? Especially since we haven't told anyone what we're doing."

"It's only one week," Bea said. She wore a heavy Christmas-themed sweatshirt but still rubbed her upper arms to warm them up. "It's easy enough for us to keep an eye on them during the day, and Pat's more than happy to take the night shift. This way, we can tell the good doctor we hired professional surveillance."

Pat showed up that evening for guard duty dressed in her typical attire—chinos, a plaid shirt, and a fleece vest on top. She was struggling to carry a big, soft, puffy object with a camouflage pattern, having trouble keeping it from dragging on the floor.

"You didn't need to bring a sleeping bag, Pat. We've got a rollaway bed for you," Angela said. "It's top-of-the-line and super-comfy. It's going to get cold tonight—high 30s, they say—but we've got blankets and pillows and a down comforter, too."

"Oh, this isn't a sleeping bag. It's something I'll happily use with the rollaway. Allow me to demonstrate."

With a big smile, Pat unfurled the puffy fabric to reveal a sleeping bag-space suit hybrid of sorts. She stepped into it and zipped it up, holding her arms out wide to emphasize its fluffiness. "It's scientifically proven to keep you warm. They even tested it in the Arctic." Then she did a few lunges to prove the suit allowed a wide range of motion. "I'll still be able to chase any bad guys that come for the trees."

"Hope you brought your rattle," Bea said with a cackle. "You look like the world's biggest baby."

Angela rolled her eyes and sighed. "Bea, since when do babies wear camo?"

"Only when they want to hide. But Pat, I'm afraid I can still see you."

"Don't you worry, Angela. As long as dear Miss Sickles keeps paying me double my regular rate, she can call me whatever she wants. Shoot. I forgot the booties. Guess I'll have to wear my shoes to sleep tonight."

"I've got plenty of thick socks," Angela said. "I think we've got some sheepskin slippers in inventory for the gift shop, too. Would you like a pair?"

"We'll have to take it out of your pay," Bea snarked. "Just kidding."

"I'll be fine with my shoes. I'm going back to San Francisco for the day tomorrow, so I'll bring my booties for the rest of the week."

"Brr!" said Bea. "Let's head to my suite for a few hands of poker, Pat. It's plenty warm there, so leave your super-sized onesie here. I don't think you'll fit through the door in it!"

A couple of hours later, Angela helped Pat set up the bed near the open French doors. Angela supplied Pat with various provisions: her favorite sandwiches, an insulated container full of hot cider, and a remote control for the giant display on the stage.

"In case you want to watch people on television projected as tall as houses," Angela said. "It's fun. You can almost imagine crawling into their mouths."

"I think I'll just surf the web on my tablet and read a good book before going to sleep. I'm still only halfway through *A Killer Uncorked*. Don't tell Bea I haven't finished reading her first mystery."

"You know that the private detective friend, Alex, is based on you, right?" Bea and Pat had met a year before at Bea's agent's office in San Francisco. Pat ran her private investigator business out of the office next door. She and Bea became friends after Bea hired her to teach her the ropes of detecting for her new mystery series.

"Now I do. When I said I hadn't finished it, technically, I meant I hadn't started it," Pat said. "Should I be asking for a cut of the royalties?"

"You'll have to negotiate that with Bea," Angela laughed. "Sleep tight. Oh, and the ballroom doors will be locked from the outside—you can still get out, but no one can come in. You only need to worry about watching the French doors and the deck."

"Roger that."

Pat read until her eyes began to droop, then crawled under the covers. Between the blankets and her puffy sleeping bag suit and the pajamas she had on underneath, she was toasty warm, but her shoes snagged the covers every time she tried to move. She kicked the shoes onto the floor and piled extra blankets over her feet. As she did, she looked out the open doors onto the deck. The inky sky was filled with stars, but no moon. The night sky in the wine country was so serene—so different from what she was used to in San Francisco. She smiled as she drifted off to sleep.

She was deep asleep, dead to the world, when she awoke in utter terror to an ear-splitting shriek. Reflexively, she threw off the blankets, swung her feet out of bed, and jumped up.

"Who's there?" She yelled to herself, spinning around and racing toward the deck to investigate. Once she got her bearings, she laughed at herself. *Oh... owl.* The vineyards of Napa Valley all welcomed barn owls, even set up little houses for them to nest in. The screechers provided the invaluable service of keeping the rodent population at bay. But no one would deny they could be very noisy.

Just country life, city gal, Pat thought to herself, smiling and shaking off her brief scare.

She noticed the thin socks she wore were hardly enough to keep her feet warm on the bare ballroom floor. After just a few moments, her toes felt like little ice cubes and made her shiver. She tucked them back under the blankets and closed her eyes, then quickly opened them again. She flicked the switch on her tablet: 3:45 a.m. The possibility of a quick dash for the bathroom popped into her head.

She tried to push the idea aside, but it was too late. All she could think about now was her bladder, and whether she could ignore it for a couple more hours.

Why did I drink all that cider?!

After half an hour of tossing and turning, Pat gave up on sleep and decided to make a run for it.

I'll only be gone a minute.

She got out of bed, slipped her feet into her shoes, and took a quick walk through the open French doors onto the deck. She watched her breath form steamy clouds as she looked around for signs of anyone lurking.

Nobody here but you and me, owl.

Pat moved quickly past the rows of pots toward the ballroom door. The bathroom was just down the hall.

The round trip will only take a minute if I hustle.

She pushed open the door and began to walk away—then suddenly remembered the door would lock behind her! She dove for it and caught it before it could clunk shut.

Phew!

She looked around the ballroom for something to prop the door.

Those tree pots are small, but they're heavy.

With a grunt, she grabbed one and placed it to block the door from closing. She slowly moved the door onto the pot… it didn't budge a bit.

Perfect.

Pat wiped off a few beads of sweat forming on her forehead. Compared with the near-outdoor temperature in the ballroom, the hallway felt almost tropical. Determined to be both quick and quiet, she started down the hall at a clumsy jog in her puffy sack. But inside the bathroom, she slapped herself on her damp forehead as she stared at an empty stall.

I'm going to have to climb out of this suit to pee. So much for 'a minute.'

Pat got out of the suit as quickly as she could, hurriedly kicking off her shoes, then pulling the suit down from her shoulders and stepping out of it. She used the toilet, then jammed her feet into her shoes and gave her hands a two-second wash.

That'll have to do. I've already been gone at least a few minutes.

She didn't waste time getting back into the suit, just balled it up and ran as quickly and quietly as she could back to the ballroom, fumbling as she tried not to trip over the dangling sleeves.

Wait—no!

The ballroom door was no longer propped.

Had the pot slipped back inside under the weight of the door?

Then she thought she heard someone rummaging in the ballroom—followed by the unmistakable sound of a ceramic pot tipping over.

Pat knew the door was locked, but gave it a desperate yank, anyway. It didn't move. She dropped the suit on the floor and raced down the hall, past the check-in desk, out the front door, and around the grounds to the outside of the deck.

"Stop!" she yelled as she got close to the deck stairs. "I see you!"

CHAPTER 4

"I don't know why I thought I could trust you," whined the professor, shaking his fists above his head. He, Pat, Bea, Angela, and Aseem were standing on the deck outside the ballroom, discussing the intrusion of the night before. The sun had been up for an hour or two and was casting a pretty light on the inn's grounds, warming the deck, though not the professor's mood. "This is exactly why I avoid involvement in commercial enterprises. Why is it so hard for you people to appreciate what's at stake?"

"I'm sorry," Pat said, her voice quavering. She was visibly shaken, a stark contrast to her normally steady personality. "I checked outside before I ran to the restroom. It couldn't have been more than a couple of minutes—"

"If you were only going to be gone for a few moments, why didn't you simply shut the doors to the deck?" the professor sneered.

"I… I should have done that. I just didn't think of it. It was the middle of the night, and all I remembered was how important it was to keep the trees cold—"

"It wasn't your fault you didn't think of closing the French doors," Angela said, placing her hand gently on Pat's arm. "We should have discussed it. But in any case, professor, it seems like little harm was done. The intruder dropped the pot that he tried to run off with."

Pat had just finished explaining that when she ran around to the outside of the ballroom, she'd spotted a slender figure running away—most likely a man, dressed head-to-toe in black, including a black cap—and had yelled at him. "I told him I had a gun. That seemed to scare him, and he dropped the pot."

"Good thinking, Pat," Bea said, giving her friend a friendly punch on the shoulder. "Maybe that tells us something about the intruder. Dropping the pot because you yelled that you had a gun seems like amateur hour to me. A pro crook would know you'd have almost no chance of hitting him in the pitch black—and if you'd really had a gun, you could've just used it instead of yelling about it."

"You're forgetting that although the thief dropped the pot, you've only recovered the pot itself and the seedling," the professor said. "The seedling seems to be missing some needles, and worse, the drip port hasn't been recovered. That means someone could have a sample of my formula."

"We haven't found it yet, professor, but that doesn't mean we won't," Aseem said gently. "The seedling and its roots were found separated from the pot and the soil, perhaps because the intruder was running so fast. We'll scour the area again and see if we can find the port."

The professor scoffed. "They were probably separated because the thief tried to yank both the port and the plant out of the pot to simplify his getaway and only managed to grab the port. Do I have to do *all* the thinking for you people?"

"Before I head back to the incubator later today, I'm going to set up motion-sensitive lights and video on the deck," Aseem said. "Even though it's only a few more days until we move the plants to their outdoor plot, we'll have that extra level of security."

"And Pat now knows she can shut the French doors if she has to go to the bathroom," Angela said.

"Nice that you're finally doing what should have been done in the first place. I hope that gets us through to the next phase without another attempted theft," the professor said. "It's clear I must get myself up here to oversee the project as soon as the seedlings are transferred to the plot. I'm going to watch these trees night and day."

"But where will you stay? Our little farm won't be close by," Angela said. "You know—because we discussed keeping them at the outer edge of our property, so no one can find it or connect it with our business."

"Then I'll need some sort of trailer—and I expect you to arrange it. Thankfully, I thought to include that clause in our agreement about ending the project if you can't maintain security or care for the plants properly."

"I'd say Angela's the best lab partner you could ask for, Gregory. These trees are growing like weeds on steroids, correct?" Bea said. "And she's been watching those pots and marking that logbook of yours like her life depends on it."

The professor nodded grudgingly. "The trees appear to be doing well. But the trailer, Miss Sickles?"

"We'll work on it."

"You might need to use a cell phone," Aseem said. "I doubt we can get a landline installed out there—and even if we could, I doubt we could keep it secret."

"Fine, as long as no one can trace the phone to me," the professor grumbled.

"Burner phone should do the trick," Pat said. "Essential P.I. knowledge. I can take care of that if you like. It'll be as locked down and anonymous as possible."

"It seems we've got our marching orders," Bea said. "Now don't you need to head back to Emeryville? Your writing's not going to finish itself."

Once the professor was on his way back to his car and out of earshot, Bea announced to the others that she wanted a "brief Jessica Fletcher moment."

"So," she said theatrically, "I wonder if any of you are pondering the same question I'm pondering."

Angela, Aseem, and Pat all looked back and forth at each other.

"Good thing someone here's paying attention!" Bea said with a cackle. "The question is, how did that intruder even know to come sniffing around here?"

The other three shrugged.

"I don't know, either. That means it's time to put our thinking caps on, people! We've got an investment to protect."

The four of them broke up into pairs. Pat and Angela headed out to the grounds to search for the missing serum port. Aseem worked on installing the camera and light under the eaves hanging over the deck, with Bea keeping him company and handing him tools as he worked from a ladder.

"OK, Bea, move around so we can test the motion sensor at different spots on the deck."

"Oh, goody, I'll test it with some of my dance moves," Bea chuckled. She proceeded to sing a few bars of a couple of her favorite tunes and demonstrate the combination of movements she referred to as "dancing."

"Ah, that felt good," she said, catching her breath after Aseem declared the sensors to be functioning correctly. "I forgot to tell you, Rebecca's not working anymore. I haven't had my morning dance in a couple of days and my joints are rusting. Would you mind taking a look?"

Back in Bea's suite, Aseem tested the tubular internet speaker and diagnosed the problem as a bad cable. He brought one back from his own suite and switched it out. Bea confirmed the fix by shouting, "Rebecca," to summon the mysterious voice inside the tube, then testing her with a request for tidbits of poker trivia. "Perfect," she pronounced. "Right as rain. Now don't you hesitate to ask me if I can help you with something, handsome."

"Coincidentally," Aseem began slowly. "I could use a little advice. Angel's coming with me for dinner at my parents' tonight. I love my parents, but they can be a bit… much."

"You're nervous?"

"They… let's just say they have big expectations. Sometimes it seems I'll never live up to their hopes. I've learned to live with it—my brother's the superstar in the family, so at least they're proud of him. But I want them to like Angel—to love her as much as I do. And to welcome her."

"What if they don't?"

"That's just what I'm worried about. Her feelings, especially."

"She's a big girl, handsome. You're both adults, right?"

Aseem nodded.

"Sometimes you have to do what's right for you, even if no one else agrees."

Angela and Pat tried to organize their efforts to find the missing serum port, but Pat could scarcely even narrow down the area where the intruder had run off. Beyond the circular driveway, the parking lot, and the barn was a vast, grassy expanse dotted with a few trees. And it had been so dark, Pat couldn't be sure exactly where the intruder had run.

They searched for a while, and Angela became frustrated—even losing her patience at one point.

"I know this is all my fault," Pat said. "I'm sorry."

"No, Pat, it's really not. Anyone could have predicted you might need to use the bathroom overnight. I'm sorry I didn't think of it. And if I sound impatient, it's not you—I'm just a bit preoccupied."

"Anything I can help with?"

"I'm meeting Aseem's parents tonight, finally. Got any advice?"

"Let's see. Shall we start with what to wear?

You might be surprised to know I like to keep it simple."

"Funny you should mention that. Aseem says his parents told him it's just a casual family dinner."

"You are more than welcome to borrow my best chinos. They might be a bit big for you, though."

Angela laughed. "Your chino game is strong, Pat, but I think I might need to go a little less casual than that. Seriously, though, I am stressed out. I just… I hope they'll like me. Aseem doesn't say much about them—just that they've always pushed him to do his best. His father's a doctor, and so is his older brother."

"Do you think they expected Aseem to be a doctor, too?"

"Aseem hasn't said so. But I think he's a little nervous about the dinner, too. He hasn't told me or anything. It's just a feeling I get. He doesn't want to disappoint them, and I don't want to let him down."

"Oh, Angela, it's hard to imagine you disappointing any man's parents," Pat said. "You're obviously a catch." Then her brow furrowed. "Unless—no, I mean, sorry—"

"Unless what?"

"Something just popped into my head. It probably doesn't mean anything."

"Tell me anyway."

Pat sighed. "Well, I met a private investigator at a conference a few years back who told me he made a lot of money on 'marital investigations'—"

"Marital investigations?" Angela laughed. "That's a relief. Aseem and I haven't made any plans to get married. We haven't even been together a year yet."

Pat tucked her lips inside her mouth and looked at her feet.

"Is there something you're not saying, Pat? Please tell me."

"The investigator was talking about background checks for arranged marriages," Pat sighed. "He told me many parents of Indian descent believe that's the best way, even when they've set down roots in the West. The investigator was from England, and said he believes it's less common in the United States, but that some Indian-American families prefer to arrange marriages for their children, too."

Angela's eyes opened wide and her jaw dropped. "Do you think it's possible—no, it can't be—that Aseem's family expects to pick a wife for him?"

"No, no, I'm sorry I said anything," Pat stammered. "It—it sounded from what my investigator colleague said that it's not that common in the US—"

"And wouldn't Aseem have mentioned it?"

"Well—I probably shouldn't say this—"

"It's too late now, Pat," Angela frowned. "Please just tell me what you're thinking."

"Well, I'm just thinking that if his family does want to arrange a marriage for him, that could be why he's nervous. Because when they meet you, it will be clear that he's not planning to go along with the arranged-marriage program."

Angela sighed nervously. "Welp, no pressure."

Angela stopped at Bea's suite on her way to meet Aseem by the reception desk.

"Don't you look pretty, girlie!" Bea said as she opened the door. "All ready for your big debut tonight?"

In place of her typical, tidy outfit of pressed jeans, a white shirt, and bright white sneakers, Angela had swapped in black jeans, a lacy, demure top, and a pair of black ballet flats. A small black bag dangled off her shoulder on a long strap, and delicate hoop earrings, a birthday gift from Aseem, hung from her ears. Her shiny hair was pulled up into a thick, high ponytail.

"I guess Aseem told you we're having dinner with his parents tonight," Angela said, stepping into the room and sitting down on the end of the bed, which was decorated with a fluffy comforter and a quilt that featured an old-fashioned New England Christmas scene. An unlit candle on the nightstand gave off a delicate pine scent. "He said casual, but I hope I'm not dressed too casually."

"Definitely not too casual in my book, Angie—and you know what a style expert I am," Bea said, doing a quick twirl, showing off her all-purpose dress-up/dress-down outfit of a track suit and beige sneakers. Her gray bowl cut sported orange tips that still hadn't completely faded from Halloween.

Angela laughed. "Thanks. I'm hoping you'll wish me luck—but that's not why I stopped by. I was thinking about what you said about the intruder, about who could possibly have known what we were doing. We've been doing so well at keeping the secret."

"We have. So why do I sense a 'but' coming?" Bea chuckled.

"I was just thinking about what Cal said—when he overheard us talking about 'tree scientist guy.' Do you remember—that day when he dropped off the load of fresh trees?"

"I remember."

"Could he have guessed we were up to something? Do you think he could have been the intruder?"

"I suppose so, but I doubt it. It's not like he could have overheard any specifics about the experiment. It seemed to me he was worried you might find another supplier of trees. He probably had no idea we might be supplying them for ourselves."

"Maybe you're right. But should we tell the professor we might have been overheard?"

"Of course not! We agreed to keep the project confidential. What good would it do to tell him we might have let the cat out of the bag? Especially since odds are we didn't, anyway?"

"You're right. It's just… it's not just Cal. I guess I don't know how I feel about all this secrecy. Isn't it better just to tell the world what we're doing? If the experiment succeeds, won't we want other people to license the technique? If it's about saving the planet, why wouldn't we want that?"

"I don't have to tell you I'm not a lawyer or a tech expert, but isn't this the whole question about the patent? Either we have a patent and we can license the invention, or we have to keep it secret."

"True. Just wondering if we—I mean, he—made the right choice. Especially since it seems unlikely we'll be able to keep it a complete secret, no matter how hard we try."

"It could be getting more dangerous, too. But the thing is, girlie, even that doesn't really matter."

"Why?"

"It's not our decision to make."

CHAPTER 5

"Oh, no, I'm so under-dressed!" Angela said.

She and Aseem had just driven through the gates of his parents' neighborhood, a Silicon Valley gated community of luxurious mini-mansions—tall, stately homes that stood close to one another on lots not much wider than their foundations. As they drove in, Aseem pointed out his older brother Sanjay and sister-in-law Preeti just ahead of them. They were getting out of their car and Angela could see that Aseem was almost as shocked by their appearance as she was.

Aseem had pulled over a few houses away so they could watch without being spotted. Sanjay and Preeti looked like they were dressed for a night at the opera or a holiday cocktail party. She was wearing a satin dress in a jeweled magenta tone with strappy sandals and what appeared to be diamond jewelry. Sanjay was wearing a dark, exquisitely tailored suit.

"Is he wearing a *tux?*" Angela sputtered. "Aseem—we can't go in dressed like this!"

"Don't worry, Angel. You look beautiful, as always. I don't know why they're so dressed up," Aseem said. "My mother was very clear that this is just a casual family dinner. They must be going somewhere afterwards."

Aseem reached for Angela's hand and gave it a reassuring squeeze. Once Sanjay and Preeti were in the house, Aseem pulled his car up closer. "It'll be fine. I promise. Let's go in." Angela studied him briefly, thinking she'd detected a touch of uncertainty in his voice.

Aseem led the way along the driveway and down the path that connected to the backyard.

"I think this is the way," Aseem said. "Sorry— they've only lived here a year. This isn't the house I grew up in. Oh, yes—there's the back door."

As they approached the steps, a young man and woman wearing black uniforms and green aprons with the logo of a local Indian chef arrived at the door, each with their arms full. One was carrying several large bags and what appeared to be a metal rack. The other was carrying several hotel pans with steam escaping from under their lids. A lovely aroma of turmeric, ginger, garlic, and other spices wafted toward Aseem and Angela.

"Are you delivering that here? It smells delicious," Aseem said politely.

"Yes, would you mind holding the door for us?" the woman called out. "Thank you!"

Aseem rushed up to grab the door and Angela hung back. "I can't go in there, Aseem. Not the way your brother and sister-in-law are dressed. And it looks like your mother planned a catered affair—"

"Of course you can. Don't worry about it. She probably just didn't want to cook—and look what I'm wearing," Aseem said. He was dressed much more casually than Angela, in typical tech worker attire: faded jeans, sneakers, and a hoodie. At least he'd swapped out his t-shirt for a button-down.

"Yes, but they love you. They have to like you —or at least accept you," Angela cried.

"Trust me, it doesn't always feel that way."

"Not helping!"

Just inside the back door was the kitchen, where the two chefs had already made progress on the gourmet meal that would apparently soon be served.

"Come through this way," Aseem said, rushing past the activity. He held Angela's hand as she walked behind him into the dining room.

"Aseem!" his father said cheerily, with a light accent to his warm voice. He was a good-looking, slightly jowly man with a full head of salt-and-pepper hair and a tidy mustache. To Aseem's dismay, his father was also dressed up, though at least he was wearing a sport coat and slacks and not a suit that could pass as a designer tuxedo. "And you must be Angela. We've heard… well, I can't say we've heard very much about you, but what we've heard is all good. Right, Aseem?"

Aseem smiled awkwardly. "Dad, you know that's just because we don't talk often."

"That's right. You're quite busy with this new job of yours."

"You're the one who's always busy," Aseem said. "Angel, my father is chief of surgery at Fremont Children's Hospital."

Angela extended her hand warmly. "What an important job. I'm sure you help so many children. Their parents must be immensely grateful."

"It's indeed quite rewarding. Sanjay, please

come meet your brother's lovely friend, Angela," Aseem's father said.

"Any friend of Aseem's is a friend of mine," Sanjay said. Then he looked Aseem up and down and chuckled. "I suppose you've been too busy to dress for the occasion, little brother? Or perhaps I should have come straight from the O.R. in my scrubs."

"Ma said casual—I asked twice," Aseem said. "Just a casual family dinner."

"At least your friend put in a bit of effort," Sanjay laughed. Angela smiled politely, feeling her cheeks grow warm.

"She's not just my friend, Sanjay," Aseem said. "She's—"

Preeti came to Sanjay's side and interrupted to introduce herself. As she shook Preeti's hand, Angela felt almost starstruck by her sophisticated appearance. Up close, Preeti was even more glamorous than she'd looked from the car, and she carried herself with an evident, enviable confidence.

"Preeti…" Angela said. "Like 'pretty'? Certainly seems more than appropriate. Your dress is just exquisite, too."

"It's *Preeti*," Preeti said, emphasizing the "ee" with forced tolerance, as if talking to a rube. "Not 'pretty.'" Her pained pronunciation of "pretty" seemed to be an imitation of how she imagined the same rube might speak.

"Of course—I'm sorry—" Angela said. She felt a damp glow surface on her forehead. Aseem put his arm around her waist and gave it a gentle squeeze.

"Are you two heading to the opera after dinner or something? Ma told me that your hospital sponsored the season. Angel, my brilliant brother is a neurosurgeon at Silicon Valley Hospital. He's following in my father's footsteps—"

"Aseem, you know Sanjay's long surpassed me," chuckled Aseem's father. "Your brother has been hired by a robotics company to help develop technology to perform surgery more accurately, from any distance—with surgeons driving the machines, of course. Quite an ambitious sideline, wouldn't you say? He's already done trial operations on patients halfway around the world. At his career stage, I was happy just to have mastered my scalpel! Perhaps you can scrape up a few rupees to invest in your brother's company. It's not too early to start thinking of your future. No, it's more accurate to say it's past time. You're the youngest, but not so young anymore, Aseem.

Sanjay, you'll promise we can buy friends and family shares before you go public, am I right?"

"Of course, Dad," Sanjay said. "Plus, you know the offer still stands for you to help us with our pediatric technology development. You could get directed shares that way."

"No, no, son, that's quite all right. I don't have the energy you do. You've practically got two full-time jobs. It's no wonder you and Preeti haven't had time to give us any grandchildren," he sighed. "It's my one request—and your mother's, most of all. Are you going to make us wait forever?"

Angela thought Aseem looked briefly relieved that the focus had shifted to his brother. But then his father added, "Of course, at least you've taken the first step in making an excellent marriage to Preeti." He looked at Aseem expectantly, but Aseem was lost for words.

"The table looks beautiful," Angela said, after an uncomfortable pause.

The long table had a dark finish and sat atop heavy, ornate pedestal legs. The place settings were elegant, with water and wine goblets and fine china, paired with silverware for multiple courses. The tabletop was decorated with candles in crystal holders and a lavish floral arrangement.

The chairs were of a similar robust walnut wood, upholstered in heavy white fabric.

"I'm sure my wife will appreciate hearing that, Angela. She takes great pride in our home. And of course, we love it when our children visit—and when we can have guests, especially dear friends of our children, such as yourself."

Aseem sighed and glanced at the large dining room table. "Angela's not just my—" Aseem stopped when the table settings caught his eye. "Why's the table set for nine?"

As if on cue, Aseem's mother walked into the room. She wore a stunning formal sari made of a luminous, ice-blue material. Beads and jewels were hand sewn into the trim, and birds were delicately embroidered throughout the middle of the drape.

Angela was so moved by the beauty of the garment that she gasped involuntarily and put her hand to her mouth. "I'm sorry," she said hastily. "Your sari is just so lovely. Is it silk?"

"The material? It's Georgette," Aseem's mother replied with a smile. "And you must be Angela."

"Ma," Aseem said, kissing his mother on the cheek, "Why didn't you tell us we should dress up? I thought you said casual family dinner. And why are there nine seats at the table? There are only six of us, right?"

"Didn't I tell you?" she replied innocently. "I thought I mentioned that Mira is in town. She's home from law school—not that Stanford is very far from here, but as you'd imagine, it's quite rigorous. She's come home to study over the weekend—"

"You didn't tell me. I still don't see why you're all dressed up."

"I just thought we'd have a little celebration. I remember how much you two liked each other growing up."

"You always say that, Ma, but Mira and I didn't know each other that well. She was four years behind me in school—"

"And, obviously, her parents are—well, the family really is quite suitable—"

"Suitable? Suitable for what?" Aseem said. Angela detected a note of alarm in his voice that was slightly less intense than what she was feeling.

"Did I say suitable?" his mother said sweetly. "I misspoke. I just meant that they're a lovely family. Isn't it nice to know families that blend so easily with ours? Socially, I mean, of course.

"Preeti, it just reminds me how your family and ours were so well-matched. Don't you remember how well we all got along, right from the start? And we all still do, of course. Such a blessing, isn't it? Since it's almost like we all got married, not just you and Sanjay."

Preeti nodded. "We've all been blessed."

"I am not sure many of today's modern couples understand this. Marriage is almost like a merger of families."

A feeling of dread brewing in her tummy, Angela looked to Aseem for reassurance. But Aseem was busy scanning back and forth from his mother and father, who seemed to have acquired poker faces to rival Bea's, to his brother, who appeared to be smirking. Sanjay quickly composed himself when Aseem caught his eye. Angela felt her face grow hotter and separated herself from Aseem ever so slightly, but he kept his arm around her and pulled her closer.

"Mother—"

"Oh, there's the doorbell," she said. "Why don't you all find your seats in the dining room and enjoy a glass of wine? The caterers have filled the wine glasses and will pass some hors d'oeuvres. Aseem, could you let the caterers know we'll be seated and ready for the appetizers in twenty minutes?"

Angela and Aseem found their name cards on

the table, at places across the table from each other. Aseem's father's place was between them, at the head. The seat to the right of Aseem had been assigned to Mira, and her father and mother were seated to Mira's right. With four seats on their side of the table, the chairs were closer together than the other side, where Sanjay and Preeti were placed next to Angela. Aseem's mother was at the other head of the table.

Angela gulped hard and stared at Aseem with wide eyes. He grabbed her arm and pulled her into the kitchen.

"I do not know why they're acting like this, I swear," he said. He put his hands on her cheeks. "Don't worry. I will set them straight."

"I don't want to embarrass you," Angela said. Tears were welling in her eyes. "You don't have to make a scene. You don't have to upset your family for me. And to think my biggest worry was they wouldn't like me—"

"Angel! Listen to me. They should worry about upsetting me, too." He pulled her in for a hug. "It will be OK, I promise. Let's just eat fast and get out of here. I won't make a scene. If I can't set them straight tonight without a fight, I will set them straight tomorrow. I promise. OK?"

Angela nodded and took a deep breath. "OK. I'm ready."

Aseem told the caterers to bring the appetizers in immediately.

"Didn't your mother say twenty minutes?"

"We want to get it over with, don't we?"

Aseem led the way quickly back into the dining room. Angela followed Aseem's lead and sat down at the table, even though the others were still mingling and sipping wine and sparkling water. His mother said, "Aseem, that's rather rude. Don't you want to say hello to Mira and her parents?" But then the servers came in carrying the fragrant first course—and immediately became confused because only two of the guests had taken their seats.

"Yes, please, go ahead and serve," Aseem said, before his mother could direct them. "Won't everyone sit down, Ma? Angela and I have had a long day. We're starved." Angela exhaled and furtively looked for Aseem's mother's reaction.

His mother looked irritated, but noted the servers standing at the ready, so she asked everyone else to take their assigned seats. "Mira, you look lovely tonight. Your seat is right next to Aseem."

Mira wore boots and a fitted knit dress that

accented her petite figure. With her youthful braided hairstyle, perfect skin, and her nearly makeup-free face, she looked even younger than her age. Mira tilted her head down to say hello to Aseem. "Nice to see you again." She leaned down to give Aseem an awkward hug.

"Aseem! Stand up and pull Mira's chair out for her!" his mother said.

"It's fine, I've got it," Mira said. She helped her parents take their seats and then squeezed in next to Aseem. With everyone finally seated, the caterers began serving the appetizer, a delicate concoction of spicy shrimp and cauliflower.

Mira smiled across the table at Angela and introduced herself. "I'm Mira."

Before Angela could reply, Sanjay piped up. "Angela is Aseem's friend."

"Sanjay, you know that she's not just my friend," Aseem said, his face growing tense with the effort required to control his temper.

"Of course," Sanjay said lightly. "We know she was once your boss, too. But hasn't all that changed, now that you're working for Gary Wheaton?"

"I must say, we are impressed," Preeti said. "Gary Wheaton is a household name—you don't even need to work in technology to know that.

Everyone at my nonprofit organization admires him."

Aseem's father beamed with pride. "You're finally starting a real career, Aseem! That Christmas stuff—well, I suppose it was fine for a while, but surely you agree it's a bit unserious... what's the word I'm looking for? Frivolous. But now you've had your fun, and it's time to get focused."

"That's not right," Aseem said. He put his glass down a little too forcefully, causing white wine to slosh over the rim. "First, Angela is still my boss. I'm only working for Gary part time. Second—"

"Isn't that a temporary thing? I thought you'd be eager to go full time as soon as you could. Is Gary Wheaton not prepared to take you on full time? That's certainly a shame."

"It's hardly a shame! I insisted that I be able to continue working with Angela at the inn."

"On the *Christmas* thing?" Sanjay said, looking flabbergasted.

Aseem jumped from his seat. "Why are you all acting like this? I know you know better. Angela is my boss and my girlfriend—the woman I love. Mira, I'm sorry you were invited under false pretenses." He held his hand up, beckoning Angela to take it. "Let's go, Angel."

Angela stood up, her face flushed, and quickly slipped behind Aseem's father's chair.

"We're leaving. But first, two things. Number one, I know you are all aware of the Betty Snickerdoodle brand—because who isn't?! And that is all Angela's doing. In fact, she's the reason I have the Gary Wheaton job. It was her success with the inn that brought his wife there.

"And since you're so enamored of technology, you should know that Angela is leading a groundbreaking, ultra-secret experiment that could literally save the world's forests. It all starts with Christmas trees—which, by the way, I know you all adore, especially you, Ma.

"I don't know where all these crazy marriage ideas are coming from," he said, putting his arm around Angela's shoulder protectively, "But understand this: This is the only woman I've ever thought about marrying. She's brilliant and I wonder every day what I did to deserve her!"

Angela gulped and looked at Aseem with awe. But his focus was on their exit strategy. Still holding Angela's hand, he led them quickly out, this time through the front door.

CHAPTER 6

The next morning, Angela went to the inn's front entrance to start designing and decorating the tree. It was early, and she'd expected to have the reception area to herself. But Bea and Pat were already there, standing by the door.

"What are you two doing up at this hour? Jackson's not even here to open the front desk yet."

"We've got a big day today, girlie. One important delivery has already arrived, and I'm expecting another any minute."

"You should check your baby trees, Angela," Pat said. "I know this sounds crazy, but I swear I heard them growing last night."

"It's a good thing we're ready to transplant them," Bea said. "I know we said a couple more days, but I think we should start moving them outside now, Angie. Some of them look like they're going to burst their pots."

"But doesn't the professor want to stand guard over them himself once they're in the ground? He said he can't get here for a few more days. And what about the trailer we promised?"

"That's the delivery I'm waiting for. I gave Oliver a call last night. I figured he'd know who could rent us that kind of thing." Oliver was a friend of Bea's and the entire Betty Snickerdoodle team, as he was a leader among the Betty Bros, one of the biggest Betty fan communities. He was also an ambitious young business owner. In the past year, he'd progressed from driving a rideshare car himself to operating a small fleet of shuttle buses and cars.

Bea watched for Oliver by the front door of the inn while Pat accompanied Angela on a quick trip to the ballroom to see the astonishing overnight progress of the little trees.

"It's amazing. I am sure my eyes aren't deceiving me this morning—those trees are definitely much bigger. Good idea to get at least some of them into the ground right away. I'm glad we had Andy Mathers pre-dig all the holes for us."

"It'll be a snap if your handsome boyfriend can help us," Bea said. "We can't bring in any outside help if we want to keep the trees secret."

"Aseem is here. He's probably just sleeping in. We had a bit of a rough night last night."

"Whoa, you two straight arrows finally went a little crazy? I'm sorry I wasn't there to see that!" Bea cackled.

"Not that kind of a bad night," Angela sighed. "Dinner with his parents was a little… stressful. I'm feeling out of sorts about it myself, but it was worse for him than for me. I hoped that decorating this big tree and the others that Cal brought over would be a productive distraction."

"Don't worry, Angie, we'll have plenty of distractions today. You can decorate to your heart's content later. Once Oliver brings the trailer, there will be lots of setup to do."

"Sounds like just the therapy I need. Aseem and I can decide on a plan for getting the trees into the ground, too."

Oliver arrived driving an SUV, leading the way for a couple of trucker friends who were hauling the temporary housing trailer on a big flatbed semi. Angela gave him directions to the outer edge of the property, where they'd set up the plot for the tree farm. Knowing it would take the little convoy a while to reach the far side of the ranch by road, Angela, Bea, and Pat decided this would be an excellent opportunity to take one of their new UTVs for a spin.

"That was the other delivery," Bea said. "The UTVs you and Aseem picked out are in the barn. They were in stock and Andy brought them over almost as soon as you ordered them."

"Aseem's going to be mad," Angela laughed. "I'm sure he thought he'd get first crack at driving them."

"You snooze, you lose," Bea said.

The three of them walked down to the barn, where Andy had delivered and stowed the two UTVs along with an open, boxy trailer that could be attached to either.

"Look at the trailer!" Angela said. "It's so cute! It's like a little red wagon, blown up. It'll make hauling the seedlings to the farm spot so much easier."

Angela started up one of the two vehicles and pulled it out of the barn. Bea climbed into the passenger seat next to her, and Pat hopped onto the jump seat in the back.

"Buckle up, ladies," Angela said. "We won't be going fast, but it could be bumpy."

They proceeded across the acreage of the ranch to the northeast corner, where the pastureland approached foothills that provided a natural edge to the property. Though Angela drove cautiously over the unfamiliar terrain, everyone felt a jolt when she hit a hidden hillock or hole.

"Phew, that was fun!" she said as they arrived at the site. Oliver and the trailer rental team were already there. They'd parked their vehicles on the side of the rarely used private access road and were preparing to unload the trailer.

"What do you think, Angela? Is that the right spot? Looks nice and flat," Oliver said.

"I think so," she said, then she leaned over to whisper to Bea, "Do you think it's close enough to the trees?" The plot where they'd plant the trees was nearby, marked off with chain-link fencing that was covered in a plastic mesh to conceal what was inside the enclosure. "So that the professor can keep an eye on them, I mean."

Bea nodded, and Angela gave Oliver and the rental team a thumbs up. They drove the rig onto the grass and were surprisingly adept at setting the trailer in place. They also set up the power generator that would provide electricity. They tested the generator and it seemed to work, then they set up the built-in furniture that turned the trailer into a miniature home. Most of the furniture flipped down from the trailer's inside walls, except for the bed, which filled most of the rear part of the space.

"It's small, but it's a lot nicer than Dr. Treedaddy's real home," Bea said. "There's even a TV and a little kitchen."

The rental team left after giving Angela instructions to pass on to Aseem about the electricity, including how to keep the generator fueled up.

"I guess we shouldn't ask you what's behind the fence," Oliver chuckled, hopping up into his SUV and starting it up.

"If we tell you, we have to kill you!" Bea said. "I'm joking. Probably."

After Oliver drove away, Angela, Bea, and Pat couldn't resist a peek inside the fence. Angela unlocked the combination padlock and looked at the five long, neat rows, each with eight holes with piles of dirt beside them.

"A little anticlimactic, I guess," she said. "I suppose I should change the lock, since Andy knows the combination to this one."

"Better safe than sorry. But that guy's so busy, hard to imagine he's got time to snoop on our tree farm," Bea said.

"We can tell the professor his home-away-from-home is just about ready to go," Angela said. "Aseem can put the finishing touches on it—like a camera to catch any snoopers."

"Leave telling the professor to me," Bea said. "He's a bit of a noodge, but I don't mind. I could use the opportunity to butter him up. I want to make sure I get that Selectric someday."

"Bea, do you think anyone else could find this place, out on this little access road in the middle of nowhere? And if they could, would the professor be able to stop them from getting curious about what's behind this fence?"

"I guess we're gonna find out, girlie."

AN HOUR LATER, ANGELA HAD DROPPED BEA AND Pat off by Pat's car. Bea had told Pat that it was time for a "surprise adventure," but wouldn't say what it was, only that Pat would "get to" drive them to it.

Pat started up her little econobox and Bea gave her the address Rebecca had provided to her. Pat typed it into the little navigation device that was perched on top of the dashboard.

"Emeryville?" Pat said. "That's kind of a long way."

"Trust me, it'll be worth it!"

An hour later, they found themselves in the lumpy, bumpy gravel parking lot of the Lucky Pines Card Club. Pat found a spot for her little car amidst an eclectic assortment of jacked-up trucks, older luxury cars adorned with fuzzy dice and shiny rims, and junkers that made her little car look brand new.

"A club? Sounds exclusive," Pat said. "I guess looks can be deceiving?"

Pat was grinning as she stared at the shabby building's unusual branding. The enormous wall that faced the parking lot was decorated with a giant mural of a pine tree, a dragon, and a poker hand—a royal flush, of course.

"You're referring to the modest exterior, I suppose?" Bea snickered. "That's nothing. Wait 'til you see the inside!"

"I dunno, Bea. I'm not sure I'm ready for another poker outing. It was clear last time that I still need more lessons. A lot more."

"Don't you worry, girlfriend. They're having a

special tournament just for us ladies today, and I'm staking you," Bea said, leading the way into the windowless building past a gaggle of smoking gamblers and security guards.

Three hours later, Bea and Pat walked back out of Lucky Pines, shielding their eyes from the late afternoon sun.

"It's just like I remember it! We called it 'Unlucky Whines' back in the day. Happy to see that's still an effective zinger to maximize the pain of a bad beat. Did you see that Russian gal's face? I almost made her cry!"

"You put the salt in the wound with perfect timing," Pat laughed, still squinting. "Why do they keep it so dark in there, though?"

"They're hoping you won't notice how filthy it is. Even the regulars would faint if they could clearly see the carpet. It would probably even scare off the criminal element. The casino sure as heck doesn't want that."

A car careened by them, spraying bits of gravel as it skidded to the exit.

"Uh-oh," Bea said. "Somebody blew their rent money."

"Whoa, Bea, my eyes are still adjusting to the light. Give me a second to be sure I can see before we head back to the car. I don't want to walk in front of a gambler in a hurry. The adventure was fun, but this definitely isn't the last place I want to see before I meet my maker."

"It's always fun when you win," Bea snorted. "But we're not heading back to the wine country just yet. Let's leave the car here and walk a little. The real adventure begins just down the street."

Ten minutes later, they were in front of the typewriter repair shop, and Bea had stopped to look longingly at the machines in the window.

"Look—that's a Selectric!" She pointed to a formidable electric typewriter in the window. The black manual antiques that surrounded it looked delicate by comparison. "Just like I used to use to write my Betty stories. When we visited the professor, he had one just like it. I wonder if this one's for sale."

"Doesn't this shop just do repairs?"

Bea sighed. "You're probably right. They're closed, anyhow. Shucks. Let's get going. I want to get where we're going before it gets dark."

A minute later, Bea and Pat were standing in the parking lot of a small building that housed a drug store and a bank branch. After scanning the area for a minute, Bea pointed to an empty bus stop in front of it.

"Let's sit a spell."

"Our adventure involves riding a city bus?"

"Not exactly," Bea said, making herself comfortable on the bench. "See that building across the street? Where that guy's entering? That's where the professor lives." A slender man, middle-aged, pressed a button on the building's keypad, then waited for someone to buzz him in. He was wearing a cardigan sweater and a tweedy cap.

"Are we here to tell the professor his trailer's ready?"

"Yep. But first, a little research. It's time for you to put your detective hat on."

"It would help if you told me what we're looking for."

"You know how the professor thinks it was our fault someone snagged a dose of his fancy tree food?"

"Yes. Technically, I thought he considered it all my fault."

"He acts like secrecy is everyone else's responsibility but his. We've had a few slip-ups, but I have a hunch he's got more leaks than we do. And now that we're moving to the next phase, I want to know what some of them are—'cause I won't be surprised if that thief tries again, and when that happens, I'm not taking the blame by default. I've got money in this thing now, and I don't want him to blame us for a breach and use it as an excuse to cut us out. It's starting to look like this wacky tree experiment might actually pay off."

"Ah, I get ya," Pat said.

"I've already noticed a couple of things, too. Watch—someone's approaching his building."

A scruffy-looking couple in dirty coats pressed a unit number on the keypad. Bea and Pat could hear the buzzer from where they were sitting, but no voice came out of the speaker, and the visitors didn't say anything into it, either—just grabbed the door once it unlocked.

"I don't think that intercom system even works," Bea said. "And here's another thing. See those huge windows on the second floor?"

"Sure. Can't miss 'em."

"Notice anything weird about them?"

"No shades?"

"Egg-zactly!" Bea said, holding her fist up to bump against Pat's. "I wonder how the professor sleeps, with all the light from the street streaming in. But there's something else. Turn around."

The two of them swiveled to look at a drab,

squat four-unit building just behind the bank parking lot. The two units on its top floor had large windows. One of them looked like it had a telescope in it.

"You think that thing's pointed at the professor's place?"

"Could be, right? If someone wanted to watch him from there, maybe they wouldn't even need one, though."

"You're pretty observant for an old lady."

"Play poker professionally and you learn to sit and observe for hours. That, and you perfect your jokes. Ready for phase two?"

Bea led the way across the street to the professor's building.

"Do you know the number?"

"201. But let's not try that one first. I have a hunch it's easy for anybody to get in this building."

Bea reached up to the keypad, and after trying just two of the five remaining numbers, someone buzzed her in—without the slightest effort to find out who she was.

Pat grabbed the door as soon as it clicked open. Bea put her finger to her lips and led the way up the stairs. As they ascended, Pat tapped her on the shoulder and tilted her head down toward a corner at the end of the hall, where the two unkempt individuals who'd entered a few minutes before had parked themselves on the floor. Bea nodded and winked her acknowledgment.

At the top of the stairs, in front of the professor's home, Bea signaled again to Pat to stay quiet. Then she picked up the mat in front of the door and found what she was looking for: a key. She grinned from ear to ear and silently pumped her fists in the air. Then she leaned gently against the door, her ear pressed to it. She held one hand out to Pat and made a jabbering gesture with her fingers.

The voices inside got louder, and then the door handle moved and the door opened several inches. Bea and Pat lurched back against the side wall.

"Surely we can come to some kind of agreement, Greg," a man's voice said. His tone was warm and vaguely pleading.

"What part of 'please leave' has confused you?" the professor said. "Furthermore, my name is Dr. Woodward. The university can fire me, but they can't erase my credentials."

"I know that, of course, Greg. But we're friends —surely you haven't forgotten that. We were practically partners, right? You can continue to call me Titus."

"Friends? How do I know you aren't the person who got me fired? You're not getting the invention as well—especially since your claims are invalid. If you'd actually been involved in creating it, you wouldn't need me to surrender it to you, now would you?"

The door quickly swung open the rest of the way, and the man in the cap and the cardigan stepped out, then turned around to face the professor. Pat and Bea stood still and held their breath.

"I'm trying to be nice, Greg. Perhaps you think this false bravado of yours is working, but it's not. I've argued to the university until now that I can intervene and keep things amicable. You don't seem to understand that I'm trying to help—as your old friend. But we're—you're—running out of chances."

"Keep threatening. It's worked well so far."

"It's not me, Greg. It's the university—and you know that neither of us stands a chance against—"

The professor tried to slam the door, but the visitor pushed on it, then caught a glimpse of Bea and Pat pressing themselves as tightly as possible against the wall, both wearing sheepish expressions.

"You've got some eavesdroppers, Greg. Unimpressive security for someone so worried about keeping secrets."

CHAPTER 7

"Aren't you going to invite us in?" Bea said.

"Why would I invite trespassers into my home?" the professor snapped, watching Titus dillydally his way down the stairs, clearly hopeful he'd overhear something useful. "Shh!" the professor added under his breath.

"Don't mind me, I'll be on my way now," Titus shouted, grabbing the door handle at the front entrance. "Good luck, Greg. I mean it—you're going to need it."

Once he was gone, the professor breathed a huge sigh and hurriedly ushered Bea and Pat into his home.

"Whatever prompted this unpleasant surprise visit, I trust you'll reveal it posthaste."

"Nice to see you, too, doc," Bea said. "And here we are, rushing to Emeryville to deliver great news. Imagine what you'd be like if someone showed up empty-handed."

The professor glowered at Bea and declined to answer. Bea nosed unabashedly around his large space.

"Where's your typewriter?" She looked at the table and noticed the Selectric had been swapped out for one of the older, black manuals and a note pad with numerous sheets curled over its spine.

"In the shop for maintenance."

"So that was it in the window."

"Yes, I allow them to display it there. They like to let passersby know what kinds of machines the shop works on. Luckily, I've finished most of what I need to do at the moment. Only a few more days' work on this old treasure and the rest I can accomplish with my pen. Just don't tell any covetous coveters that I've put their inheritance to work."

"Speaking of work, professor, we're ready for the next stage of ours. The baby trees have outgrown their cribs. And speaking of cribs, your trailer is ready for you to move in."

"You can't plant them until I arrive! The treatment protocol must move to phase three and it must be done with utmost precision. They've outgrown the drip ports now. I'll need to set up the trunk injectors to infuse the trees with the next formula. You'll simply have to wait a few days—as we planned."

"I'm not sure that's possible. Didn't you warn us about the pots killing the trees if they're too congested? We may have been too successful in our part of the experiment. I'm kind of surprised you don't look more grateful. Don't worry, you can thank me later!" Bea added with a cackle.

"I must finish here," the professor said, putting his gray, wrinkled face in his hands. "I suppose there's only one solution, sub-optimal though it is."

Pat retrieved her car from the casino lot, parked in front of the building, and pressed the button for the professor's unit. Upstairs, Bea and the professor had started preparing boxes full of "trunk injectors" that looked like Brobdingnagian hypodermic needles.

"Turn around," the professor said sharply. Bea and Pat complied and turned their backs to him, though Bea didn't bother trying to suppress a snigger. The professor filled the injectors in the first two boxes, which held ten each. "OK. These are ready to go." Bea and Pat took the two boxes down to Pat's car. When they returned, two more boxes were ready to go.

"Remember, attach these only if the trees must be transplanted. This diagram shows you where to place them," he added, handing them a piece of paper with a crude drawing and a small, manual drill. "You will need to drill a small hole, too. DON'T move the trees unless you absolutely must! We're at a delicate stage, and it would be vastly preferable for me to handle this process myself. Hold off unless you're sure the trees have outgrown their pots. But above all, it's most important that the new treatment begin within twenty-four hours of transplantation."

"Aye-aye, cap'n," Bea said.

"Why am I getting the sense you still don't appreciate what's at stake, Miss Sickles?"

"Why am I getting the sense you still don't appreciate that what's at stake is my money, Dr. Woodward? Here's an idea: Why don't you focus on getting yourself out to the wine country as soon as you can? You know, the trailer has a nice pull-down desk. You could bring your pad of paper and work there, and then you wouldn't have to worry about us little people bungling the tree IVs."

"I'm planning to. Now to that end, please leave me to my work."

∼

"LONG DAY," ASEEM SAID, WALKING INTO THE INN lobby to find Angela putting the finishing touches on the big, bushy Christmas tree. He'd just come from the farm plot, where he'd finished transplanting the experimental trees. The job needed doing, and, much like Angela, he'd needed a distraction from brooding about the upsetting prior evening with his family. "You hungry? Up for an early dinner?"

"Actually, I am," she replied. She'd helped him with setting up a camera on the trailer and with moving the plants into the enclosure before returning to her tree-trimming. "Tired, too. And I could use a shower. Looks like you could, too," she added with a smile. Aseem had smudges of dirt all over his hands and face.

His phone rang, and he pulled it from his pocket and turned it toward Angela. The screen showed Sanjay's picture. He hit the ignore button.

"Fifth time he's called today."

Angela sighed. "Not counting the three times

he called on the drive back last night, I'm guessing? Still don't know what to say to him?"

Aseem and Angela had hardly said a word on the ninety-minute ride back to the inn the night before. Aseem had been too angry to say much, except to repeat to Angela that his family was behaving strangely, and that he was sorry. Angela had been in a state of shock, but reached for his hand at moments to squeeze it. She knew he was even more surprised than she was by how the evening had gone.

"That's about the size of it. How about The Little Burger Joint? Meet you back here in twenty minutes?"

"That sounds great," Angela said. "But wait… who's watching the seedlings?"

"We are," Aseem said, smiling. He held up his phone again and showed Angela the live stream from the camera he'd hooked up to the trailer. It was pointed right at the fence gate. "There's a motion-sensitive spotlight, too. And I put the new lock on. Give me your phone for a sec, and I'll add the stream to it. Can't hurt to have more than one of us watching."

"Perfect."

"By the way, maybe Pat could move to the trailer tonight. The heater works great, and I got the television going. We can send her up there with a selection of DVDs. But if she doesn't want to, I'll be happy to stay up there until the professor takes over."

Forty minutes later, they were in "The Little Burger Joint," which was more of a California-style café. The menu featured burgers of all sorts, but mostly healthy ones made of vegetables, falafel, and turkey, along with the kinds of sides millennials love: sprouts, fries, milkshakes, and large portions of irony. It fit in perfectly with the trendy shops that had proliferated on the main street of their Napa Valley community and had quickly become a favorite of Angela and Aseem's.

"Are you ready to talk about it?" Angela said, dunking a sweet potato fry into ketchup and mayonnaise. The restaurant had a pleasant ambient aroma of fried food and spices.

"I'm more worried about you. Please, don't hold back, Angel. Say whatever you're thinking. I'm just so sorry. Please believe me, I don't know why they were acting like that. Especially Sanjay and Preeti. My parents are always tough on me—on me and Sanjay. But Sanjay dishing it out? That's a new thing."

"I bet you're hoping it doesn't become an old thing," Angela smiled.

"And Preeti was so rude. I don't see them often, but Preeti's been nothing but polite and kind. Like I said, my parents are tough on me, always. But this was new, Angel, I swear. Plus, that whole thing with Mira—I have no idea where that came from! I barely know her."

Angela looked at him carefully. "I suppose… could it be because of how happy they are for Preeti and Sanjay? And how they love Preeti's family? Maybe that makes them think they should also have a say in who you, you know—"

Aseem laughed. "Angel, Sanjay might be their golden child, but trust me, he would *never* have let my parents pick his bride. He is far too stubborn for that. He and Preeti met when he was in medical school in Los Angeles. Her family still lives there. In fact, my parents might not even have seen hers since their wedding more than three years ago."

Angela took a sip of her vanilla milkshake. "Hmm. I think I get it. Maybe it's because you're the youngest that your parents are extra… protective. Maybe that's not the right word, but I get it about the expectations. My mom's like that sometimes, and I think it's because I'm her only child. It's like I'm her life's work."

"Maria? She's nothing like that. She's like your

cheerleader—or your best friend," Aseem said skeptically, before taking a big bite of his turkey burger.

Angela let loose a big laugh. "My mom's all supportive now, but didn't I tell you how she reacted when I quit my corporate job? We fought for weeks and then she didn't speak to me for three months. *Three months!* I would call her up to try to break the ice and she would say, 'If it's a matter of life and death, I'm here for you. Otherwise, I love you—but I don't want to talk to you.' All in Spanish, of course—'*si es una cuestión de vida o muerte, mija.*' Just to remind me that my Spanish is terrible!"

"Come to think of it, our parents would probably get along perfectly."

"Probably too perfectly. Imagine how they'd gang up on us if we actually did get—" Angela stopped herself. "You know what I mean."

Aseem reached across the table and picked up her hand. "I know what you mean. And whatever we decide, whenever we decide, it will be up to us. Even if it means we have to gang up on our parents."

Angela snorted and wiped milkshake off her upper lip. "I guess we wouldn't have any fights about Christmas, since your parents think it's trivial and all."

"That's the other crazy thing. My mother loves Christmas. I bet she'd challenge you to a tree-trimming competition," Aseem said, smiling and practically shouting. "Of course, she would lose!"

Angela made a heart symbol with her hands and giggled. "That reminds me of something—the trees. Do you remember you blurted out something to your family about our experiment? The one that we're supposed to keep completely secret?"

"I know. My father bragging about my brother's stupid surgery robots got under my skin."

"Stupid surgery robots probably have patent protection, though."

"The thing is, we don't really know any of the professor's trade secrets—except that we grow the trees inside first, then transplant them, and we feed them his super-secret serum. We know nothing about the serum itself, or other modifications he makes to the seeds. So why's he worried about us saying we're doing an experiment? It can't be that easy to copy it, can it?"

"When Cal dropped off our trees, he accidentally overheard me and Bea talking about the experiment. He heard me say 'tree scientist.' He seemed rattled," Angela said. "I told him that of course we still planned to buy trees from him. I wanted to say we'd give him some of our trees if the experiment worked—you know, to reassure him. But Bea reminded me we agreed in our contract not to tell anyone. It's so frustrating, when I can't see how we can keep the existence of the experiment a secret, anyway. The professor's so worried someone will figure it out. And what if they do? Thanks to him, no patent protection. Isn't that worse? We're doing something that could help so many people, maybe the entire planet, and his goal is to restrict access to it— forever. It doesn't seem right that we can't even talk about it."

"Especially since the professor himself likes to talk about it when he's in the right mood," Aseem said sardonically.

"What do you mean?"

"When I saw him at the office making his investment pitch, he was bragging to everybody about his discovery and how it would save the environment. It's possible, I suppose, that he thought that everyone there was automatically under a confidentiality agreement."

"Aren't they?"

"Not really. I mean, we all understand the need to help entrepreneurs protect their secrets, so we're sensitive about it when people present their business concepts. With so many people coming in to pitch, though, we can't sign confidentiality agreements at that stage. No early-stage investor does."

Aseem paused for another bite of burger, then put the sandwich down with a pregnant look.

"Besides, the professor wasn't just talking about it in a pitch. He bragged about it to anyone he met wandering in the hallways, including plenty of people who aren't part of those pitch meetings and aren't expected to keep what they hear secret."

"Wow."

"Exactly. The professor is worried about us, but he's the one who told a bunch of money managers and motivated tech geniuses how his invention would transform housing, retail products, paper, and who knows how many other industries."

"And if any of them happened to be greedy—"

"They all definitely are," laughed Aseem. "And not just that. You and I still have a hard time figuring out how letting slip to our friends that 'we're working on a tree experiment' translates to 'someone's going to copy it.' That's what the professor is afraid of, right? But odds are, the people he blabbed it to are a lot more likely to be able to reverse-engineer the invention than anyone we know."

Angela and Aseem were all relaxed smiles as they walked back into the inn lobby, where they found Bea and Pat had also just arrived.

"We cleaned up—played a tournament in Emeryville and got first and second place. Not too shabby," Pat said.

"And I'm giving you first prize, Angie," Bea said.

Angela clapped. "Yay! Am I going to be rich?"

"Not exactly. I'm keeping the cash, just giving you the special girlie prize. You can make better use of a spa day than I can. This is why I don't like playing in ladies' tournaments. The prizes aren't really my style."

"Oh, I'll be happy to use that, but I plan to share it with you. It'll be my turn to show you a fun adventure that's outside your comfort zone."

Bea shook her head and chuckled. "You'll also be glad to know we informed Dr. Treelove that we're ready to transplant the seedlings."

"Ah, so that's why you went all the way to Emeryville to play. You'll be happy to know we had a big day, too," Angela said. She then explained how she and Aseem had finished setting up the trailer, installed a camera, trimmed the big lobby tree, and Aseem even transplanted all the seedlings.

"That's great!" Bea said. "Except for one thing. The professor got himself into a full panic about the trees needing a special injector at this stage. He gave us two boxes to take back with us. He was hoping he'd get here in time to do it himself, but it's a good thing he gave us the stuff. Since he says the injections must start within twenty-four hours of transplantation, he's going to have to trust us."

"We could start on it tonight, if you like," Aseem said, yawning. "Maybe we do the first ten we planted? The spotlight shines directly on the trees closest to the gate. Pat, if you wanted to stay out at the trailer tonight, it's all set up. I could run you up there in a UTV and we could attach a few injectors."

"Let's just do it first thing in the morning," Angela suggested. "We have until noon to get the first ones done within the twenty-four hours. Plenty of time. But Pat, do you want to stay in the trailer tonight? We fixed it up nicely."

"I'll stay there with you," Bea said. "You said

you wanted more poker lessons. We could do that and eat pizza."

"Great plan!" Angela said. "I'll order your usual pizza. Bea, you and Pat go grab whatever you need for your sleepover. Aseem and I will bring the boxes with the injectors inside for safekeeping until tomorrow. Then we'll fire up the UTVs and shuttle you out there."

CHAPTER 8

The sun was barely up when Angela attached the little wagon to the back of the UTV, filled it up with the boxes of injectors, grabbed coffee for all, and headed across the pasture to the tree farm site. She'd expected to have to wake Bea and Pat up, but they were awake and squabbling.

"Angie, did you bring iced coffee?" Bea said. "There's not enough caffeine in the world this morning—"

"You seemed to be sleeping fine when you stole all the covers," Pat said. "You're a little smaller than I am, but you're surprisingly strong."

Angela's eyebrows headed for her hairline as she tried not to laugh. Pat was not tall, but she was sturdy, and Bea was probably half her size.

"I see you doubting, Angela," Pat said. "But those spindly legs of hers are strong!"

"This ought to help." Angela handed each of them a steaming latte. "Sorry, Bea, you have to settle for hot today. But it has milk. I brought blueberry muffins, too."

The three of them relaxed on the bench seats of the UTV and enjoyed their breakfast and the rising sun that was warming the late fall air.

"It really feels like we're out in the middle of nowhere, even though we're still on the ranch," Pat said.

"That's why I didn't want to leave you out here all by yourself," Bea said.

Pat looked at Bea curiously, seemingly touched by her friend's gesture. "Aww, and here I thought you just wanted to play poker. Thank you, my friend." She held her fist up for a bump against Bea's.

"I'm glad that's settled. Are we ready to start the tree therapy?" Angela said. The three of them huddled over the wagon and reviewed the professor's drawing. "Doesn't look too hard, does it?"

Angela unlocked the gate and tugged it outward to prop it open. She looked at the combination lock and decided to lock it. "Can't be too careful, I suppose."

"Yep, Jack the Ripper could stumble upon the world's puniest, most secluded farm and lock us three ladies inside!" Bea chortled, slapping her thigh. "Could you blame him, though? I mean, look at us!" Bea did one of her clumsy spins. She finished it with a dramatic hand gesture, as if to show off the elegant contours of her mall-walker ensemble.

"Very funny, Bea," Angela smiled. "I just want to be sure we don't lose the lock or forget to reset it on the way out." Then she looked around the plot and the large fence that surrounded it. "Doesn't seem like it would be too easy to climb out of this thing if we got locked in, either."

"Or to climb in," Pat said. "It's got to be ten feet tall."

"Eleven," Angela said, pulling an injector out of a box. "Had to special order it. It's heavy-duty, too. With this, the lock, and the video Aseem set up, I think our little tree babies are pretty secure."

"I feel secure, too, Bea," Pat said. "You don't have to stay out here with me tonight. I'll be fine on my own."

"As long as you're sure. The professor should be here tomorrow, anyway—at least we hope."

"OK, how 'bout one of you help me with the first tree?" Angela said. "The chart says we're supposed to insert the injector right where the lowest branches protrude."

A few hours later, their project was finally done. Angela locked the gate and suggested they head back to the inn for a late lunch. "I'm doing a final tasting of samples from the chefs for Thanksgiving dinner. There should be plenty for the three of us, and it'll be fun."

"Are you sure we can leave the trees? Especially now that we've loaded them up with drugs?" Pat said.

Angela showed them the video stream on her phone. "We can monitor them on the go. I think it's fine to leave them a while as long as we monitor the video—and as long as you'll be back before it gets dark. Overnight's when any tampering is most likely to happen, right?"

They bundled themselves back into the UTV, headed back to the inn, and stowed the wagon back in the barn, then headed to the ballroom. Jackson was putting finishing touches on some Christmas decorations Angela had laid out and helping the culinary team by setting up a table for the tasting. Bea, Pat, and Angela pulled up chairs.

"How many people are we expecting for Turkey Day?" Bea said.

"I put out the word to all the families that came for Halloween," Angela said. "Plus any others who might not be able to prepare a holiday dinner easily—you know, police and fire, people who have to work. I put a notice on our website, too. We're still getting calls—in fact, Jackson tells me another family signed up this morning. Oh, and Bea, you'll be happy to know Sergeant McGregor and his wife are coming."

"Oh, joy," Bea said. "One less thing to be thankful for. Maybe two. I haven't met Beef Jerky's wife yet."

"I thought you and McGregor were getting along better. You're backsliding. You promised you'd try to be nicer."

"Puh-leeze! Everyone else says I'm going soft!"

"They don't live with you."

"Good one, girlie. Knowing I can take credit for your sassification takes some of the sting out of my decline."

After trying the delights the chefs had whipped up, the three ladies pronounced themselves satisfied—and ready for a nap.

"Didn't even have that much turkey," Pat said

with a big yawn. "Just a few bites of breast and I'm ready to snooze."

"Probably had nothing to do with sampling two kinds of potatoes plus apple, pumpkin, and pecan pie," Bea cackled.

"Fresh air will help," Angela said buoyantly. "Let's rally! We could go for a walk."

"I think fresh air's a good idea, but I'll get mine up at the tree farm," Pat said. "I'll sit out by the gate until it gets dark. Once I'm in the trailer, that motion-sensitive light Aseem set up will alert me to any intruder, right?"

"Heck yeah," Bea said. "It's like the kind they use to keep prisoners of war awake."

"Question for you two," Angela said, walking toward the French doors and pointing to where the potted tree they'd brought back from their first visit to the professor stood. True to his word, it had grown to about five feet tall before they stopped treating it. Now it looked lonely and small on the large deck. "What do you think we should do with that tree? Since we stopped the treatment, the professor says it will grow slowly, like a normal tree. It's not big enough to use anywhere inside the inn."

"We could plant it with the others," Pat said. "Just have to dig another hole."

"Might be interesting to see how the growth of the experimental trees compares," Angela said.

Jackson piped up as he cleared up the tasting table. "Sorry—couldn't help overhearing. I'm just thinking a little decoration there would be nice, especially with our Thanksgiving celebration in just two days. That little tree fits fine on the deck. And you know how the weather can be this time of year. If it's warm, people might want to step outside to chat after dinner."

"That's a great idea, Jackson, especially because our first Christmas guests will arrive this weekend," Angela said. "Can you take care of trimming it?"

"Of course. And one more thing—Miss Sickles, Dr. Woodward called for you," Jackson said. "He said to tell you he'll be ready to move into the trailer in the morning. I invited him for Thanksgiving dinner, too."

"Perfect," Bea said. "That means just one more night in Siberia for you, Pat."

It took Pat about half an hour to make her start for the tree farm, what with setting her phone up with the tree farm live stream, grabbing a change of clothes, and waiting for Angela to pack her a hefty supply of leftovers and another jug of delicious cider. "Here are the fixings for hot cocoa, too," Angela said, popping the box of Pat's provisions onto the passenger side of the UTV. And a supply of holiday DVDs. You remember how to get there?"

"Yep, just head for the ridge to the edge of the property. Couldn't be easier."

Still yawning, Pat said her goodbyes and made her way across the wide-open field to the tree site. The sun was going down, creating a soft glow behind the foothills. She parked the UTV by the trailer and went inside to grab one of the two chairs. After setting it down near the gate, she took a stroll around the perimeter of the little tree garden.

She walked along the tall fence to the edge of the property, where the short side of the fence stood nearest the private access road. It was a narrow road with gravel sides, and as Pat looked in both directions, there were no signs and no connections to public roads in sight. She trudged around the other side of the plot, back to the gate and the welcome sight of the chair, which she immediately plopped into.

Phew. I only wish I had a comfier chair. At least the sun's almost down. Once it sets, I can grab a nice nap inside.

Pat yawned again and tried to pass the time

considering which of the DVDs Angela had packed most caught her fancy. She was still undecided when, despite her best efforts and upright position, she nodded off in her uncomfortable chair.

WHEN A SHRIEK STARTLED HER AWAKE, SHE HAD NO idea how long she'd been asleep. She looked up to see a barn owl, a doomed rodent in its talons, taking flight on its huge wings toward the inn, illuminated in the night sky by the rising moon.

"You again?" she laughed aloud. "You sure are loud, but there's no denying you're a majestic creature. Well, maybe you're not the same owl that woke me up last time, but I bet you could be." She remembered how that owl encounter had led to her ill-fated trip to the bathroom. "At least this time I didn't leave my post. Watch over me, noisy wise one!" she said, picking up the chair and heading into the trailer for the night.

∽

"LEXIE?" ANGELA SAID, PICKING UP HER CELL phone from the nightstand and staring at it blearily. "Why are you calling at this hour?"

Lexie Greene was a reporter for the *Sacramento Bee.* Her relationship with Angela had begun, inauspiciously, nearly a year before. At that time, Lexie was still working as a junior reporter at the *Wine Country Grapevine,* writing about local events. While covering BettyCon, Lexie had made the mistake of aiming her saucy allure in the direction of Aseem. But as the fates would have it, Aseem had proven immune to Lexie's charms. Lexie had also redeemed herself by authoring a bestselling crime book with Bea—another home run for Betty Snickerdoodle, Inc., so a truce between her and Angela was forged. The acclaim her book attracted had also catapulted Lexie into her job at the *Bee* and the big leagues of journalism.

"You won't like it. But you'd like it even less if I didn't warn you," Lexie said. "There's a story launching on our website this morning. I sent you a preview. Check your email."

Angela sighed. She put her cell on speaker, then rolled out of bed and slid her feet into her slippers. She sat at her desk and opened her email. Lexie's message was right on top. She clicked on the link and gasped as she read the headline and first paragraph.

S.O.S. Targets Secret Betty
Snickerdoodle Grow Operation:
Eco-terrorism Group Claims Hit
on Napa Complex
by Lexie Greene

(SACRAMENTO, CA — November 27)
The clandestine international
eco-terrorism group that calls
itself "S.O.S." has taken
credit for an attack on an
apparent experimental farm in
the Napa Valley wine country,
the *Bee* has learned.

Accompanying the article was a photograph of a crude sign attached to a very young tree, of the same variety and size as the trees in the Christmas tree farm. It was handwritten with a thick marker, in the shaky style of someone writing with their non-dominant hand.

Innocent lives will end because of your ghastly efforts to alter the will of Nature! The cost of your arrogance will soon be clear. Stop, in the name of morality. Let this life be the last that is sacrificed on the altar of your unchecked ego and hideous greed!

—*S.O.S.*
   STEMS OVER STUFF

THE TREE IN THE PICTURE LOOKED TO ANGELA LIKE the ones she and Aseem had transplanted. But it appeared to be ill or dying, its trunk bent to one side, its once robust branches hanging wanly down, its needles mostly gone. The sign had been affixed to the injector. The color of the liquid inside the tube looked slightly different than Angela recalled.

It doesn't look like one of ours, but it is a decent fake.

"That liquid—" Angela started to question the photograph, but stopped herself from revealing anything. "Lexie, why would you publish this without validating it?"

"Hey, I could ask you why you didn't give me the scoop on your secret farming operation."

"I'm not confirming or denying that this tree is on our property," Angela said. "But if we did have a 'secret grow operation,' wouldn't telling you be the worst way to keep the secret?"

Lexie laughed. "You have a point. But look, I got the message direct from SOS. I had no choice but to do the story. Predictably, my editor insisted we try to be first with it. I don't know if any other news outlets got the same email we did, either. I'm sorry, Angela. But at least you have a chance to get ahead of the story—a brief chance."

Angela thanked Lexie and started to hang up.

"Lexie—you still there?"

"I'm here."

"Maybe we can help each other. If I had some knowledge related to the tree in the picture—and I'm not saying I do—could we speak off the record? I mean, if I found out something that might confirm or refute the story, for example."

"Nicer to work together, right? So yeah, we can speak confidentially. What have you got?"

"I'm not sure yet. But I'll be in touch if I find anything out."

"Standing by. But Angela, one thing I must be clear about," Lexie said. "I can't promise to hold off publishing anything I get from other sources —'cause, you know, it's my job."

"I get it."

Angela hung up and considered what to do

next. No one else was up. Could someone have gotten past Pat and into the tree plot? That seemed unlikely. Angela looked at the video stream on her phone: from the angle of the video camera, everything looked fine. Untouched. She decided that it probably wasn't one of their trees. But since she was awake now, it couldn't hurt to get dressed and take the second UTV out to the farm site, to confirm for herself, and maybe for Lexie, that the photo wasn't real.

CHAPTER 9

Angela was relieved to find the gate of their tree farm still locked. She felt surer that the ill-fated tree in the picture couldn't be one of theirs. Someone, somehow, had known enough about their trees to fake the whole thing.

Would that really be better, though?

For the moment, she decided it would. It would mean that someone had learned a lot about their experiment—enough to imitate it. But that seemed less bad than another breach of the experiment she, Bea, and Aseem were overseeing, and especially preferable to having to admit that to the professor.

She thought about waking Pat, but dawn was just breaking. The time on her cell phone said it was not even six-thirty. She gave Pat a few more minutes to snooze.

The morning air was crisp and clean, but chilly. Angela shoved her hands into the pockets of her hoodie and took a meander around the tree farm. She walked to the edge of the property, to the private access road, and looked in each direction.

It would be hard to find this place even if you wanted to. Right?

She walked along the road, the back fence of the tree plot to her left. The fence loomed large. If someone managed to find it out here in the middle of nowhere, Angela wondered how tempting it would be. The privacy screens blocked all view of what was behind the fence. The chain link was securely attached to posts embedded deep in the ground. It was the tallest chain-link fence she'd ever seen. It didn't seem to invite climbers.

She looked back at the trailer, at the light and the camera Aseem had installed. That super-bright light would surely scare off any trespasser. And the light was far too bright for Pat to sleep through.

The more she thought about it, the more certain she felt that the tree in the picture couldn't have been one of theirs. She felt herself relax as she made her way back to the front of the plot, to the gate.

Just one last step to confirm my theory. Then I can let Lexie know that she was duped by some effective fakery.

Though she felt a little guilty about it, the thought of telling Lexie she'd been duped made Angela chuckle.

She unlocked the gate and walked into the little farm. The trees in the front row looked healthy and strong.

Not just healthy—beautiful. They're beginning to look like quintessential Christmas trees. And they've grown even more already!

Angela basked for a moment in the prettiness of the young evergreens and the success of their experiment. It was thrilling to think their gamble was working. If the project continued like this, they'd have plenty of trees for BettyCon in January—fresh trees, lush trees, in-no-way-artificial trees. She leaned in to one and inhaled its piney perfume.

But then she walked to the right side of the little farm, glancing toward the back of the plot, the farthest right corner. That last tree—was it listing? Were those needles on the ground?

Angela inhaled sharply and trudged down the row to confirm the terrible truth: The tree was dead. And on its trunk was affixed the same threatening sign she'd seen in Lexie's article.

Angela sighed.

How on earth did S.O.S. find us? And how did they get in here?

After waking Pat, Angela decided they should head back to the inn and pick up Bea before deciding what to do next.

"Let's drive both UTVs back and leave one there for Aseem. That way, he can bring the professor up to the trailer if he arrives while we're back up there."

Pat nodded her head somberly. "I'm so sorry, Angela. I just can't imagine how they got in. Is it possible the light didn't come on? I'm sure it would have woken me up."

"I think so, too. Maybe it malfunctioned. I'll ask Aseem to check the video. Then maybe he can figure out how someone got in without unlocking the gate, too."

"The lock might have been pickable," Pat said. "Definitely not easy, but I know some P.I.s who have that rare skill. Even the best would have trouble in the dark, though." Pat grabbed a clean tissue from the trailer and gently picked up the lock. "I can't tell if there's more than one set of prints on it by looking at it. I didn't bring my fingerprint kit with me, but I could go home and get it."

"I'll grab another lock back at the inn. We can swap out the lock again and store that one where no one can touch it."

After returning to the inn to retrieve Bea and the replacement lock, they made their way back to the tree plot. Bea immediately wanted a closer look.

"Look at the ground," she said. "Those are new footprints."

"Yep. Boots. Average size. Could be a kinda tall girl or a kinda short guy," Pat said.

"Brilliant," Bea cackled. "You learn that in detecting college?" Pat looked a little wounded. Bea punched her lightly on the shoulder. "Just kidding, girlfriend. We know this wasn't your fault. We gotta maintain our sense of humor."

"Here's something else," Angela said. "Look at the injector. Doesn't the bit of liquid left in it look different from the ones on the other trees?"

"Looks darker to me," Bea said. She was still looking at the ground near the dead tree, and something else caught her eye: an unusual imprint on the ground near the fence. Then she noticed there were three more.

"Look at that," she said, walking cautiously near the spot, avoiding stepping on both the marks and the footprints. "Angie, grab some pictures with your phone."

The imprints Bea spotted were four rectangular impressions in the dirt, two about a foot apart in the soil nearest the last row of trees, and a similar set about three feet away, close to the fence.

"Could they have been made by a stepladder?" Pat said.

"Just what I was thinking. I think we should look on the other side of the fence," Bea said. "I bet someone—or more likely a couple of someones, probably young, strong someones— brought two tall stepladders. Lightweight ones."

"Like fiberglass," Pat said. "Or aluminum."

"Sounds right. One guy climbs up one ladder on the outside of the fence. The other guy hands him the second ladder, and he hoists it over in this corner. Maybe he has to have it opened up first, so it's gotta be light. Then the guy steps off the first ladder, over the fence, and onto the second ladder."

"That way, they don't even need to unlock the gate," Angela said.

"Those aluminum ladders are so light, maybe even one person could do it with two ladders," Pat said. "But what about the spotlight?"

"It would only come on after dark," Bea said. "Maybe they came before dark. But even at this end of the plot, you would have seen them from your post by the gate, wouldn't you, Pat?"

Pat put her head down and hemmed and hawed a bit before saying, "I guess it depends on how quiet they were."

Angela and Bea both looked at her, confused, but then Bea let loose a cackle. "I know what happened. You fell asleep."

After a few weak denials, Pat eventually admitted she'd nodded off— "but I don't think for more than a few minutes."

"Really? Was it dark when you woke up?" Bea said with a knowing grin.

Pat frowned. "I'd rather not say."

"Why didn't I think to send Paprika and Dames up with you?" Angela said. Paprika and Dames were two miniature dachshund puppies that Angela and the inn more or less shared with Connie, who'd brought their mother, Bijou, to live with her at her property next door. Paprika and Dames were by far the liveliest of Bijou's four puppies, and still very puppy-like at about nine months old. "Those two never doze anymore, and they bark at everything."

"You can always ask the professor if he wants canine company," Bea said. "I doubt he's an animal lover, but you know those pups do their best to win anybody over."

"Speaking of which, look—" Angela said, pointing across the open pasture at the other UTV, approaching them in the distance, carrying two men and pulling its little wagon, which had a small suitcase and a hard-sided attaché case jostling inside it. "Here he comes with Aseem."

A minute later, Bea, Aseem, Angela, and Pat were standing with the professor, all of them staring at the poor, sick tree and the sign attached to it.

"You're oddly quiet, professor," Bea said.

"I'm engaging every last gray cell to deduce how to get you people to understand what is at stake," the professor huffed. He removed his glasses and squeezed the bridge of his nose between his thumb and index finger, then pulled a cloth out of the pocket of his droopy cardigan and used it to methodically clean the lenses. "It's a simple, obvious concept. Still, none of you seem to fathom why we simply must safeguard this experiment. We have the opportunity to save the planet. Yet for you simpletons, it's too much to ask for you to lock the gate to protect these precious specimens. They're just a bunch of spare Christmas trees to you."

"Listen, doc, we wouldn't be investing thousands of dollars of *my money* for a few extra Christmas trees. Why is that simple, obvious concept so hard for *you* to fathom?"

"We're talking about *murder*," the professor snarled, "and all you can think about is *money*?"

"It's not all I can think about," Bea said. "But surely even an ivory-tower type like you can see that investing money focuses one's attention."

"We should be focusing on who killed this tree. You dolts contributed with your inattention. But someone poisoned this tree—someone who knew how to do it. Smell this," he said, tipping the injector vial of one of the healthy trees in Bea and Angela's direction.

"Sweet. Smells like syrup," Angela said.

"Now smell this." The professor tilted the vial of the dead tree toward them.

"I don't smell anything," Bea said.

"Exactly. And look at the darker color. I believe this is a powerful herbicide called Formort. It's usually used for killing individual trees quickly by injection. It's designed to do it swiftly, without damaging any nearby trees, because little of it ends up in the ground. Arborists kill mighty trees this way, giants fifty or a hundred years old. This quantity would far exceed the poison needed to kill normal trees of this size."

"Someone wanted to be sure it worked—and worked quickly," Bea said.

"Yes. And perhaps someone realized that these trees—" The professor stopped himself.

"Perhaps someone knew that these trees would be stronger than normal trees. That's what you were going to say, right, professor?" Angela said. Aseem smiled at her encouragingly. "Someone knew something about your protocol."

The professor shrugged and resumed scowling. He picked up one of the droopy branches of the dead sapling. "Poor thing. A martyr for his kind."

Bea tried and failed to suppress a snort. "Should we give it a hero's burial? Pat plays a mean Taps on her kazoo!"

"I do?" said Pat, causing Bea to unleash a cackle.

"Despite your crass sarcasm, you might have a point. There's a chance the poison will leach into the soil. Because of our trees' accelerated metabolism, we can't assume that what's true for normal trees will hold for our specimens. By removing that risk, we can at least do *one thing* right to protect them. Maybe you people could at least manage to get a sturdy lock for the gate as well. Too much to ask?"

"We've done a lot right. We're going to double-check for prints, but it doesn't appear that the gate was ever unlocked," Angela said. "The attackers seem to have come in over the fence. They knew what they were doing."

"They chose the furthest corner of the camera's range. And at that angle, they could have just barely evaded the motion-sensitive light," Aseem said. "It didn't occur to me that anyone would try to climb over such a high fence. It would have required plenty of planning. They'd have to have known in advance what equipment they'd need to scale it."

"Which makes one wonder who knew to plan such a thing, huh, doc?" Bea said. "Someone would have to know how to find these souped-up saplings. And they'd have to have a reason to care about them."

Aseem nodded. "S.O.S. doesn't take on small fry. How would they hear about a little private investment at an inn in Northern California, a tiny experiment with as low a profile as possible? They had to have heard of this through a big-time connection—connections none of us have, but *you* probably do. Like an environmental organization, or a university—"

"That's right!" Bea said. "*We're* not the ones who have ex-partners and our former university employer threatening us about our little world-saving enterprise—you are. Or are you forgetting what Pat and I observed at your humble abode just days ago?"

Angela's phone chimed. She glanced quickly at a text on the screen. "You know, professor, we're planning a lovely Thanksgiving celebration here. Since you'll probably still be here, would you like to join us? Someone could relieve you on watch duty for a dinner break. You could invite a family member—"

The professor shook his head quickly. "Pfft. Thanksgiving. Please. Just because you can't stay focused on our priorities doesn't mean I can't."

"No family?" Angela said kindly.

"Family ties are profoundly overrated and many people are better off unfettering themselves as soon as possible," the professor said. "Besides, you persist in missing the point. If—when—we complete our objectives, we can rightly call Nature herself our family, which is exactly how things should be. Provided you can do a remotely adequate job of concealing our efforts from parties like S.O.S.—"

"You keep blaming us, but the only plausible explanation for S.O.S. finding this spot is that you were followed, or through your university ties, or some other contact of yours," Angela said, growing uncharacteristically impatient. "We can still avoid all of this stress and risk. There's still time to file a patent application. A patent would protect the invention, even if someone tries to steal it. Why is that *simple, obvious concept so hard for you to fathom?*"

Bea failed to suppress a chuckle and said "good one, girlie" to Angela under her breath. Angela's phone rang and she pressed the ignore button, then tapped it again to read a text. Her brow furrowed slightly. She tapped out a quick reply.

"A patent would also allow us to market it aggressively—and maybe groups like S.O.S. would see we're on the same side," Aseem added. "Actually, don't you think it's curious that S.O.S. doesn't see that already—"

"You people still haven't read up on Robert Kearns and his windshield wipers, have you?

Patent protection is a fiction that hypnotizes prey into trusting its predators! We cannot let that happen with the entire planet at stake."

"It doesn't seem like we can change your mind today, professor," Angela said soothingly. "And I'm sure you heard my phone. There's something I need to handle back at the inn."

"Good. All of you, leave me be—I'll hide out in the trailer and guard the experiment with the vigilance you people have failed to provide," the professor said, hustling out of the enclosure. The others followed behind. "If it's not too much to ask, don't tell anyone I'm here. And find a safe place for those supplies before you go!" he sneered, pointing to the wagon attached to the UTV.

"Don't you want your burner phone?" Pat said, but the professor just ignored her as he stepped up and roughly grabbed the door handle.

"Guess he doesn't want to be reached," Bea snickered.

"Guess he doesn't want to get into the trailer, either," Pat said, smiling and dangling the key.

Bea let loose another bark of laughter and slapped her knee. "Guess he thinks everyone hides their keys under the mat."

As the four of them piled into the UTVs,

Angela whispered to Aseem that Jackson's text said a group of people were at the front desk, asking about the trees and the "secret grow operation." Angela and Aseem quickly agreed to vary their route back, staying closer to the foothills to avoid being spotted. Bea and Pat went with Aseem in one UTV, and Angela led the way in the other. As they approached the inn, they peeled behind the casitas and the main inn building. That way, Bea and Pat could use the side entrance to reach Bea's suite, and Angela could zoom around the back way to the barn without being seen from the lobby. After she tucked the UTV in the barn, Angela went straight to the front desk to deal with the unwanted visitors.

"May I help you?" Angela said sweetly. "I'm Angela Garcia. I manage the inn."

"I'm Titus Melville," the visitor said. "I'm a professor at Avalon. This is Brandon… my… my technology assistant, and this is his—"

"I'm a friend, Margaret," piped up the heavily made up, middle-aged woman who accompanied them. She wore jeans and a sweater, both a little too small, and her hair was tucked under a puffy, oversized newsboy cap. Titus wore the same cardigan and cap he'd worn the day Bea spotted him in Emeryville. Brandon was in his twenties, a few inches shorter, and about thirty pounds heavier. He wore a thick sweatshirt and sweatpants and a look on his face that said he felt out of place.

"We read the story about the tree in today's *Bee*," Brandon said. "Doctor Melville is a botanist. We thought perhaps we could see them—the trees."

Angela laughed in a cool, calm way that would have made Bea proud. "Oh, yes, we saw it, too. Who knows where they got that crazy idea. We're not growing trees here."

"Actually, we're looking for Gregory Woodward," Margaret said, peering over the front desk.

"Jackson, we don't have a guest by that name, do we?" Angela said.

Jackson typed several phrases into his computer. "Nope—and I've checked through December. No Gregory Woodward."

"That's unfortunate," Titus said. "We're here about a legal matter. We want to help Dr. Woodward. It won't behoove him to avoid us, so if by chance—"

"Do any of you have business cards?" Angela said. "If this Gregory Woodward contacts us, Jackson will be sure to let him know you're looking for him." As she spoke, Angela gestured in a nudging way toward the door. The two men reluctantly headed in that direction, the woman squinting at Angela and hesitating.

"Perhaps since we're here, we can book a room at your lovely inn—"

"All booked through January," Angela said sweetly. "Sorry. It's our busy season, as I'm sure you can imagine."

"Thank you, Miss Garcia. I understand. Do you mind if we walk your lovely grounds for a bit?" Titus said as they stepped outside. "We drove more than an hour to get here, and it would be nice to stretch our legs before doing it again."

"Of course. Take your time."

Titus stared for a moment in the direction of the parking area.

"You know, I couldn't help noticing that car when we parked," he said, pointing at an older silver sedan. "It looks just like our friend Gregory's."

"That one? That's a very common make and model, isn't it?" Angela said. She caught herself staring at a visible dent on the rear fender of the car and stopped herself. She hoped it wouldn't identify the car as the professor's. "Well, if you're looking for a nice, low-key hike, I recommend the trail that runs from near the little barn on our property up to Heavenly West, the property next door. You'll have picturesque wine country views along the way. And the weather's just perfect for a brisk walk."

"That does sound lovely. Shall we?" Brandon and Margaret nodded and the three of them headed down toward the trail.

Angela watched them approach the barn, then saw Titus turn around to look for her. She slipped back toward the inn entrance as if heading inside, pretending she didn't notice him, then popped her head around to see what he was doing. She saw him lead Brandon and Margaret away from the barn and the trail and toward the deck off the ballroom. Angela watched him climb the steps and moved a little closer. She saw Titus inspecting the potted tree, looking curiously at the soil and the roots and ignoring its stunning decorations.

She started walking over and waved at him, catching his attention just as her cell phone rang.

"Can you hold on a sec?" she said into the phone.

Then she watched as Titus sheepishly turned from the tree and the trio headed back to the trail, looking back a few times to see if she was still there.

She smiled and waved, and when they were clearly on the way toward Heavenly West, she returned to the caller.

"Sorry, Lexie. Thanks for waiting. Good timing. I wanted to ask you a question about S.O.S."

"That's why I'm calling. I've got news about them, but why don't you ask your question first?"

Angela hesitated, wishing she'd let Lexie speak first. "Off the record, right?"

"Of course."

"Would S.O.S. kill a tree to make a point? I mean, would they consider it a worthy sacrifice to try to frame one of their terrorism targets?"

"I doubt it. Are you saying that's what happened?"

"How about you tell me your news now?"

Lexie chuckled. "Getting cagier, girl. Taking lessons from Bea, I see."

"Why am I sensing you don't want to tell me?"

"Don't worry. It's not you, Angela, it's me. It's just—let's just say that publishing that S.O.S. story hasn't helped me fight the naysayers who think I'm in over my head in my new job."

"What do you mean? Oh, wait...."

"Yeah. S.O.S. called my boss. They say it wasn't them."

"Who was it, then?"

"That's the next thing I have to figure out—and fast. I hope I don't have to retract the story before I can pull together a corrected version. A connected friend is helping me trace the email and the picture. I'll let you know when I find out anything more. In the meantime, let me apologize in advance."

"For what?"

"They assure me they didn't send the email. But now—now that they've read about it in the *Bee*—they want to know more about what's going on at Betty Snickerdoodle's Christmas Inn & Ranch. So you will probably hear from S.O.S.—"

"Oh, no!"

"Please believe me, I truly am sorry—"

"No, I mean—I think S.O.S. is already here!"

CHAPTER 10

Think, think, think!

Angela frowned at the vehicle approaching, with its clear "S.O.S.: Stems Over Stuff!" signage on both doors. She knew that if Titus and company saw that car parked at the inn, there'd be no discouraging them from nosing around.

She glanced up the hill toward Heavenly West, where she could still barely make out Titus, Margaret, and Brandon. She relaxed a little. At least they were still walking away from the inn.

Angela blew out a deep breath, hurried out to the road, and stood at the street entrance to the inn. Sure enough, the woman behind the wheel— she looked to be about fifty, with two salt-and-pepper braids—signaled that she planned to turn into the driveway. Angela waved her down and stood in front of the entrance. The driver rolled down her passenger-side window.

"Hello, I'm Angela Garcia, manager of the inn. I'm afraid… I'm afraid we're completely booked through the holidays."

You've got this! Besides, you're practically telling the truth—the inn will be full in just a few days….

But despite her positive self-talk and the crisp late-fall air, Angela felt a bead of sweat form on her brow.

"I'm Michelle Healey," the woman said. "I'm not here for a stay. As you can see from the signs on the side of the car, I'm with S.O.S.—the strategy division. Did you see the story today in the *Bee?* Since it affects both of us, I'd like to talk with you about it. I mean—assuming you have nothing to hide."

"Of course. Nothing to hide," Angela said with a weak smile.

She looked up the hill toward Heavenly West again. To her horror, she saw Titus, Brandon, and Margaret had turned back toward the inn. Angela looked around the parking area and quickly came up with an idea. There were more cars than usual because of deliveries and added staff for the

Thanksgiving event. Angela looked at her own car, which was parked next to Aseem's. The empty spot to the right of hers was reserved for delivery trucks.

"We've got a lot of arriving guests, and we're going to have some parking issues later today. That's my car—why don't I back it out? Then you can take my spot. I'll park in the loading zone. The front desk can move mine if need be."

Michelle nodded and Angela jogged to her car and backed it out in a flash. As soon as Michelle moved her car into the spot, Angela parked as close to its right side as she could. She hoped to make it less likely that anyone could read the sign on that side. Her car door only opened a few inches before bumping into Michelle's. Trying desperately to look casual, Angela groaned as she squeezed out of the slender opening on the driver's side.

"Oops, guess I got a little close," she laughed. "I'll move it after we chat. Why don't you come with me this way—around to the side entrance? I'm sure you'll want to meet the owner of the property as well."

"Good. I was hoping to meet Ms. Snickerdoodle."

"She goes by Bea. Right this way."

They reached Bea's suite and Pat answered the door. Angela introduced Michelle to Bea, then excused herself for a quick chat with Pat in the hallway.

"Was the guy you saw at the professor's place in Emeryville—his former colleague—named Titus?" Angela whispered. "Would you know him again if you saw him?"

"Yes and yes," Pat said. "I believe he'd recognize me, too."

Angela explained that Titus and his two friends were stalling their departure from the inn, snooping as they walked the grounds, and that she wanted to make sure they didn't run into Michelle —or Bea or Pat.

"This is where your private detective skills come in handy, right?"

"Yep. I'll go watch for them. I'll be sneaky. And I'll text you as soon as it's safe to bring Michelle back to the parking lot."

"One more thing. If you can manage it, I think the S.O.S. signs on her car door are magnetic. I parked so close to her that the passenger side one will be hard to see, but if you have an opportunity, maybe the one on her driver's side can 'accidentally' slip onto the ground?"

Pat chuckled. "Consider it done."

"And maybe Jackson can tell them they need to leave to free up parking—could you ask him?"

Pat got to work and Angela went back inside Bea's suite to join the meeting with Michelle.

"Angie! Just in time. Michelle here was just explaining how the *Sacramento Bee* story was totally wrong—that S.O.S. never sent the paper that picture. That picture of a dead tree wasn't even taken by any of their people. She wants to know who sent it to the *Bee* as much as we do. And S.O.S. has nothing against Betty Snickerdoodle, am I right, Michelle?"

"We didn't take the picture," Michelle said. "And we want to know who's trying to get attention in our name. But if you have some kind of experiment going on here with trees, well, I'll need to know more about what it is before I'll say we have nothing against you."

Thanks to Pat and Jackson, Titus, Brandon, and Margaret were nudged on their way, none the wiser about the visitor from S.O.S. who shared their interest in the professor's arboreal project. Since Michelle kept her visit brief, Bea and Angela were relieved to get the all-clear text from Pat—just in time.

"Glad we got rid of her fast," Bea said.

"If you call 'watching her leave despite our

attempts to stall her' getting rid of her," Angela said. "Besides, I doubt we're rid of her for long," Angela said. "Her comment about 'property boundaries easily found on the internet' wasn't all that reassuring."

Evading Michelle's questions while adhering to the terms of their confidentiality agreement with the professor had proved all but impossible. They'd wanted to show Michelle that they were on the same side, but wound up pushing her in the opposite direction.

"If we were to invest in a tree experiment," Angela had ventured, "it certainly wouldn't be one that harmed trees. We love trees! If there's anything we want around here, it's *more trees*."

"Especially Christmas trees," Bea chimed in.

"And we care about the environment," Angela added. "We're trying to use more live trees. We've thought about artificial ones, but they're made of plastic—"

"Why not just skip 'using' trees?"

"Our business is Christmas," Angela said, her face scrunched.

"Business," Michelle scoffed. "Sounds like more wasteful *stuff*. Trees are living things. More important than *stuff*."

"Sticking to the matter at hand," Bea said, "now

that you've been here, you can see there are no evergreens planted."

"Then I suppose you won't mind me exploring the perimeter of the property. From what I've seen online, it extends for acres, out to the foothills, where nothing's been built as yet."

"You must have seen that the outer edge is undeveloped, and the only access is via a private road," Angela said. "Sorry, but for liability reasons, we can't permit you to drive on it."

Michelle smirked. "If you think we're afraid of trespassing, you haven't read enough about us."

Though Angela tried, mainly by reminding Michelle that they could help each other find out who impersonated S.O.S., it proved impossible to steer the conversation in a peaceful direction. Michelle was unmoved and when she got up to leave, Angela felt relief when her phone chimed with the text from Pat. She and Bea joined Pat in the parking lot, and as they watched Michelle drive away, they wondered aloud what her next move would be.

"Look—she's not going back the way she came. You don't think she'll try to find the tree farm, do you? I knew we should have teamed up with the other property owners to put gates on the ends of the access road."

"Who knows? Nothing more to be done, Angie. At least we kept her and Titus apart for now," Bea said. "Good job, Pat."

"You're right," Angela said with a sigh. "With Thanksgiving tomorrow, our busy season kicks off. I've got so much to do between tomorrow and Christmas and then BettyCon in January. I just hope we get through this tree experiment without any more drama."

"You'll let me know if I can help, right?" Pat said. "I'm here through Thanksgiving, anyway."

A FEW HOURS LATER, ANGELA THOUGHT OF A WAY Pat could help. Since she was busy working with the chefs and the servers on last-minute touches for tomorrow's Thanksgiving dinner, Angela asked Bea and Pat to check on the professor and make sure Michelle hadn't made good on her trespassing threat.

The late afternoon sky was dusky. As they approached the trailer, Pat turned the UTV's headlights on, and though they were still about a hundred yards away, they could see the professor hurry to the window, pull back the curtains and look around anxiously, then turn off all the lights and hide.

"Let's not engage the professor for a surveillance operation anytime soon," Bea snorted.

They pulled up beside the trailer and Pat knocked on the door. The professor ignored them.

"Yo, Greg," Bea called from outside the trailer, "you got visitors. Mostly friendly."

He peered out of the window closest to the door, his anxious, bespectacled face clearly visible to Bea and Pat. His face softened when he recognized them, and he opened the trailer door and stepped out.

"Sorry, I was afraid you might be—you know—"

"Your friend Titus?" Pat said, ignoring a cautious glance from Bea. "He's not here. Have you seen anyone else up here?"

"No, why? And of course I didn't mean Titus. I meant it might be the person who attacked that poor tree."

Pat walked from the trailer to the edge of the fence, near the private road. She looked both ways and shrugged.

"We were wondering if S.O.S. might have shown up here," Bea said. "One of their operatives came by. We didn't tell her anything, but she seemed intent on snooping. Turns out they didn't take that photo. They knew nothing about you, or the experiment—at least, that's what she says. But now that their impersonators have put ideas in her head, she wants to find out if we really are putting stuff over stems by tampering with trees."

"I wonder if they'll bring one of their organized groups up here," Pat said. "You know, walk along the road with protest signs."

"Why would they do that?" the professor said, regaining his arrogant footing. "Their raison d'être is attention. That and bullying greedy corporations. The two go hand-in-hand, of course. If she wanted to make you uncomfortable, she'd set up a protest in front of your inn, not here in no man's land. I must say, under normal circumstances, I might be on S.O.S.'s side—not the side of the money."

"Generous of you to sacrifice a little integrity for our enterprise," Bea said with a snort. "But let's say you're right that S.O.S. would prefer to protest down at our inn. Don't you think they'd want to make sure we're really growing Frankentrees first? They'd be shooting themselves in the foot if they were caught protesting the wrong villain, especially since they like to break laws while they're at it."

"At least you don't have to worry about that S.O.S. lady bumping into your old pal Titus, professor," Pat said. She didn't seem to notice that her confident assertion was followed by a slight wince on Bea's face. "We figured it would be a bad idea if Titus and his friends learned that the S.O.S. lady was sniffing around here, but we outsmarted them."

"Titus was here? On your property? That's curious," the professor said. "Can't imagine how my flabby brained former colleague made the connection to the inn—unless he recognized *you*, Miss Sickles, when you dropped by my home uninvited. Perhaps he identified you as that literary giant Betty Goldendoodle."

"Ha! Good one, Greg. But I doubt it. See, I was in hiding until recently, and only my truest fans would know me on sight. Somehow, I doubt Titus is one of them."

"You don't have to worry that Titus figured anything out, professor," Pat said. "Bea and Angela kept the S.O.S. gal busy until I could shoo away Titus and Brandon and their friend Margaret—"

"Brandon was with him?" the professor said, furrowing his forehead. "And someone named Margaret? Are you sure?"

"Yeah, when Titus introduced Brandon he said,

'He's my technology assistant, but he used to be Dr. Woodward's teaching assistant.'"

"Well, that's not right. Brandon's not—it doesn't matter. What matters is I can't stay here after all—not right now. I've got to get back to Emeryville tonight—there's work to do and I can't do it here. I'll need you to shuttle me back to the inn immediately."

"Guess I'm camping out in the trailer again tonight," Pat sighed. "Good thing I left a spare pair of underwear under the mattress just in case."

"Poor Pat," Angela said. "I know she was looking forward to her turkey dinner."

Angela was sparkling, playing hostess in the ballroom to the inn's Thanksgiving guests. The service was unfolding just as she'd planned it.

The ballroom was decorated in Angela's classic, opulent Christmas style. A majestic, artfully trimmed tree stood in the corner, imparting a subtle fragrance of pine. An eight-foot wreath with an enormous velvet bow hung above the fireplace, where a blaze crackled and popped. A video of a yule log, accompanied by holiday music, played on the enormous video display on the ballroom's stage, and children were dancing on a large square of parquet set in front of it. The tables were decorated with harvest flower arrangements, and an impressive buffet of appetizers was set out in front of the fireplace. Angela looked festive and beautiful in her favorite midnight blue cocktail dress and posh stilettos, her hair in a loose, pretty updo.

"One of us can bring Pat a plate later," Bea said. "But remember what happened last time. Not too much turkey! And we should include a big jug of coffee."

Bea had taken a different approach to a festive appearance. She was back in the green and red felt elf costume she'd worn on Halloween. To celebrate the start of the season, she'd dyed over the orange tips of her white hair with red and green. They poked out from the band of her belled elf cap, which jingled lightly when she moved.

"Bea, you know that Andy Mathers' sister Helen and her family will be here for Thanksgiving dinner. Aren't you worried poor Finn will think you're a witch again?"

"I think that little germ carrier should be worried about scaring me. I forgot to get my flu shot."

"It's Thanksgiving. There will be families here. Try to channel your inner Betty."

"You're always telling me to be sweet," Bea

whined. "Why don't you tell those pint-sized Petri-dish people to grow up?"

"That's funny coming from you," Angela snorted.

"I'm old and rich. Immaturity is my privilege."

"I bet you weren't all that mature when you were a professional poker player, either."

"You know that's different, Angie. Back then, immaturity was an occupational asset. Anyway, I'm not going to scare the little pipsqueak again. I've found a solution," Bea said, holding up her cane, dramatically presenting it to Angela as if it were Excalibur.

Rejuvenated by a new routine of daily dancing and her restored enthusiasm for writing, Bea hadn't needed the cane for nearly a year. But she still relied on it for special occasions—like when she wanted to trick opponents into thinking she was meek and frail, or like today, when she needed the perfect prop.

"See? I turned it into a candy cane again." The cane was wrapped from top to bottom with wide, diagonally placed white and red satin ribbons. The cane did, indeed, look like a giant candy cane. "Even that color-blind child will recognize it as the accessory of an elf—not a witch."

"I hope so," Angela laughed. "My mom's

already at the table with Aseem. Let's say hi. She's been looking forward to seeing you."

"Don't get up," Angela said, leaning over to kiss her mother on the cheek. Bea plopped down in the empty chair next to Aseem and Angela sat between Aseem and her mother. "Are you two enjoying yourselves? What do you think of the food so far, Mamá?"

"Exceptional," Maria said. "I'm so proud of you." Angela's mother wore her Thanksgiving best: dark velvet slacks, a silky blouse, and a sweater decorated with fall leaves and pumpkins.

"Me too," Aseem said. He was dressed up a bit, too, in slacks, a neatly pressed shirt, and an autumn-themed tie.

"Aww, thank you," Angela said. "Aseem, Bea and I were just talking about Pat. Would you be willing to run a plate out to her later? I know she's sad to miss out on dinner."

Aseem took out his phone to send Pat a text. "I just told her to let me know when she's ready."

"Where is she?" Maria asked.

Angela looked at Bea and then at Aseem, then quietly explained the basics of the tree experiment that Pat was watching over. "The thing is, we have to keep it secret. OK?"

"Of course. But to be honest, *mija*, I saw Lexie's

article in the *Bee.* I was waiting for you to tell me because I didn't want to pry. So it's true?"

"Partly," Angela said, lowering her voice to nearly a whisper. "Do you think the other guests know?"

"People were talking in the parking area, but I don't think they really believe it. They look around here and they don't see a tree farm. And they know and love Betty Snickerdoodle, while S.O.S. has a reputation for violence. But Angela, what's true about the story? I mean, if you don't mind me asking."

Angela kept her voice low. "Mamá, like I said, we do have an experimental tree farm— not much of a farm, really, just a tiny plot of trees. But that picture in the *Bee*—a woman from S.O.S. told us the picture wasn't even theirs. Someone posed as them, using their name to draw attention to our experiment. So now S.O.S. is interested in what we're doing, and whether it's something they actually *should* protest. That's one reason Pat's watching the farm, instead of joining us. She's watching for trespassers from S.O.S.," Angela said. "Another thing that's true is that whoever submitted the picture to the *Bee* also sabotaged our tree. By that I mean they *killed* it deliberately! And they had to scale an eleven-foot fence to do it."

"I see why you don't want to leave the trees unattended," Maria said. "Especially on Thanksgiving. Whoever's behind it might think this would be a perfect day to try again."

"Egg-zactly," Bea said. "Like I always say, Angie, your mom's one smart cookie."

The ballroom filled up and the atmosphere got merrier. The chefs filled the buffet with main courses and sides, and servers walked from table to table to make sure new arrivals had a chance to taste everything. Angela was in her element as she worked the room, making sure everyone had a wonderful time, even cajoling the recalcitrant elf, Bea, to tag along with her. Maria was just returning to her seat with a big plate loaded with desserts to share when Bea and Angela came back to the table.

"Those look great, don't you think?" Angela said. "Pat loves that pecan pie—let's be sure to save a piece for her. Aseem, do you think she's ready for your special delivery?"

"I've texted her twice and she hasn't answered. Maybe she has the phone in her pocket and can't hear the text chime. I'll go outside and try to call her. It's too noisy in here."

As Aseem stepped out of the ballroom doors, in walked Sergeant McGregor and his wife. Helen and Hal and their three children followed behind.

Bea ducked her head behind Angela. "Oh, no! Hide me, girlie!"

"Who are you avoiding, Bea? McGregor or little Finn?"

"Both!"

"C'mon, head elf. Let's greet our newest guests."

Bea grumbled but reluctantly tagged along. Sergeant McGregor had done his best to dress for the occasion. He was wearing brown slacks, a white shirt, and a brown jacket that was a size too small. The buttons of his shirt seemed to be protesting as well.

"You look nice, McGreggy, but I'm not sure those are the best Thanksgiving eating clothes," Bea cackled. "Your buttons already look like they're going to make a run for it. Don't worry, you can take as big of a doggy bag with you as you like."

"You must be Mrs. McGregor. Welcome," Angela said, shaking the woman's hand warmly. "Your table is on the other side—a prime spot near the French doors. Enjoy the view." McGregor's wife, a small, shy woman, smiled in return.

The McGregors walked across the room and Angela and Bea greeted Helen and Hal and their children.

"I guess Andy couldn't join you today after all?" Angela said.

The littlest child was hiding behind his mother's leg once more, but popped his head around to answer Angela. "Work."

"That's right," Helen said. "Andy had to work for a little while. He'll join us later." Then she leaned down to her boy and said, "Come on out from behind me, Finn, and say hello." His sister rolled her eyes. She looked uncomfortable in an outdated holiday dress and tights. The older brother, in a slightly wrinkled button-down shirt and chinos that were a little too short, scanned the room for other people his age. The little boy emerged reluctantly, a tear threatening to roll down his cheek. "Now shake Miss Sickles' hand."

Hesitantly, the little boy extended his tiny hand. Bea declined to shake it, instead offering him a look at her cane. "Don't worry, kiddo. See? I brought this just for you. Doesn't it look like a candy cane? I hope you can see now that I'm an elf, not a witch."

The little boy nodded and smiled a bit and looked at his sneakers. His parents and Angela simultaneously said, "Aww," and Angela ruffled the boy's hair affectionately.

"Besides," Bea said, hunching over the candy-cane cane, "even if I am a witch, the kitchen's pretty far from here, and so is the oven!" Then she let loose one of her standard cackles. To adult ears, it was merely an irritating noise, akin to nails on a chalkboard, and a hint that Bea was just having fun. But it seemed to have a terrifying effect on the poor little boy.

Angela looked at Bea with exasperation. "Helen, I hope you know Bea was just kidding."

"I *was* just kidding. Honest, kiddo," Bea said to Finn. But the little boy was now crying hard and paying her little attention.

Helen looked at her husband crossly. "Hal, this is all your fault! I'm sorry, Miss Sickles, my husband likes to act out the characters when reading old fairy tales to the kids, and I'm afraid your laugh sounds just like his version of the witch from Hansel and Gretel."

"I'll be darned," Bea said. "Care to share your rendition, Hal?"

"No!" said Helen and Angela simultaneously.

"I guess I shouldn't have mentioned the oven again, kiddo. My bad." Bea looked more impatient than sorry, but the boy's crying seemed to subside, even though he still gripped his mother's leg.

Aseem hurried back into the ballroom. "Pat's not answering her phone. I think I should go up there and check on her."

"Let's all go," Bea said. "I could use fresh air."

Angela turned to Maria and said, "Mom, could you hold down the fort here for a while? Jackson's out at the front desk if you need him."

The three of them hurried out of the ballroom, but a moment later, Bea returned and rushed over to Andy's family's table to talk to Finn.

"Between you and me, kid, I'm sorry. But listen, this is kind of a big deal for me. I don't normally do apologies," Bea said. She was leaning close to the boy's face. He was cowering behind his mother's arm. Bea looked at Helen, who smiled weakly and shrugged.

"How'd you like to wear my hat for a while? I bet you'll make an even better elf than me. Better yet, you keep it. Just promise me—this is important—that it'll be our secret. People keep saying I'm going soft, and I can't have that. I've got a reputation to uphold."

Helen put the hat on Finn's head, which brought a smile to the boy's face. "Perf!" Bea said. Then she made an exaggerated zipping motion across her lips and said, "Don't forget our secret," and the child's grin spread. That pleased Bea and she started to cackle, but managed to tamp it down. Her obvious struggle to suppress herself made the little one laugh.

"Good talk, kiddo," she said, holding her small, bony fist up to the boy's tinier one for a bump, then hurrying out of the ballroom to catch up with Angela and Aseem.

Bea, Angela, and Aseem piled into the UTV, Aseem behind the wheel.

"Thanks for taking my hint," Bea said.

"What hint?" Angela said.

"About all three of us going up to find Pat."

"I thought you were just trying to get away from that poor child," Angela said. "Or maybe McGregor."

"Excellent side benefits. But I wanted us all to go together for safety in numbers. What if Pat's in trouble? Definitely didn't want to send your handsome boyfriend in there all by himself."

Angela sighed. "I had the same thought. Let's think positive, though. We'll probably get up to the tree plot and find Pat left her phone in the trailer and can't hear it."

"Or maybe her battery's dead," Aseem chimed

in. "She'll probably be mad we didn't bring any food!"

The three of them laughed nervously, then fell into silence as the UTV bumped across the pasture. Sunset was just a couple of hours away, and the light was fading. Angela zipped her hoodie and pulled her legs up under her.

"Not the best outfit to be outdoors in," she said.

Aseem offered her his jacket to cover her legs, but she shook her head. "I'm OK for now."

"Hope we don't have to chase any bad guys, girlie," Bea said. "'Course, if Aseem catches 'em, you can always stab 'em with your shoe to keep 'em in line."

After what seemed like ages, the trailer and the little tree farm came into focus.

"No lights on in the trailer," Aseem said. "Could Pat be taking a nap?"

As they got closer, they could see that something was wrong. The fence gate was ajar. Pat's chair was still posted outside it—but she wasn't in it and was nowhere to be seen.

Aseem parked the UTV near the trailer and ran over to the gate, Angela and Bea trailing behind.

"Oh, no!" Aseem yelled from a few rows into the enclosure. "I think it's—"

"Is that... is that Andy Mathers?" Angela gasped.

She bent down for a closer look at the dead man lying face down in the dirt between the third and fourth rows, not far from the fence gate. His head was turned partly to the left, his face covered with dirt and half-buried at the base of the young tree amid scattered needles and broken branches. A huge syringe, like the ones they were using to feed the saplings, was stuck into a gash on the right side of his neck. A dried river of blood trailed down into his shirt, some blood forming a stain on the surface of it. His outfit was the same branded shirt, chinos, and cap that Andy had worn to the Halloween party.

"It's him!" Angela said. "That's his uniform from the home and garden company. Should we turn him over? Just to be sure we can't revive him?"

"He's not moving in the least," Aseem said. "He's got to be dead. And look at the color of his hand."

"Don't touch him, Angie," Bea said. "Don't move him. Don't get any fingerprints or DNA on him."

Angela stood up, her face pale, on the verge of tears. "Poor Andy! I can't believe our trees were the work he had to do today. Surely it could have waited." The tears started to come. "We're going to have to tell his family that he's dead—and on Thanksgiving." Aseem put his arm around her to comfort her.

"I know, girlie," Bea said softly, patting Angela on the arm. "But we should leave him for a minute. We can't help him now—and we still don't know where Pat is."

Angela gulped and her eyes widened as she realized she'd forgotten about Pat. The three of them decided first to check the rest of the tree plot. Aseem put a finger to his lips and whispered, "Just in case whoever did this is still here. Follow behind me and let's stay quiet."

The three of them started to creep down the left side of the fence. With the first step, Bea's elf shoe jingled softly. Angela and Aseem turned back to look at her and motioned her to stay put. Bea frowned but complied.

Aseem and Angela stepped carefully along the fence, peering down each row as they went, Angela struggling a little as her heels occasionally sunk into the softer areas of the plot. Bea watched them studiously at first, then turned her attention to the ground near Andy's body, looking for clues. She noticed some blue-green needles among the ones on the ground and leaned over carefully to pick them up. As she did, one of her shoes jingled, and she shrugged sheepishly at Angela and Aseem at the other end of the enclosure.

"It's OK. Looks all clear," Aseem said. "Should we check for Pat in the trailer?"

"Wait!" Angela said. "Did you hear that?" She leaned toward the fence near the corner, nearest to where the property met the private road. "I thought I heard a moan."

CHAPTER 12

The three of them rushed out of the gate, then turned left around the fence and back toward the road. Aseem led the way, followed by Bea. Angela trailed behind, wobbling desperately on the tufted, uneven terrain in her stilettos.

"It's Pat!" Aseem yelled.

Pat was lying on the ground, mostly hidden by tall grass. She was tied to the fence near the end of the enclosure, close to the road, blindfolded and gagged. Another oversized syringe, similar to the one found in Andy's neck, was on the ground next to her. It had a little blood on the tip but was otherwise clean and empty. A few tiny drops of dried blood led from a small wound in her neck to below her collar.

"Are you OK?" Bea said, rushing to Pat, bells tinkling. Aseem started to untie her.

"Wait," Angela said, catching up to them. "We should take some pictures before you move, Pat." Angela and Aseem took out their phones to make sure they captured the entire scene. Aseem ran back to Andy's body to do the same, while Bea and Angela freed Pat and made sure she truly was OK.

Once Pat was untied and they were satisfied that they'd taken enough photos, the four of them warmed up in the trailer while Pat explained what happened.

"Andy showed up and said the professor had sent him with more doses of tree serum. He had a box—I never saw what was inside, but I thought it must be the serum," Pat said. "I'd never met Andy, but since you told me he was the young guy who dug all the holes and that he brought lots of supplies, and since he was wearing the store uniform, I figured it was him."

"His older sister and her family are at the inn right now having Thanksgiving dinner," Angela said, tears welling again. "He's supposed to be joining them later."

Angela leaned on Aseem's shoulder. Bea

touched Angela's hand and then said, "Pat, tell us the rest of what happened."

"It's hazy after that. I remember letting him into the tree plot. He didn't have the combination to the lock, but I figured that was because you hadn't had the chance to tell him you changed it, so I let him in the gate. Was that right, Angela?"

"Of course, Pat. Don't worry."

"Then I think—it's fuzzy—he started checking all the trees carefully. We chatted for a couple minutes, but he was really focused on the trees. I thought he wanted to be left to it. I walked out of the enclosure and headed to the trailer. Then I guess he must have come up behind me as I was opening the door. I remember a hand on my face, covering my mouth. I got woozy. Then, maybe—" she touched her neck softly, "I think I might have felt a prick in the neck?"

"That must have been the tree syringe," Angela said.

"That syringe is so big, but I don't think I felt more than little poke."

"That's because you're a tough cookie," Bea said.

"Not tough enough to fight him off. I was so woozy. I didn't think drugs worked that fast. For a second, I was aware I was in the grass. It's all blurry —wait, I think maybe I got pricked after I was in the grass? No, that doesn't sound right. Maybe it had to have been before he moved me. I just don't remember getting to the other side of the enclosure. I'm sorry, it's all hazy. I guess he tied me to the fence and gagged me while I was unconscious."

"So after that, someone else—maybe more than one person—must have shown up and attacked Andy? I know I probably shouldn't ask," Angela said, "but you don't recall anything about that, do you?"

"Definitely not. I don't remember hearing anything," Pat said, touching the red spot on her neck. "It's so frustrating. Wait—I remember at one point feeling like I could wake up—I thought I heard clinking, like glass. But then it was lights out again."

"Let me put something on your neck, Pat. Even small puncture wounds can be dangerous," Angela said. "There's a first aid kit here in the trailer."

"It's nothing," Pat said. "Just feels weird. A little itchy."

Bea chuckled, earning a frown from Angela. "Sorry, I just never thought people got stabbed in the neck with a syringe in real life. Especially a giant tree syringe. It's straight out of James Bond!"

"Do you think I got injected with the same stuff that killed Andy?" Pat said.

"That wound in Andy's neck is so big, he could have been killed by that and not the drug. Plus, wouldn't the syringe have been filled with tree serum?" Aseem said. "Would tree serum knock a person out? I wonder if that stuff's even poisonous for people."

"We'll have to wait and see if Pat has a growth spurt tomorrow," Bea cracked.

"The syringe on the ground near you looked clean, Pat," Aseem said. "Maybe Andy brought fresh syringes for the trees and a little of some kind of human drug to use if he needed to be sure no one saw what he was doing. That could explain why the needle has hardly any blood on it."

"So Andy didn't want to kill me, but was up to some shenanigans he didn't want me to see? Maybe that's why the wound doesn't feel like much," Pat said, rubbing her neck again. "Then we think someone came along while I was knocked out, someone who wanted to kill Andy? Angela—while you're in that cabinet, could you grab my phone? Maybe it wasn't such a good idea to stow it there. I'm sure glad you came looking for me."

"Whoever killed Andy might not have known

who they would find up here. Maybe they didn't expect to find anybody at all," Angela replied.

"Hmm. In that case, maybe I'm lucky Andy knocked me out and tied me up out of sight," Pat said. "But now that I say it, that doesn't sound right. I mean, if I'd just gone back into the trailer, would Andy have left me alone?"

"It seems to me that it probably wasn't Andy who knocked you out, girl," Bea said. "I think we're overcomplicating things. My guess is that someone came here looking for someone else—or, more likely, something else, as in the tree plot. They probably thought they might have to put someone out of commission for a while. They could guess someone might be guarding the trees. They were ready to sneak up and knock that person out. It was the second person—poor Andy —who was a surprise."

"That would explain why they didn't kill you," Angela said. "As long as they were sure you didn't see them, they didn't have to."

"I wish I could remember," Pat said, putting her face into her hands. "Now I'm not even sure if I remember being stuck with the needle."

Angela found Pat's phone and the first aid kit and pulled out some gauze, which she moistened with bottled water and used to dab Pat's neck.

Then she put some antibacterial cream on the wound. "You're right, it doesn't look deep." She squinted as she looked at it closely and covered the spot with a bandage. "It almost looks superficial. But I don't think it would hurt to get it looked at."

"I'll be fine," Pat said.

"We can't say the same for Andy," Bea said. "Someone's going to have to tell his family."

"McGregor's at the inn," Aseem said. "Isn't that his job? In fact, shouldn't we call him?"

"How will he find us? He doesn't even know this place exists," Angela said. "Besides, what about the professor and our secret? How much should we tell him about our experiment?"

"Good point," Bea said. "Angie, you just gave me an idea. Could you and Aseem look for any notes the professor hid here in the trailer? Pat and I will go take another look at dead Andy, just to confirm he's the guy Pat let into the enclosure. If you find anything related to the experiment, let's take it with us before McGregor and his Keystone Kops get their noses in our business."

"We can tell already that nobody raided this trailer," Aseem said. "Or at least if they did, they were awfully neat about it. There isn't even a footprint."

Pat had a look on her face like she was racking her brain again, then she put her chin down and frowned.

"It's OK, girlfriend," Bea said. "I predict you'll remember something later. Right now, let's just be glad you're all right. Now how 'bout a look at our dead body?"

Inside the tree plot, Pat looked at the corpse and said she was certain it was the same man she let into the gate. Then Bea noticed something else: the drip syringes were missing from many of the trees in the first few rows.

"Andy's killer for sure used another to stab Andy. But then what? The killer grabbed as many as he could carry and ran off?" Bea said. "Looks like as many as ten are missing."

When the two of them returned to the trailer, Angela and Aseem confirmed the professor had left nothing behind related to the experiment. He'd left nothing behind at all.

"I haven't seen Andy's box anywhere, either," Aseem said. "Whoever killed him probably took it."

"Someone's trying to crack the professor's code," Bea said. "And that brings me to my next idea. Pat and I will go to Emeryville to the professor's place. Assuming you're OK to drive, Pat."

"I feel fine," Pat said. "Are you thinking whoever did this might look for him there? He seemed to think it was important to get back to Emeryville yesterday. And now it looks like he took all his stuff related to the experiment with him, too."

"That's why I want to be sure he's all right. While we're gone, Angie, you and Aseem—I know you're not going to like this part—you'll have to tell McGregor about Andy. Our little operation is going to turn into a crime scene. Can't be helped."

Angela's face crumpled and she sighed. "At least that means McGregor will have to tell Andy's family. But how can I tell him what happened without telling him about our experiment? And isn't he going to want to talk to you and Pat?"

"Easy peasy. You don't even have to lie—much. Tell McGregor we don't know how the experiment works, all we know is that it's a new food for trees and it's supposed to be secret. Mostly true, right? Then tell him I took Pat to urgent care, and that we don't know where the professor lives. OK, those are lies. Just keep reminding yourself it's for the safety of the professor—and for the good of our tree project."

"That way, we can warn him, protect him—"

"What I really want to protect is my *investment* —and my access to that Selectric! But don't get me wrong, the professor is growing on me. I kind of like that hoity-toity little wingnut."

"If we get to him before McGregor finds him, we'll be free to do whatever we need to do to keep the secret safe—and the professor, too," Pat said soberly.

"Exactly. Just two freelance detectives on the case, right, my friend?" Bea said. "In light of the somber occasion, I'm working hard to keep my emotions in check. But I can't lie, it's gonna be fun!"

~

BACK AT THE INN, BEA QUICKLY CHANGED INTO HER standard get-up—plum-colored velour track suit, beige sneakers—before leaving for Emeryville with Pat. Angela and Aseem stowed the UTV in the barn, then stood at the inn entrance, preparing themselves to reveal the shocking news about Andy.

"Angel, do we agree that we won't say anything to the family?" Aseem said. "We should just speak to McGregor and let him handle it, right? He's got the experience and training for this."

Angela nodded. "Experience. You just reminded me how Sergeant McGregor always complains we've quadrupled the murder rate around here. Something tells me that's going to come up again."

Aseem thought for a moment. "How about this. We could have Jackson go into the ballroom and ask McGregor to come out and meet with us."

"That's good. Then we don't risk being overheard."

"What can I do for you, Ms. Garcia?" McGregor said, joining them in the lobby's plush seating. He had a warm smile on his face and was smoothing his mustache with his thumb and index finger. "I was just about to dig into your fine desserts."

"I'm sorry to spoil your Thanksgiving dinner, Sergeant," Angela said. "But I'm afraid we've got some bad news. A terrible crime has been committed on our property. It's—I'm afraid it's murder."

"Murder?" McGregor laughed. "You're pulling my leg, right? I didn't hear anything."

"I wish we were joking. You didn't hear anything because it happened at the outer edge of the ranch, acres away from here. We've—we've been doing a project up there. Sort of an agricultural experiment—it's a low-profile thing."

"Huh. I guess those online stories were true? I read what that reporter Lexie Greene said. Looks like she's hit the big time at the *Bee.* You're going to have to tell me about this 'secret grow operation' of yours," McGregor snickered. "'Secret grow operation'—sounds like the kind of funny business Sickles would get involved in."

"There's not much to tell," Angela said, trying to stick to Bea's instructions. "Despite Lexie's colorful description, it's just a little plot. Like a big garden with some saplings. We offered a bit of land to a professor who's developing a new… a new plant food. It's all—it was all supposed to be about helping the environment," Angela said wistfully. "The professor wants to keep it secret. He tells us very little. What's important now is that a man was killed near the trees, and unfortunately, his family is here, waiting for him to arrive for Thanksgiving dinner. They're seated near you—three kids and their parents. The children's mom is the man's sister, and his name is Andy Mathers—"

Angela stopped mid-sentence because Finn came tottering around the corner, moving as fast as his four-year-old legs could carry him. Angela noticed he was wearing Bea's jingling elf cap and smiling with glee. The sight of him in the cap made Angela smile, too—but then she remembered the awful news that was about to ruin his family's dinner—and much more.

"Finn, where are you going?" Angela said, leaning over the arm of her chair as the boy came running in her direction.

"To meet Uncle," Finn said, racing joyfully past her toward the doors. "Uncle!"

Angela and Aseem spun around, then stood up and watched as Andy Mathers bent down and scooped up his nephew mid-stride.

"That's right. Uncle's my name, fun's my game," he said, grinning and shaking the boy gently above his head, prompting a torrent of giggles.

Andy was wearing normal casual attire, not the uniform he'd worn when they met him before. Angela gasped and Aseem's jaw dropped.

"You look awfully surprised to see me," Andy laughed. "I hope I'm not too late. Have you run out of turkey?"

"Um—you might not want to shake him too hard," Aseem said in an unnaturally chirpy tone. "I saw him eating a lot of pie."

"So—so, you must be done working?" Angela said. "You're—you're not in your uniform."

"Oh, I lucked out and had time to go home and change. I was doing prep for our big rush tomorrow. Black Friday tree sales—real ones already on the lot, plus artificial ones we had to pull out of inventory. Got pretty dusty, so I went home to clean up before coming over."

Angela looked nervously at McGregor, then at Aseem.

"Oh, I apologize," Andy said to McGregor, who stood up to shake his hand. "I'm Andy Mathers."

McGregor looked at Angela briefly with eyebrows raised, then introduced himself. "Nice to meet you, Andy Mathers," McGregor said, lingering over the name and deliberately catching Angela's eye. "Happy Thanksgiving."

Unsure of what to do next, Angela blurted to Andy that his family was in the ballroom and told him to head right in for his share of turkey.

"Don't mind if I do," Andy said cheerfully. He put Finn down and took his hand and the two of them headed to the ballroom.

"Well, that's good news," McGregor said dryly. "I guess he's not dead after all. Maybe there's still a chance I'll get some pie."

"I'm sorry, Sergeant," Angela stammered.

"Someone who looks just like him, wearing his same work uniform, is lying dead at the edge of our property."

"Yes, I know it's going to be a while before I get my dessert—if I get it at all," McGregor said, his jolly mood replaced with bitterness. "I'm going to have to examine the crime scene. I'm going to have to drag the coroner out on Thanksgiving. And I'm going to have to get Officer Babiak to come help me, and then I get to tell him he's watching the scene all night. I'm sure they're both going to be even more thrilled than I am. I must say, you and Miss Sickles are doing a great job of creating work for our little law enforcement community. Speaking of Beatrice, where is she?"

"She—she took Pat to urgent care. Pat was watching over our—the professor's—project, and she was attacked, too. At first, she thought it might have been the victim—the man we thought was Andy—who attacked her. She didn't see anyone else. She was knocked out and tied up while he was killed, so she has no idea who killed Andy—er, the victim. When she woke up, she had a prick on her neck. We thought someone injected her with an anesthetic. Andy—the man who looks like Andy—was using syringes to feed the professor's trees."

"How do we get to this secret garden of yours?"

"We usually take a UTV. It's a straight shot across the fields. You can go on local roads until you hit the private access road. But that takes longer because it's not very direct."

"I guess you two better run me up there in the UTV. I'll need to leave my wife the car. Give me a minute to tell her this fantastic news and call the other two." McGregor lumbered back into the ballroom.

"Tell her we'll pack slices of all the pies to take home for you!" Angela called after him.

"I know we should leave the detective work to the professionals—" Aseem said.

"Do you mean McGregor or Pat and Bea?" Angela said.

"Not sure," Aseem laughed. "But I can't help wonder whether McGregor thinks Andy is a suspect."

"McGregor gave me a weird look. Does he think it's weird that Andy's alive or that we're more annoying than ever? Probably both. Plus, the bigger question: It's not Andy's body in the plot, so whose body—"

"Happy Thanksgiving, Angela," came a voice from behind them. "I hope I'm not too late for turkey. It's a busy day in the tree business, I'm sure you know. Love what you've done with this one," Cal Banks said, admiring the dazzling decorations on the tree he'd provided for the reception area.

Angela turned to greet the red-headed tree vendor. "Welcome, Cal," Angela said, warmly extending her hand to Cal's strong, calloused one and accompanying him down the hall, toward the ballroom doors. "I'm sorry—is your hand all right? I hope that didn't hurt." As she pulled her hand away, she noticed a large square of gauze taped across Cal's entire palm. A small blood stain had spread underneath the bandage.

"This? Oh, it's nothing—a rope burn from hoisting trees. Forgot my gloves today. Happens the first day of every season. After all these years, I still haven't learned."

"Glad it's not serious. And don't worry, there's still plenty of everything left. Head on in and find your wife and daughters at a table close to the big tree in the corner. Another one of yours, of course."

"It makes me feel good that you still like my trees, Angela," Cal said. His eyes looked misty, despite his rugged appearance. "I give them my best, and I know they might not be perfect—"

"But they are perfect, Cal! You give your best and your trees *are* the best."

"So I shouldn't be worried about the tree on the deck? The live one? I know that's not mine."

"Oh, no—is that what this is about?" Angela said. "That tree was a gift. It seemed too small to plant, but too big to have inside. That's why it's on the deck." Then she placed her hand reassuringly on Cal's arm. "I want you to know I love your trees and only wish you had more. You already know I'll buy another batch before Christmas, and if you have any left in January, I'll be delighted to take them off your hands."

"As long as you need me and my trees, I'm happy," Cal said gruffly, brightening a little. "Happy Thanksgiving, Angela."

"To you, too, Cal."

Angela smiled as Cal's family enthusiastically beckoned him from the other side of the ballroom. She headed back to the reception desk feeling lighter, but as she rounded the corner, what she saw stopped her in her tracks.

Aseem was standing at the front desk with the last four people she expected to see: his parents, Sanjay, and Preeti. They were all dressed elegantly for the occasion, his mother and Preeti in silky dresses and pumps and holiday jewelry, the men in slacks and blazers. Aseem's mother held a large padded envelope with a bulge in its center. It appeared she was trying to hand it to Aseem, but he wasn't responding.

Angela stood motionless with her hand over her mouth. She caught Aseem's eye and saw he was just as stunned as she was.

"Ma, Dad—what are you doing here?"

"We came for dinner," his mother replied. "We thought we could have a nice Thanksgiving at Angela's beautiful inn, and at the same time solve the problem of you not returning our calls."

"I'm sorry," Angela stammered. "But our Thanksgiving dinner is reservation only. It's sold out, and I don't believe I saw you on the list."

"But we do have a reservation." She smiled and turned to face Jackson. "Do you have a party of four under 'Dickens'?"

Jackson nodded. "I do. Prepaid, but they haven't checked in yet."

"That's us. I assumed that if I tried to make a reservation under our own names, you'd tell us the dinner was sold out even if it wasn't. I know you're angry with us, Aseem, and I am sure you also must be, Angela. You deserve an explanation. This was the best way we could think of to get a chance to apologize."

Preeti walked closer to Angela, smiling tentatively. "I'm hoping we have a chance to chat today—and maybe start over? You look lovely, Angela. Your dress suits you perfectly."

Angela opened her mouth to speak, but no words came. She looked down at her feet—and noticed, for the first time, that her velvet stilettos were covered in dust from tromping around the tree plot. She felt embarrassed to notice there were even flecks of dirt all over her shins.

"Aseem, I'm going to change my clothes. I just realized I'm not appropriately dressed for—you know, for that thing we have to do. I'll be right back."

"Yes—Ma, Dad—Angel and I have something we have to do, and I should change, too. Since you've got a reservation, Jackson can show you to your table in the ballroom. Enjoy your dinner."

"Can we talk later?" Sanjay said, squeezing his brother's bicep.

"I don't know if we'll be back in time, Sanjay. But if we are—sure. Maybe."

"Don't leave without this—it's for you, my son," his mother called, holding up the padded bag.

"Jackson, can you hold onto it for me?" Aseem said, then hustled off to his suite.

CHAPTER 13

Following Bea's instructions, Pat pulled her car up in front of the typewriter repair shop. "Look! A perfect spot!"

"There's one a lot closer to the professor's building," Pat said. "But I guess this makes sense for surveillance purposes."

"Egg-zactly. Plus I wanted to check on my future writing companion," Bea said, pointing at the professor's Selectric, in its place of honor, under a light in the shop's window. "Yippee, safe and sound."

"Let's hope the professor is, too," Pat said.

They began the short walk to the professor's dismal building. In the distance, illuminated by a streetlight, Bea spotted the same pair of rough-looking characters they'd seen last time, once more poking buttons on the keypad, hunting and pecking for someone to let them in. After a few tries, they found a taker. From a few yards away, Bea and Pat heard the door buzz.

"Hold that, would ya?" Bea called out to them. Pat jogged ahead and grabbed the door from them. As she held it for Bea, Pat gave her a questioning look.

"Just in case," Bea whispered. "In case he's not home to buzz us in, I mean." Pat nodded.

The two who let them in quickly found their same huddling spot on the floor in the back corner of the first story. Pat and Bea ascended the stairs to the professor's unit. Pat knocked softly on the door. No response came, so she knocked again.

"What do you think?" Bea whispered, picking up the corner of the mat. "Shall we give it a go? Would be a shame to come all this way for nothing."

The building was quiet. They looked down the stairs furtively and decided to take a chance. Bea slid the key in the lock and turned the handle. The door opened with a creak.

"Let me go first, just in case," Bea said. "You've already been attacked once today."

"Aw, shucks," Pat whispered. "Let's do it together. And be careful."

Pat stood just behind Bea's left shoulder as she pushed the door ajar.

"Oh, boy," Bea said. "This looks like my old pad after it got tossed by Cash."

Cash was a crook who turned Bea's life upside down the year before by stealing a Betty Snickerdoodle manuscript. Though it forced her out of the secretive life she loved and resulted in the demise of her beloved Selectric, the episode had worked out much better for Bea than for Cash, who wound up in jail. Bea wound up cranking out bestsellers again and buying the inn.

The professor's place had been upended as rudely as Bea's old cottage. Right away, Bea noticed things were missing. Some of the supplies Bea remembered seeing under the lab table were gone, and there were fewer items on the tabletop, too. Bea and Pat looked toward the professor's little kitchen table. The stacks of typed pages that had been piled near the table were no longer there. The pages that remained had been rifled and littered all over and folded, crumpled, or ripped into pieces.

"Are we too late?" Pat said.

"I'll say," Bea said soberly. She'd turned to the left, toward the shabby futon sofa, which was opened flat under the massive loft windows. "Look."

"Yikes!" Pat gasped.

The professor was lying on top of the futon sheet, his face pressed down into a decorative pillow. The gray hair that hung from the side of his head was crusted to a dark red bloodstain. Now lifeless, his body looked even smaller than when he was alive. His right arm hung from the side of the futon and the left was twisted unnaturally behind him.

"That's an odd position for sleep," Pat said. "Do you think someone surprised him? Could have been someone who knew about the key."

"Not just an odd position—he's still wearing his bow tie," Bea said, peering into his face. "Someone hit him with something heavy—and sharp, too. That's quite a gash."

Pat leaned down for a look of her own at the large lump and gaping, sticky wound in the professor's temple. "He might have been dead awhile. I'm no coroner, but he doesn't look that stiff. Maybe rigor is wearing off."

Bea pointed at the shelves that held the prized Remingtons and Royals. "I think we know what the murder weapon was." The last typewriter in the row was missing. There was a silhouette of its base in the dust in its empty spot on the shelf. She stepped closer to the shelf and noticed a flat, rectangular box behind the typewriter that had been second in the row, and now was first.

"I'm gonna need that," she said to Pat. "I'm too short—can you grab it?" Pat reached up and snagged the little orange box with a surprisingly delicate touch. The print on the outside said that it contained a replacement ribbon for an IBM Selectric. "All yours," she said. It rattled softly as she handed it to Bea.

"And look at this." Bea pointed to a round scrap of fluffy cotton cloth that sat on the small end table beside the futon. The cloth had a brownish-yellow stain in the center. Bea rubbed it between her fingers and remarked that it reminded her of fluffy cloth diapers of her childhood. She picked it up carefully, making sure her fingers didn't touch the table, and put the cloth in her pocket.

"This too," Pat said, pointing to a box on its side in the corner. It was still full of empty syringes and drip ports. "Surprised they left it behind."

"The papers the professor was working on contained details of the experiment," Bea said. "Whoever came in here must have been looking for them. They wouldn't need those empty syringes if they had the complete instructions."

"Especially if—especially if this is the work of the same person who hit your tree farm. They've already got the syringes they stole from the trees —and whatever was in Andy's box, too."

"That was exactly what the professor was afraid of," Bea said, leaning down to examine some of the pages that remained scattered on the floor. "There's hardly anything left of his notes. Remember those stacks? Would have been a job just getting them out of here. No wonder they left behind anything they could easily purchase later, like the empty syringes."

She showed Pat a page with a big "X" across all the typed text, numerous lines crossed out, and notes written in the margin. "These are all X-ed out. Some are just random to-do lists, like this one. Item two: Selectric repair. I wonder if we could get that gem out of hock. It can't do Professor Woodward any good now."

"Now I get why you wanted that replacement

ribbon," Pat said. She bent down and picked up a thick piece of paper off the floor. "Does this mean the professor was an engineer?" The discolored parchment stated, in an ornate, gothic typeface, that Gregory Woodward had earned a Doctor of Philosophy in Biomedical Engineering from Avalon University of California.

Bea looked up from shuffling through pages on the floor and took the diploma from Pat. "Huh. Biomedical engineering—isn't that like pacemakers and stuff? I thought he was some kind of botanist. Wonder how he got into plants? I've never been an academic type myself. Are you expected to stick with what's on your sheepskin? Look at the stains on the back. I bet he kept it on the kitchen table and used it as a placemat for all those dirty coffee cups. He wasn't exactly cherishing it."

"Hard to know if he's dissing his degree or the place he got it. Here's something else you'll like," Pat said. "If you want to get that typewriter out of the repair shop, I bet all you need is the receipt. And guess what I just found?"

"Hot diggity! I've got something, too," Bea said. She held up an appointment card with the name of an attorney on it. "Trusts & Estates. Fancy address. Too much to hope for that ol'

Greg partook of his services before getting brained?"

Pat shrugged. "We done here?" Pat said, tucking the papers she thought looked useful into her jacket pocket. "What do we do about his body? Should we call the local cops?"

"Soon. But there's something else we should do first. Let's slip out of here real quick and quiet, so no one in the building realizes we were here."

~

ASEEM, ANGELA, AND SERGEANT MCGREGOR scarcely talked as the UTV bumped across the fields. Aseem drove slowly and carefully. The sun was down, and the UTV's headlights were hardly a match for the dark country night.

By the time they approached the tree plot, Officer Babiak was parking a police van on the side of the private road. He got out and pulled a tripod with a large light from the back. "Should I place it here, Sarge?" he called to McGregor. He tentatively placed the light near the bland compact car the victim had left by the side of the road.

"We can start there," McGregor yelled back. He pointed at the tripod. "Is that all the light we'll have for the scene? Aseem, any idea how long we'll be able to leave this little cart's lights on?"

Aseem shrugged. "Not long, I expect. Battery life for the UTV's headlights isn't great. But watch." He parked the UTV near the trailer and hopped out. As soon as he got within radius, the motion-sensitive light on top of the trailer illuminated the area in front of it, plus the front and side of the fence around the little farm.

"Not bad," McGregor said, pointing to the gate. "Victim's in there? Still pretty dark behind that fence."

Angela nodded and pointed at the far end of the fence, near where Officer Babiak was standing. "And we found Pat right over there. There's a depression in the grass. See the syringe?"

McGregor nodded and looked back at the top of the trailer. "What about that camera? Any video we should be looking at?"

Aseem's eyes widened. "In the shock of finding Pat and Andy—er, the victim—I forgot about the video camera." But then he stared at the camera, noticing something was off. "It's been tampered with. See how the lens was tilted upward?" He pulled out his phone and began tapping on it to access the video.

"Someone could have done that with a pole of some sort."

"Look!" Angela said, walking closer to the end of the trailer that was closest to the road. She knelt down and spotted a rod that was tossed behind the trailer. The end of it was just barely visible. "I think that's a rake. Someone could have poked the camera with that, right?"

Sergeant McGregor walked over toward her for a closer look. "Good eye. Where's that go?" He stood at the end of the trailer and pointed at the ground on its far side. There was a long stretch of grass that ran for a hundred yards or more, until it approached the base of the foothill. "That looks like a path." The grass had been pressed down and parted slightly, forming a narrow route. "Maybe a new one."

"I don't know what's on the other side of the hill. Undeveloped property, I think," Angela said. "At least, I think that's what was there when I last looked at the property lines. That was more than a year ago, when Bea bought the place."

"I've got good news and bad on the video," Aseem said. He set the video on quadruple time and turned his phone around so that McGregor and Angela could see the display. The video showed only a bit of the top edge of the trailer and the sky above it, which changed subtly as the sun set. "That's the view after the camera was moved. But before that, we can see our victim talking with Pat."

Aseem rewound and showed the footage of "Andy's" arrival at regular speed.

"Definitely not Andy," Angela said. "I don't recognize that man at all. But that uniform's just like Andy's."

They watched "Andy" get out of his car carrying a large box. He and Pat seemed to have a friendly chat before Pat opened the gate for him. They both disappeared briefly into the enclosure. Then after several minutes of no action, the camera turned skyward.

"According to Pat, she was in with him and the trees for a few minutes," Angela said. "The killer must have arrived and moved the camera just before she came out of the enclosure. She told us she remembers someone coming from behind her as she was entering the trailer. Bea thinks the killer was prepared to knock one person out, because someone would have been guarding the trees. But then the poor victim must have surprised the killer—"

McGregor cocked his head and grinned slyly at Angela. "Guarding the trees? Sounds like this experiment of yours is a little more valuable than just a new flavor of tree food, Ms. Garcia."

"It really is just tree food," Angela stammered.

"Tree food's big business," Aseem added. "It would be normal to have someone watching this kind of experiment, even though it would be overly cautious. You'd have to be sure the experiment conditions were not disrupted—"

McGregor chuckled. "You two can save your stories for now. We'll get to the truth in short order. And as far as Beatrice's opinion goes, we're going to gather evidence first and then we build our theory, not the other way around. But for tonight, it's too dark to do this right. We're not going to touch anything we don't have to," McGregor said. "Except you can keep working on that vehicle, Babiak. The light on the trailer's illuminating it OK."

Officer Babiak was already carefully looking through the glove box with a gloved hand. "Found a registration, sir. Says the car belongs to—"

"Keep it to yourself for now, Babiak," McGregor said.

Angela frowned. "You sure you can't tell me who it's registered to? What if it's someone we know?" She leaned a bit to her right, trying to subtly make note of the car's license plate.

"We'll let you know if we're interested in your recollections," McGregor said roughly. "And you can tell Sickles we won't be needing help investigating this time."

The coroner arrived in her van and while she unloaded a gurney from the back, Angela stared at the victim's car's number plate, repeating the digits silently until she was sure she'd memorized them.

"Angela, Aseem, you stand here at the gate, in case I have questions for you," McGregor said. "Babiak, I need that light now. Place it near the gate. Only the coroner and me in here. We need to leave the scene as untouched as possible so we can scour it tomorrow in daylight."

The coroner and McGregor snapped pictures of the body from every angle. McGregor called to Babiak again for help, and he pulled the coroner's gurney over from the side of the road. Then Angela heard her phone chime and stepped away to take a look: a new text from Lexie.

```
What's going on? Heard you got
cops and coroner up at your
grow op.
```

Angela sighed. Why did it always seem like

there was no escaping Lexie's nosy nose? Plus "grow op"—why does Lexie have to be so intentionally irritating all the time?

But then it occurred to Angela that if Lexie was after something, she might be willing to provide some help in return. She tapped out a reply.

```
Can't talk now. Will call
later. Promise.
```

"Angel! Angela—look at this!" Aseem called from the gate. "Look at what they've found."

Angela started to run past Aseem toward the corpse. The body had been rolled over as the team prepared to lift it onto the gurney. From the gate, Angela could already see that a sheet of paper with large text on it, stained with blood, had been under the victim.

"Hold up," McGregor barked. "I already said I don't want anyone else in here. It's hard enough to try to keep this scene intact."

"But that was found on our property," Angela said. "Surely I have a right to know what it was."

"Don't worry, I'll send you a picture. And you can get a closer look when we finish our examination in the morning."

~

"IT LOOKS LIKE NOBODY'S HOME," BEA SAID.

She and Pat were back on the sidewalk, standing under the streetlight in front of the professor's building. They were looking across the street at the parking lot at the four-unit apartment behind it, the one with the unobstructed view into the professor's big windows.

"Nobody's home or nobody lives there anymore?"

"Shall we go find out?"

They crossed the road for a closer look from the parking lot, but it was hard to make out anything in the dark.

"I can't see the telescope," Bea said. "Hard to know if it's there or not with the lights out. Let's see if we can get inside."

They lucked out at the door of the building. A young woman with a fedora and a chain running from her earlobe to her nose was exiting just as they arrived. Bea launched her sweetest little old lady routine.

"Oh, miss," she said softly, hunching over. "Can you tell us, do you live in the apartment that overlooks the parking lot?"

The young woman looked warmly at Bea, but then looked at Pat as if unsure what to do.

"My name's Chris," Pat piped up. "I'm a private detective, and I'm helping Miss Eunice find her lost dog."

"That's right, Christine, thank you," Bea croaked. "I came to drop off my typewriter at the repair shop last week. Little Petal got off her leash right near the bus stop. A bigger dog started chasing her, and, well, I couldn't run fast enough." Bea stopped for a dramatic gulp. "I thought she might come back here. This building, and that apartment especially, with its big window, seems like it would have a great view of the street. We would like to ask whoever lives there if they saw my poor Petal. We already tried to ask the people in that one," she added, pointing at the professor's building. "But nobody was home."

"What does the dog look like?" the girl said.

Bea said "fluffy and white" at the same time Pat said "dachshund."

"Sorry, sorry, I was confusing Petal with another client," Pat said. "Pet-finding is my main line of business."

"Chris, how could you forget what my precious Petal looks like?" Bea said, looking stricken and as if she might cry. "I thought you were the right person to help me, but now I'm not so sure. Oh, my poor Petal, all alone in the cold—"

"There, there," the young woman said, rattled by Bea's display of emotion. "I'll try to help if I can." She held the door open and the three of them stood on the tile floor of the building's dim, utilitarian lobby. "You mean that apartment, at the top of the stairs? That door in the back?"

"Yes, dearie."

"No one's actually lived there for a while. A man was renting it as an office for his company. I think he might have left, but I'm not sure. He wasn't there all the time."

"Why don't I go up and see if he's there?" Pat said. "You stay here, Miss Eunice. I know the stairs are hard on your bad hip."

Pat bounded up the stairs and winked at Bea from the top.

Bea hunched over and gradually turned her body toward the door so that her back was to Pat, and the young woman followed her cue. Pat pulled her picks out of her pocket and began working the door's lock as soon as she was sure she wouldn't be observed.

"Thank you for keeping me company, dearie," Bea said, affecting her creakiest voice. "Have you ever had a pet go missing?" Bea put her head down and jiggled her shoulders slightly, as if starting to cry.

The young woman patted Bea awkwardly on her back. "I haven't been lucky enough to have a pet since I moved away from home. But I'm sure it must be frightening to lose a pet—I mean, you know, temporarily."

Bea stole a quick glance up the stairs to gauge Pat's progress, then laid the emotion on thick. Shaking her shoulders vigorously, she dug in the pocket of her track suit and found a half-disintegrated tissue. She blew her nose with a resounding honk that coincided with Pat opening the apartment door.

"Thank you, sweetie," she said, dabbing her eyes with the tissue. "I hope my poor Petal is only gone temporarily—"

"The door was left open," Pat yelled down the stairs as she emerged from the empty unit. "Nothing inside."

"I guess we should be going, then," Bea said.

Pat reached the bottom of the stairs and thanked the young woman. "Miss, would you be willing to give us the name and number of the landlord? Maybe they'd rent the place to us for a week while we look for Pearl—"

"You mean Petal!" Bea howled.

"I'm sorry, Eunice, I meant Petal!"

"Of course. I'll write it down for you." The young woman returned from her first-floor unit with a small, square note. "Good luck finding your furry friend."

"Thank you, dearie."

Bea and Pat were silent until they were back in Pat's car and out of earshot of anyone.

"Nice job with the lock, but no calling me Eunice ever again," Bea grumbled. "It starts with 'ewe,' and I'm no sheep."

"Come to think of it, it also ends in 'nice,' and you're not—"

"OK, OK, I get it." Bea frowned at first, but then a little chuckle bubbled up. "That was a pretty good one, girlfriend."

"I'm sorry about 'Eunice.' It was the best I could come up with on the fly. Be glad I didn't go with my first instinct. I almost called you 'Mylanta.' Anyway, when this is all done, we can pick alias names for future cases."

"Future cases! I like the sound of that. Don't forget, I need lock-picking training, too."

Pat started the car and headed toward the freeway that led back to the wine country. "You're gonna like the sound of this better. There was a little card in the slot on the door with the name of the tenant. The landlord must have put it there, and whoever used the place forgot to remove it when they left. I got a picture of it."

"Don't keep me in suspense. What's it called?"

"GreenGene: a ThriveCore Company."

"Bummer. Doesn't ring any bells."

CHAPTER 14

After several hours with McGregor at the tree plot, Aseem and Angela were both exhausted. Luckily, by the time they made it back to the inn, the local Thanksgiving crowds had gone home, and the few overnight guests were tucked in. The inn was quiet.

"That poor junior cop," Aseem said. "He has to stand watch all night. McGregor wouldn't even let him nap in the trailer."

"To be fair, it isn't exactly proven that anyone can guard the plot effectively from the trailer," Angela said. "At least Officer Babiak can go in there to warm up occasionally. And at least McGregor was true to his word. Look—he sent me the picture he promised."

She turned her phone around to show Aseem the display. He was sitting on the bed in her suite, on top of a wooly throw and a quilt with an antique design of red reindeer and snowflakes on a creamy background. Angela sat at her desk.

The image on the phone was of the paper they found under the body in the tree plot: another missive from "S.O.S." It was written in marker as before, apparently with the writer's non-dominant hand.

Your arrogance knows no bounds but you will soon learn fear! Nature forgives much, but when you go too far, she will have her way with you. You are lucky to be warned. Ignore us, Her defenders, at your peril!
—S.O.S. STEMS OVER STUFF

"Hard to believe S.O.S.'s impersonators had the nerve to try again," Aseem said. "That message is even more threatening. Didn't they see Lexie's correction to her story?"

"They say that nobody reads corrections, especially when the story's juicy."

"I suppose tree terrorism and secret

experiments at sweet Betty Snickerdoodle's inn qualify as juicy."

"Now that this one's tied to a murder, it's only going to get juicier," Angela said. "Speaking of Lexie's juicy stories, I promised her I'd call. You're welcome to stick around."

"No, thanks. I'm beat, anyway. Plus, I should probably go to the front desk and pick up that package my mother left for me."

"What do you think it is?"

Aseem snorted. "She wrote 'for your future, with love' on it. I assume it's another stack of brochures from her financial planner. No matter how many times I tell her I am, she never believes I'm saving money."

Aseem gave Angela a kiss goodbye and headed back to his own suite. Angela texted Lexie to be sure she was awake. Lexie responded by calling her immediately.

"Never a dull moment up there," she said as soon as Angela picked up.

"Too bad you moved to the state capital for excitement," Angela said. "Bad call?"

"I'm lucky your hotbed of crime is only an hour or two away. Speaking of which, what's the latest? Police scanner reports made it sound like… murder?"

"Off the record?"

"Sure."

"Yep. Murder. Now can I ask you a question? What's up with that friend of yours who was tracing the email from the S.O.S. impostor?"

"Old boyfriends. They say they want to help you, but then they make you wait. Don't worry, I'll find a way to give him a little motivation. He won't even know it's happening. You know what I mean, right?"

Angela didn't reply.

"Of course you don't," Lexie laughed. "Girl, you're lucky you've got Aseem, 'cause your game-playing skills could use some sharpening."

Angela was glad Lexie couldn't see her scowling. "You don't have to tell me I'm lucky to be with Aseem. You of all people know that, of course."

"Touché. Maybe I deserved that. Listen, I'm sorry I don't have an answer yet on the source of that email. I'll nudge tomorrow. There's something else I have to tell you, though."

"Let me guess. You're coming here to cover the crime for the *Bee*."

"Yep. You know it's my job, right? But you don't have to help me any more than you want to.

I found the property lines on the internet. I think I can find your experimental grow op on my own."

"Good. I'm not supposed to tell you, but I can't help it if you find it on your own."

"Maybe I'll see you there tomorrow."

"You'll still have to convince McGregor to let you have a look at his scene. He might be a harder nut to crack."

Angela disconnected the call and frowned. Her kind and honest nature was something she liked about herself, but Lexie's insinuation that she lacked feminine wiles still annoyed her. Then she remembered the license plate number of the victim's economy car, which she'd so carefully memorized, intending to ask Lexie if her contact could dig up the car's owner.

An idea popped into her head and she picked up her cell phone. She scrolled through her contacts and touched a number, then tapped out a text. Her phone rang immediately.

"Nice to hear from you, beautiful," the man's voice said. "How can I help you?"

"Hi, Drew," Angela replied. "That was fast."

"It's not every day you get a call from the one that got away."

Angela smiled and felt a little glow bloom on

her cheeks. "How's the FBI life? Where are you these days—can you even say?"

"California. That's about as much as I can narrow it down this time. The case is a good one. We're on the verge of putting some really bad characters out of work."

"That makes me glad. I feel safer just knowing you, Drew."

"Aw, shucks, ma'am."

"It sounds like you're awfully busy, but do you think you might have time to do me a little favor?"

"That depends. Do I still have a shot with you someday? Or is Aseem 'the one'?"

"We're going strong," Angela said. "I'd be lying if I said I didn't love him. But, you know, we're not married or anything."

Drew laughed. "A slim chance is better than none. Tell me what you need."

Angela told Drew about the staged S.O.S. attack, how Lexie had heard from S.O.S. denying responsibility, and the latest wrinkle of another attack that looked like S.O.S. was behind it—and how this time, a human was the victim.

"Would you believe that Lexie also asked me for help tracing the email?" Drew said. "Of course, she just wanted it for her story. Now that I know lives might be at stake, I'll put a rush on it."

"And here I was thinking you were helping me because I'm so charming," Angela giggled.

"Don't worry. That's exactly what I'm going to tell Lexie," Drew said. "Now what's that license plate you want me to run?"

~

THE NEXT MORNING, ANGELA GOT UP BEFORE anyone else at the inn, dressed quickly in jeans, a long-sleeved t-shirt, and a thick sweater, and headed to her favorite café on Main Street to pick up fancy coffee drinks for herself and Bea. They'd decided to get up early and review what they'd learned the night before, since they wouldn't be able to speak freely once McGregor and his team rejoined them at the tree plot. Angela started with the bombshell that the dead body wasn't Andy after all.

"My news has no silver lining. My idea to go to the professor's place was mostly a bust," Bea said. She had shifted her standard ensemble for a slightly more Christmassy version: a red velour track suit and green sneakers. "Whoever's after the professor's idea got there before we did. They'd turned the place over and it looks like they got all his notes."

"That *is* terrible. Do you think they got enough to reproduce the experiment?"

"Hard to know. They didn't leave much behind, though."

"At least maybe we could change his mind about the patent now. I know—we could offer to help him! He could dictate and we could type, and we could get the patent application in before the thieves try. We've still got the advantage of having actual results that show it works."

"I think our chances of changing his mind are worse than ever," Bea said, chuckling. Then she explained that she and Pat had found him splayed on his futon, dead.

"You might have led with that, Bea."

"My bad. Anyway, I've got an idea for how we might be able to get our hands on what they stole. We gotta take a trip back to Emeryville, though. And not at night."

"I like that idea. I've got something else I want to do up there during the day, too. It's also kind of a surprise for you. Shall we plan to head up there after McGregor finishes with us? You, me, and Pat —this afternoon?"

"Deal."

"By the way, Bea, did you call the Emeryville

cops about what you found? The professor's body, I mean?"

"Yep. Pat still had that burner phone the professor never used. We called in an anonymous tip, and since we did it from outside his building, no one will ever know it was us. Just an unidentified caller from the streets of Emeryville."

"Are you concerned you and Pat would be suspects?"

"Technically, we were trespassing. Mostly, I don't want the hassle of being interviewed. And I'd like to prevent McGregor from connecting the dots as long as possible. The professor's dead, and nothing can fix that, but maybe we still have a shot at protecting the experiment. We can try to make some progress before the investigation calls more attention to the good, dead doctor and his work."

"Good thinking, especially since McGregor says he doesn't want our help this time. He got the victim's registration out of his car and wouldn't even tell me his name."

"And you keep saying I shouldn't call him Beef Jerky anymore!" Bea cackled. "I guess I don't need to tell you: No letting McGregor know that we know the professor is dead." Bea made a zipper motion across her lips.

"No need to tell me. And about the victim, I memorized his license plate. Drew Faulkner said he'd run it for me."

"Foxy Drew Faulkner! Did you flirt with him, girlie? Don't worry, I won't tell your handsome boyfriend."

"I didn't flirt! I was just polite, of course," Angela said. "Maybe I flirted a little."

Bea let out a cackle and held her fist up. Angela reluctantly bumped it with hers.

"Speaking of Drew, Lexie had already asked him to help figure out who sent that message to the *Bee* claiming to be S.O.S. I told him what's been happening up at our tree plot, and why we really want to know who it is. He said he'd check into that for me, too. Oh, and by 'what's happening up here,' there's more big news. Another S.O.S. message was at the scene. McGregor and the coroner found it when they lifted up the victim last night." She pulled out her phone and showed Bea the picture of the paper sign McGregor found under the victim.

"Stakes are getting higher for S.O.S. Wonder how ol' Michelle is gonna feel about that," Bea said. "Once Lexie publishes this one, S.O.S.'s nature-defending, do-gooder narrative is gonna be a lot harder to sell."

. . .

ASEEM WORKED IN SILICON VALLEY EVERY FRIDAY, so Bea, Angela, and Pat headed up to meet McGregor and his team at the tree plot without him.

"Where's your gauze pad?" Angela asked Pat as they climbed into the UTV.

"Don't need it. Look—you can't even tell I got stabbed," Pat said. "Not a scratch left."

"But we told McGregor that you and Bea were going to urgent care. You need to have an injury. He thinks that's why you weren't here for questioning last night." Angela hopped out of the vehicle and jogged back into the inn for a fresh bandage.

Bea cackled and applauded as Angela ran off. "See, Pat, we'll make a liar out of her yet!"

Angela returned with a square adhesive bandage, which Pat slapped into place. Angela turned the ignition key and they made their way across the field.

"Nice of you people to get out of bed by the crack of noon," McGregor said as they arrived. He and Officer Babiak were standing outside the tree plot's gate. Babiak looked like he was waiting for instructions. McGregor ignored him and scrolled through notes on his phone.

Angela looked at her phone incredulously. "It's

8:30."

"Girlie, you forgot to add, 'And we don't work for you,'" Bea said.

McGregor mumbled something that sounded almost like an apology. "Not much sleep for any of us last night. Here's what we need from you—"

"We'll be happy to help as ever, Sarge," Bea said. "But we would also like some help from you. As Angela told you, this tree plot is an experiment —and we promised to help our friend the professor with it. It was very important to him—"

"Save your breath, Sickles. A man was murdered here. You don't get to pick and choose whether you help us find out who did it."

"Tell us the bare minimum we can do to help you, then, and I won't bother reminding you that you're supposed to help protect taxpayers' property, too, right?"

Angela sighed glumly, but Bea and McGregor seemed, surprisingly, to settle into a truce. Officer Babiak pointed out that there were many footprints in the tree plot—probably including Bea's, Angela's, and Pat's. McGregor said that while he worked to gather evidence inside the enclosure, the junior officer should start by eliminating the non-suspects based on their footprints.

"Can you ladies help us get impressions of the shoes you wore in here recently?" the junior officer said. He walked away from the gate toward an untrodden area closer to the trailer and beckoned Bea, Pat, and Angela to join him.

"You'll need Aseem's, too," Angela said. "And Bea and I were wearing different shoes yesterday. See those high heel marks? Those are mine. What about you, Pat?"

Pat confirmed she was wearing the same shoes as the day before. She stepped on an untouched spot away from the scene, and the cop took photos and confirmed the footprints matched several inside the enclosure.

"Thank you, Pat. Angela, Bea—we'll take pictures of the other footprints and compare notes back at your inn later. We'll do the same with Aseem," Officer Babiak said.

"Sickles! Get over to the gate!" McGregor barked.

Bea rolled her eyes and moved as slowly as she could without losing her balance.

"Sickles?!"

"Coming, Sargent," Bea said, dragging the phrase out for a good ten seconds.

With one step to go to the gate, she adopted her customary spry pace. She popped her head into the opening and shouted cheerfully, "How may I help you, good sir?"

If McGregor perceived her mockery, he ignored it. He was staring at the trees in front of him, mouth open. He was standing a few rows in, where the row of trees whose serum supply had been cut met the rows that still had their syringes.

"These trees grew half a foot at least overnight. I'm sure of it."

"That's crazy!" Bea howled. "Trees can't do that. Maybe you should take a nap in the trailer. You might be delusional from lack of sleep."

"I can see that the trees are injected with something, Beatrice," McGregor said, prompting a scowl from Bea. Bea purposely left the full version of her first name behind decades ago. Hearing it always got under her skin, a rare trigger which McGregor had learned to exploit. "This is no ordinary tree food. I think I see why someone found this worth brawling—or killing—over." He gently lifted a branch from one of the trees, which appeared to have been broken half off. "What exactly are you tinkering with up here?"

"We'd like to know more about who our trespassing victim was and how he died, including what was injected into him. Perhaps we can help one another."

"Babiak, show Angela that picture of the vic's registration." Outside the fence gate, Babiak tapped a few times on his phone and then turned the display toward Angela.

"Got it!" Angela yelled, snapping a picture of Babiak's phone with her own.

"Your turn. Spill," McGregor said to Bea.

"We invested in an experimental method for growing trees more quickly. I provided land and cash for the supplies. We met the inventor through the incubator Angie's boyfriend works at. Everybody calls the inventor 'the professor.'"

"I'm gonna need a name."

"We'll get the coroner's full report?"

"I'll do my best."

"We're under a confidentiality agreement. I'm not supposed to tell you anything. Do you promise to keep it to yourself? No doubt that intrepid reporter Lexie Greene will be around here soon—"

"You know I don't tell reporters anything, Sickles—"

Angela's phone beeped. She gasped as she read an incoming text.

"Bea, Pat—we've got to get back to the inn."

She hopped into the driver's seat of the UTV and Pat hopped onto the back. "C'mon, Bea!"

"Pleasure doin' business with you, Sarge," Bea said, climbing into the vehicle. As Angela started up and turned the UTV around, Bea shouted back, "Oh, and the professor's name was—er, is—Gregory Woodward."

"Where can I find him?"

"I'm not sure—maybe Berkeley? Or try Avalon University of California."

CHAPTER 15

"I love a good getaway ploy, girlie, but what's the emergency?"

"Jackson texted me. There are protesters at the inn claiming to be S.O.S."

"I thought that lady from S.O.S. said she had nothing against you," Pat said.

"She said her organization didn't send that picture to the *Bee*, but she also said she had to know more about our tree project before saying S.O.S. had nothing against us," Bea said. "And since we wouldn't tell her anything, it makes you wonder if she could have learned something from someone else."

"Maybe it's S.O.S., maybe it's not. But whoever it is, their timing is terrible. Our first wave of

Christmas guests arrives for the weekend today! Our whole team has worked so hard to make sure everything's perfect," Angela moaned. "We don't need a protest crew messing it up. The guests have been emailing me for weeks to tell me how much they're looking forward to kicking off the Christmas season here."

"Don't worry, Angie. If we can't get the protesters to leave, we can always tell McGregor they're here. Maybe he'll round them up and take them in for questioning. After all, we've been receiving threats in the name of their organization. Wouldn't they be automatically on his suspect radar?"

"That might work," Angela said, her face softening. "Shoot. Maybe I should have told him about the protesters before we left. All I could think about when I got Jackson's text was getting back here fast to deal with them. Since we've been assuming the S.O.S. notes were from an impostor, it didn't even occur to me that McGregor might want to talk with them about the murder."

"Plenty of time to tell him later. This way, we get to do our own questioning first," Bea said, rubbing her hands together and grinning.

The UTV bounced over the field as Angela pushed it to its limits. Pat was pushed to hers, too, as she hung onto the handlebar in the back seat for dear life. Soon they were close enough to see the inn—and the crowd of about twenty protesters walking in front of the entrance. They were carrying signs illustrated with caricatures of pine trees with big, weeping eyes and messages like, "Merry Christmas, MURDERERS!" and "How Many of Us Must DIE for Your Fun?" in huge letters. Half of the marchers were morosely singing "Give Trees a Chance" while the other half shouted out the messages on their signs.

"It's even worse than I thought," Angela cried. She hastily stopped the UTV near the inn entrance and marched toward the crowd, Bea and Pat trailing behind her.

"Who's in charge of your group?" Angela said to the crowd. No one responded. "You're not allowed to block access to this property, and I'm pretty sure you are committing slander with those signs!"

"Go, girlie!" Bea said.

The protesters continued to ignore Angela. "You think it's fun to go to jail? It'll be less of an adventure when you're connected to a felony!" That momentarily got the attention of a few of the demonstrators. "As of this moment, S.O.S. has claimed responsibility for *two* felony crimes. If you're thinking it's just gonna be a little trespassing charge you can brag about on social media—"

"You're bluffing!" one of the agitators yelled. "We know you murder trees. You're trying to deflect attention."

"Did you see the story in the *Bee?*"

"You're a step behind, lady. They printed a correction. S.O.S. didn't do that crime."

"Maybe you're a step behind. Tell me who sent you here and we can both find out. Was it Michelle Healey?"

The protestors' concern they might be connected to something more than a nuisance crime proved fleeting. None of them reacted to Angela's question. They just resumed marching, chanting, and singing.

"Michelle's name didn't seem to ring any bells," Pat said.

"Could be she's too much of a muckety muck to deal with the street-walking riffraff," Bea said.

"Should I call Michelle and let her know what's happening?" Angela said. "Maybe she doesn't know about the murder. She might not want to risk S.O.S. being directly connected to it."

Bea let loose a bark of laughter. "Puh-leeze, girlie. Why give her a heads up? Would she tip you off that she was sending a bunch of troublemakers here to ruin our Christmas?"

"Good point. But I do know two people I *should* call."

"McGregor?" Pat said.

"That's the second one." Angela pulled out her phone and snapped a few pictures of the protest, then tapped it to make her first call.

"I'm just on my way to your place," Lexie said through the speakerphone.

"You'd better hustle. A bunch of S.O.S. protesters are here, and I'm pretty sure they'll be rounded up for questioning soon."

"Why? Protesting's not illegal."

"You know I can't go on the record with why, but trust me, there's another S.O.S. story in it for you. If you get here in time, maybe you can sweet-talk the cops and get access to the scene."

"I hear that Officer Babiak's still single," Bea yelled in the speaker's direction. "He's probably no match for your ninja flirt tricks, Hot Pants."

A FEW HOURS LATER, THE PROTESTERS WERE ON their way with McGregor to the cramped holding cell at the police station, Lexie was on her way to another big S.O.S. story, the early arrivals for the first Christmas season weekend at the inn were on their way to their suites, and Angela, Bea, and Pat were on their way to Emeryville in Angela's car.

"Nice touch, letting Lexie do the dirty work on S.O.S., Angie," Bea said.

"I figured it was a win-win. She needs a story, and since we don't want to give away anything new about the tree farm—"

"Might be kinda moot with the professor dead, though, no?" Pat said. "I mean, someone got his papers and those syringes from the farm. Maybe the enemy already has all they need."

"Since we've got the baby trees, we still have the only known proof of the process. And we don't know for sure the professor included everything needed to reproduce the innovation in those documents. If there's a chance to protect the secret, I still wanna try," Bea said. "Besides, if Lexie does the digging on S.O.S. and not us, that's one less thing we have to lie to McGregor about. We want what the politicos call plausible deniability."

"Exactly," said Angela. "We need Lexie to write another story that will flush out Michelle— or whoever's behind the protest. If S.O.S. *didn't* kill that man in our tree plot, Lexie's next story tying S.O.S. to the murder should get Michelle's attention. This way's a lot better than us trying to talk to Michelle. If we approached her, she might get more out of us than we'd get from her."

"Smart thinking!" Bea said. "Now that you've saved the day once more, Angie, how 'bout you tell us why you wanted to go to Emeryville?"

"Like I told you, it's a surprise, but I think you're going to like it," Angela said. "I'll give you a hint: it's all about girl time. It's been a hard couple of days and we could use a little fun, right? Your question reminds me, though—why did you tell McGregor you thought the professor lived in Berkeley?"

"Berkeley's the next town over. Close enough that he might not figure out I lied, but it might keep him out of Emeryville for a while so we can nose around." Bea suddenly scrunched up her face as if smelling a dead fish, and her shoulders quivered.

Angela glimpsed her out of the corner of her eye and struggled to stay focused on the road.

"Bea, are you all right?" Angela said, with an air of panic.

"Ahhhhh-chooooo!" Bea's sneeze seemed to last about fifteen seconds and shake Angela's little SUV. Then she let out another piercing cackle.

"Woohoo, that was a good one. Uh-oh, here comes a dribble."

Bea put the back of her right hand up to her nose and snuffled loudly.

"Correction, here comes a deluge!"

She rummaged around in her velour jacket's pocket and pulled out a couple of balls of used tissue, accidentally bundling them with the stained cloth she found at the professor's place. She blew her nose with a loud honk, then inhaled deeply and rubbed her nose repeatedly with the wad.

"Hoo-oo-oo-eeeee," Bea said, her head rolling around on her shoulders. "I'm feeling dizzy all of a sudden. That was some sneeze, I guess...." Her voice trailed off and her chin dropped to her chest. The ball of tissue and fabric fell to the car floor.

"Bea!" Angela and Pat shouted at once. Angela sped toward the next freeway exit and looked for a safe place to pull over. She spotted a gas station and careened into it, tires squealing, but by the time she stopped the car, Bea was awake and guffawing.

"Where's the fire, girlie?"

"Bea, you passed out. Straight out of the blue," Angela said.

"I guess I did. Just suddenly felt so sleepy."

"Can you hand me the tissue you were using?" Pat said. "It fell down by your feet."

"You sure you don't want a fresh one?" Bea cracked. "I bet Angela has one. She's always prepared."

"Nope. Pass me your gooey rags."

Bea handed the used blob to Pat, who held it gingerly and pulled out the stained cloth. "Bea, this scrap you found at the professor's was mixed in with your tissue." Pat put the remnant a little closer to her nose to sniff it, but immediately pulled it away. "Whoa," she said, eyes wide. "I got a little woozy just from that one sniff."

She looked at the cloth more closely. "There's a company name and a logo on it. Bos-Curae is the company. And there's a staff with a snake around it, inside a triangle." She reached from the back seat to the front to show the scrap to Angela and Bea.

"Take a look—but not too close."

"I thought it smelled a little sweet when I blew my nose," Bea said. "But you know how I like to keep a mint or two in my pocket."

"The logo looks medical," Angela said. "'Curae' must be 'cure,' right?"

"Yep, and that's the *caduceus*," Bea said.

"Another good Jeopardy! answer. I never understood how a stick and a snake became the symbol of good doctoring."

"I can ask Aseem about the company. His brother and his father are both doctors, so maybe they can help. It's probably time for him to stop giving his family the silent treatment, anyway. They obviously wanted to apologize when they came for Thanksgiving. Aseem was relieved that helping McGregor gave him an excuse to avoid them. Can you hold the cloth up again, Pat?" Angela took a picture of the scrap and texted it to Aseem.

"You know, there's one other thing to ask those doctors in his family, Angela," Pat said.

"What's that?"

"Can they tell what's on the cloth? Because it just made Bea pass out... and I think I recognize the aroma."

"Ohhh," Angela said, eyes wide.

Aseem texted Angela back that he'd try to help, then sighed. Sanjay had called again an hour earlier. Maybe it was time to bite the bullet and talk to him.

Sanjay answered on the first ring. "Happy to hear from you, little brother. You know I'm not big on worrying, but Ma's anxiety is eventually contagious."

A little pang of guilt jolted Aseem, but he shook it off.

"You enjoyed your Thanksgiving dinner, I hope?" Aseem said. "Angel—Angela—worked so hard to make it perfect."

"It was better than perfect," Sanjay said. "Please tell her I said so. We *all* thought so."

"I will. Sanjay, I'm calling for some help. Angela sent me a picture of something. It looks like a medical item. I was wondering if you know what it is. There's a company logo on it, too."

"I'll be happy to take a look. But you have to promise you'll let me explain about the dinner party. And apologize—because it was almost all my fault. Did you open the package yet?"

"No. It's just some financial planning stuff, I'm sure."

Sanjay laughed. "It's definitely not financial planning stuff. Open it. If only because it will settle forever the debate over which of us is Ma's favorite."

Aseem sighed. "OK. I'll open it later. Can you look at the picture now?"

"Huh. That logo—Bos-Curae—it isn't a medical

company I've worked with. Sounds vaguely familiar, though. Maybe that's just because of 'curae.' No, wait—that triangle around the logo could be a V. I think this must be a veterinary medicine company. Remember when I did that medical device internship? Maybe I recognize it from those animal trials. Why was Angela interested in this?"

"I don't know," Aseem said. It was technically true, though he had a guess or two involving crime scene evidence that he knew he shouldn't share. "But thanks. I'll let her know. And I'll open Ma's package."

"You can't hang up now. You promised to let me explain about the dinner party—"

"I will—just not right now." Aseem clicked off and hit redial on Angela's number.

As Angela pulled off the freeway toward Emeryville, her phone rang and she saw Aseem's picture pop up on the screen.

"We're just arriving in Emeryville," she said cheerily. "You're on speakerphone."

Bea and Pat chimed in with "Hi, handsome!"

"I talked to my brother about that logo. He said it was a veterinary brand. He had an internship at a medical device firm during medical school and thought he recognized it from animal trials. He started asking why we wanted to know, so I had to cut the conversation short."

"Maybe that stain is an animal anesthetic," Pat said. "Bea took one whiff and passed out for a minute. And I thought I remembered the smell when I took a sniff. If it's an anesthetic… maybe it's what the killer used to knock me out."

"Do you think you could ask your brother about that? Will you be talking to him again soon?" Angela said sweetly.

Aseem sighed. "I wasn't planning to. He was getting curious about why I wanted to know about the scrap and, you know… But I'll think about it. Maybe we can find out ourselves using the internet, Angel. You and I could research it tonight when we're both back at the inn."

"Sounds good. See you later. We're just arriving at our destination," Angela said, blowing a kiss at the screen and disconnecting. "Start looking for parking, ladies. We're just a few blocks away."

"I bet great minds think alike, Angie. I think I know where we're going," Bea said. She waved at the window of the typewriter shop as they drove by. "Hi, my love!"

"Who are you talking to?" Angela said.

"Betsy 2—she's right there in the shop window."

Angela giggled, then turned down the next street.

"Huh. I thought you'd keep going down the main street—"

"Nope, I guess I surprised you after all. And look—we lucked out. There's a spot right in front."

By the middle of the block, it was easy to see that the street was a demarcation of sorts, roughly signaling where gentrification of the neighborhood began. The building Angela parked in front of looked shiny new, as did the restaurant next to it, and the condominium further down. On the other side of the street, development was underway on another modern structure.

"Hahaha, good one, girlie," Bea said, looking at the business's pink and lavender sign, which said *Queens and Goddesses Spa Retreat.* "That's the place I won you the gift card from in the poker tourney."

"As you like to say, *egg-zactly!*" Angela said. "That's the surprise. Manis and pedis for the three of us."

Pat's eyes grew wide and her face turned

white. "You want me to expose… *my feet*? And let someone… *touch them*?"

Bea let loose a cackle. "Oh, Angie, too bad. When you said 'girl time,' I thought you meant poker at Lucky Pines. I already promised Pat we'd play. Didn't I, Pat?"

Pat nodded vigorously and exhaled with relief. Angela frowned. "But they'll have to charge the gift card for all three of us, anyway. It's too late to cancel."

"Don't worry, we'll get you a new gift card. I'd love to go to the spa with you… someday. Today, you enjoy your girlie time, and we'll regroup when you're done. Hey, I know—see if they'll give you an upgrade in place of me and Pat. Treat yourself to a leech wrap or a piranha gnawing or something fancy like that. Call us when you're done, and we can meet you back here. The cardroom's just a few blocks down the main street."

"OK, I guess," Angela said, crestfallen. "If you're sure."

"I'm afraid it's how it has to be," Bea said, looking skyward. "It wouldn't be right to let Pat down, especially after her recent ordeal."

"Good point. I should be more thoughtful,"

Angela said. "You two go have fun, and I'll call when I'm done."

As soon as Angela slipped inside the door of the spa, Bea turned to Pat and said, "You're very welcome, girlfriend."

"I never thought I'd be so happy about heading back to that grubby cardroom."

"Don't worry," Bea said, chuckling. "You're getting out of the spa torture—I mean, treatment—and you don't even have to play poker. First, you're gonna try to reach the landlord of that apartment across from the professor's place again. Then we'll get my new Selectric out of the infirmary." She pulled the piece of paper the girl at the low-rise apartment building had written the landlord's number on out of her pocket and handed it to Pat, who dialed the number on her cell, then left a message on voicemail.

A half hour later, Bea and Pat emerged from the repair shop, Pat carrying the Selectric. They still hadn't heard back from the landlord. The sun was setting and the air was getting chilly.

"I guess that was a slight flaw in my plan," Bea said, rubbing her upper arms. "Didn't occur to me that the landlady wouldn't call us back right away. You'd think she'd want a new tenant."

"GreenGene probably prepaid some rent. We

could look for a coffee shop to wait in for Angela —or even head to the cardroom… if you want." Pat grimaced and leaned to the side, as if imagining carting the heavy portable typewriter the half mile or so to the poker hall.

"Don't worry, you won't have to drag that thing like a pack mule. I've got a better idea."

A few minutes later, they'd crossed the street and the parking lot and were standing to the side of the four-unit building. They were mostly hidden by some ill-tended shrubbery, the typewriter tucked behind their feet. It didn't take long before a young man in a knit beanie hustled out the door, distracted by the phone he held to his ear. As the man walked away, Pat rushed over and grabbed the door. "Got it!"

Bea grabbed the typewriter and hauled it with a grunt behind Pat into the building. Upstairs at the vacant apartment, they noticed that the label on the door saying GreenGene: a ThriveCore Company was still in its slot. Pat put her ear to the door and concluded no one was inside, then worked magic with her picks again. Soon they were inside the small, practically empty efficiency.

Bea flipped the light switch just inside the door.

"Oops. I probably shouldn't have touched that.

Fingerprints, right?"

Pat shrugged. "We can wipe that before we leave. Let's just try not to touch anything else."

"Sounds like a plan. I thought we might get lucky and find another clue in here—if not, at least we can stay warm while we wait for Angie."

The main living area had the large window they'd noticed from the street, the one with the direct view into the professor's loft. There was a kitchenette and a built-in table or desk of the utilitarian office variety, one side screwed to the wall, the other end resting on a cylindrical pillar, but no drawers and no chair. A door from the living room into the bedroom was partly open, and there was a bare mattress on top of a plain, rusty frame. After checking out the apartment's limited contents, Bea and Pat stood by the big window, watching the street below. It was getting dark fast and the streetlights were coming on.

"What time is it?" Bea said, after they'd watched for a while and noticed nothing. "Doesn't it seem like we should have heard from Angie by now?"

"She's probably just getting extra spa treatments, like you suggested—poor thing," Pat sniggered. "The outing's not a total bust, though, Eunice. We can watch for your poor, dear Pearl after all. Look, I think I see her," she laughed, pointing down at an empty spot on the street.

"The dog's name's Petal! How can you forget my beloved imaginary pet?" Bea cried. "Ain't you got no feelings?"

Pat chuckled, but then something outside caught her eye. "Oh, wait—now that's interesting. Shut off the light!"

Bea reached behind her and flicked the light switch on the wall, then the two of them stood at the edge of the window in the dark and peered out.

"That guy right there—he looks kinda familiar. I mean—his outfit does," Pat said. "Not that it narrows it down too much, but he's got the same general physique as the guy I chased from the ballroom a couple weeks ago."

"The one who tried to steal a baby tree? Who might have gotten one of the professor's drip thingamajigs?"

"Yep. The thing is, I can't really make out his face with the hoodie tied so tight."

"That's by design," Bea said. "Standard issue crookwear. But look—he seems to be coming this way."

"Is that a good thing or a bad thing?" Pat said.

"We'll know soon enough."

CHAPTER 16

Angela emerged from the spa feeling refreshed, despite a lingering touch of regret that Bea and Pat hadn't joined her. She felt so relaxed, she wasn't even worried about the unfortunate mishap with her phone.

She'd been working so hard for so many weeks: preparing the inn for its first Thanksgiving celebration and Christmas bookings, planning for BettyCon in January, and, of course, helping with the tree experiment. The pampering session at the spa had cleared her mind and boosted her spirits. The generous pour of champagne probably helped. The slight fizzy feeling she owed to the bubbly might also have contributed to her phone landing in the foot bath, but Angela decided she wouldn't let a drowned phone spoil her relaxed mood. Sure, the timing was frustrating. She'd dropped the phone to its watery death while trying to read a text from Drew Faulkner. It seemed he'd found out something about who'd sent that first picture to the *Bee* claiming to be S.O.S.—information she was anxiously waiting for.

It doesn't matter, Angela thought, realizing a little patience was in order. If her phone didn't dry out by the time she got home, she could read Drew's message on the old spare phone she kept for emergencies like this. Drew was going to send her the name on the victim's car registration, too, but she didn't need it now that Officer Babiak had shown her. ("John Nixon," which hadn't rung a bell anyway.) The only real problem was that she couldn't call Bea and Pat. Thankfully, the poker place was nearby. She could simply walk down to retrieve them the old-fashioned way. A few hours without a cell phone never hurt anyone.

Angela left her car in front of the spa and headed toward the main street to the poker hall. She looked to the left first: the typewriter repair shop was just steps away. Then to the right: she could see the professor's dreary building. Her curiosity was piqued. She couldn't resist a quick scan of both places before heading to the cardroom, though she wasn't sure what she hoped to find.

The typewriter shop was already closed, so Angela turned and headed back toward the professor's building, wondering what she'd look for if she got inside. Bea and Pat had already alerted the cops that the professor was dead. The place would surely have been cleaned out already. And even if it hadn't been, Bea and Pat must have searched it from top to bottom. She trusted them. Yet though she kept telling herself these things, and there clearly was no reason to go inside, temptation was getting the better of her.

Like Bea, Angela hadn't lost hope that she and Bea and Aseem would be able to figure out the professor's secrets before anyone else. If they did, they could patent the technique and build a business around those miraculously fast-growing trees. How fabulous would that be? Bea would be delighted, of course, if her investment panned out. For Angela, though, the primary allure was the pride she felt as she imagined herself leading a business that did well while doing so much good.

At the door of the professor's building, a tenant who was leaving let Angela in. As she walked up the stairs to the professor's door, she could feel and hear her heart thumping.

I know this is a waste of time. I probably won't even be able to get inside.

But when she got there, she was thrilled to find the door ajar. Without stopping to wonder why, she pushed it.

"Ms. Garcia," Sergeant McGregor said gruffly. "Fancy meeting you here."

Angela gulped. "Sergeant McGregor—"

"Whatever you have to say can wait for your interview," McGregor said. "Detective McMahon here is handling the investigation of Professor Woodward's homicide. Funny—you said Berkeley, not Emeryville. Person might think you were trying to slow me down."

"Technically, that was Bea, not me. And I'm sure it was an honest mistake. We're not far from the Berkeley border, right?"

"And yet here you are—and you knew exactly where Dr. Woodward lived, right down to the correct door."

Angela felt her face heat up.

"Don't worry, you don't have to say anything on behalf of Beatrice—except perhaps to tell us where she is. I assume she's with you. I called the inn, and that's what your front desk manager said."

A debate instantly flared in Angela's mind. If she told McGregor that Bea and Pat were down the street playing poker, he and McMahon would pick them up and they'd all have a long night at the police station. She knew for sure that Bea wouldn't want that. But on the other hand, if she kept it a secret, Bea and Pat would have no idea where she was—or how they'd get home.

"No—no, that's not right," Angela said. "I mean, she was going to come with me, but she changed her mind. She and Pat went off to do something else, and I don't know what or where." Angela was feeling good about her bluff. She'd started off with a bit of a quaver in her voice but was pretty sure it smoothed out as she talked. At least she hoped so.

"OK, we're done here. Let's go," McGregor said. Detective McMahon nodded. "And by the way, Ms. Garcia, I hope you're getting a clear picture of the Emeryville police. This is a real city department, and they're not going to put up with any of Beatrice's shenanigans."

"I… I don't know what you're talking—"

"Save it, Ms. Garcia," Detective McMahon said. "I've heard all about you and your boss and your inn, and all the murders and all your meddling.

When we get down to the station, you're simply going to tell us everything you know, OK?"

Angela nodded. "I will get one phone call, won't I? It's just—my cell is dead."

Detective McMahon laughed. "You can call anyone you want. You're not under arrest—at least not yet."

Inside the empty GreenGene apartment, Pat and Bea put their ears to the door, Pat hunching over slightly to the level just above the doorknob, and Bea crouching under her. They were convinced the man in the hoodie had walked to the door of the squat, four-unit building, and now they were listening in case he was headed up to the apartment they were standing in.

Bea whispered, "I hear something. Stand back and get ready to take a picture with your phone."

Pat backed up and pulled out her phone. She tilted it, tapped on it, and then held the phone in front of her face, finger in ready position.

Bea kept listening for a moment or two until she heard the sound she expected: fingers prying up the metal tab and scratching at the paper insert that labeled the apartment as the home of GreenGene: a ThriveCore Company. She moved to the side of the door and hissed at Pat, "3-2-1, now!"

Bea flung the door open. The young man's face, what little of it was showing through the opening in the tightly tied hood, was frozen at first with shock and confusion. Pat snapped the picture. The man figured out what was happening and bolted back down the stairs and out the door.

"Dang it, I wish I had my cane. It would have been fun to hook his foot and send him flying face first down those stairs."

"Hard to believe you're worried about going soft."

"No need for comments from the peanut gallery," Bea cracked. "Just tell me you got the picture."

"You know I did. I thought it was Brandon at first," Pat said, turning the phone toward Bea. "But now I don't think that's right. Do you recognize him?"

"Yep. I'm pretty sure that was the real Andy Mathers."

Angela had hoped to speed up the interview by cooperating. She assured the cops she was ready to answer questions as soon as they all arrived at the police station. But then McMahon and McGregor left her cooling her heels in the interview room, alone, for thirty minutes. By the time the two cops were ready to start, Angela was visibly anxious about Bea and Pat. She asked the cops if she could quickly use the phone, telling McGregor and McMahon that she intended to call Aseem. She figured this was better than alerting McGregor that Bea was nearby.

"Hi, honey," she said brightly, giving her best effort to maintain a cool demeanor. "Remember those two people I was meeting for dinner here in Emeryville—my old friends Trixie and Tricia?" Out of the corner of her eye, she saw the gears turning in McGregor's big head, and knew instantly that she'd underestimated his ability to solve her little puzzle. But by then it was too late.

"Yeah, I dropped my phone in the water at the spa. Would you mind calling them—T and T—and letting them know I'll be late? Maybe you could even meet them—I'm sure they'd appreciate the company. I know it's a long ride from Silicon Valley, but you'll still probably get there before I will."

"Let me talk to him," McGregor said, grabbing the phone and barking into it. "Aseem, this is Sergeant McGregor. If you're on your way to Emeryville to see this 'Trixie' and 'Tricia,' and if one of those two is actually Beatrixie Sickles, you need to tell me right now."

Angela strained to listen and thought she

heard Aseem say, "No, of course I don't know where Bea is. I give you my word. I've been on the Peninsula all day." She knew he was lying by telling the truth, since he didn't know *exactly* where Bea was *yet*. The thought made her smile, but she looked down quickly and fought it back.

"I'll be back at the inn soon to talk to you, Aseem. Monday morning at the latest. You, Trixie, and Tricia better be there and ready to tell the truth. *The whole truth!* And that includes anything I should know about that incubator of yours and how you met Gregory Woodward in the first place. Got it?"

"Of course," Angela heard Aseem say, followed by, "anything to help—"

But McGregor hung up and cut him off. "Shall we get started with some truth-telling, Ms. Garcia?"

By the time Pat had tried Angela's phone three times, with each call going directly to voicemail, it was getting chilly by the big window in the spartan apartment, not to mention exceedingly boring. The end-of-day rush of workers and shoppers heading home was waning, and the streets below were all but empty. Pat called the day spa to see if Angela was still there but got an automated after-hours message.

"I hope we won't be sharing that old mattress tonight," Bea said, tilting her head toward the glum little bedroom.

"At least there aren't any covers for you to steal," Pat said. Then she noticed Bea wasn't laughing. The expression on her face was serious.

"Don't worry, Bea. I'm sure there's a perfectly logical explanation why Angela hasn't called."

Finally, Aseem's call lit up Pat's phone.

"Angela dropped her phone in the water at the spa. And somehow… I don't know how, but somehow she crossed paths with McGregor. She couldn't tell me how it happened, since she was with McGregor and a local detective and using the landline at the police station in Emeryville. I'm already on my way to get you. Don't worry. Just tell me where you are."

Pat told Aseem about the parking lot right across from the professor's loft, and she and Bea settled in to wait another half hour for him to arrive.

"Can't believe Lazybones McGregor sprang into action so fast," Bea chuckled. "I thought we'd at least have the weekend to try to solve the case ourselves."

"He's probably sick of you making him look incompetent."

"Too bad. Usually showing him up is more than enough reward, but the professor's secrets are much bigger fish to fry. I don't even care that much about the murder—OK, of course I can always use a good idea for my next mystery book, and I'm definitely going to use a typewriter to the head on one of my victims. But I've got some serious cabbage riding on that experiment! I hope there's still time for us to find the culprits and the stuff they stole before the cops do."

Aseem pulled into the parking lot and Pat and Bea hurried out of the apartment building to meet him, Pat lugging the cumbersome typewriter. They both hopped in the back, but Aseem asked Bea to sit up front.

"Aren't we picking up Angie?"

"She's got to get her car home, and she let me know she didn't want us to show up at the station. I think she figured we'd all be there all night if McGregor found out we're here in Emeryville," Aseem said, brow furrowing. "I just wish Angel had her phone for the ride home."

"She'll be fine. Maybe McGreggy will be considerate enough to give her a police escort back to Napa. He'll have to drive back, too, right?" Bea said. "Pat, why don't you take the front seat? I'll sit back here with my Betsy."

Pat gladly hopped out and joined Aseem up front. "I agree with Bea that she'll be fine. But we can always retrace our steps to look for her if she doesn't show up within a couple of hours."

The rush-hour traffic had dissipated and when they were nearly home, they stopped at Bea's favorite fast-food joint for several bags of tasty, unhealthful snacks. While they were waiting in the drive-through line, Aseem's phone rang. He looked at the screen.

"I don't recognize the number," he said, but he answered the call anyway.

"It's me," Angela said. "I'm leaving Emeryville now. Detective McMahon had a burner that he let me use for safety's sake."

"I hope I was right not to come by the station —" Aseem said.

"Absolutely. I wish I could have spoken more freely, but McGregor and McMahon were hovering. I've got lots to tell all of you about my police adventure."

"We're at the drive-through. Can we pick up something for you? Then we can convene in my suite—I thought it would help to hash everything out with the white board."

"Perfect. I'm about forty minutes behind you."

Aseem, Bea, and Pat arrived at his suite and

settled in. He set the bags of snacks on his desk like a buffet, then rolled his white board into the middle of the room. The board was filled already with his two to-do lists, one for the incubator and the other for the inn. He unlatched it and flipped it over so that they could use the blank back side. Bea and Pat grabbed sandwiches and sat on the fluffy, Christmassy blanket at the end of Aseem's bed, giving them a perfect view of the board.

"I suppose we could start by jotting down our open questions," Aseem said, marker poised. He started by writing, "Whose body did we find?" Bea piped up that Angela actually had the answer, because Officer Babiak had shared it with her at the scene that morning.

"OK, but *we* still don't know."

"True. And it didn't ring any bells for Angela, either."

Aseem cupped his chin with his fingers, then erased what he'd written. "Let's be more organized."

He divided the top half of the board into four columns, which he labeled "CRIMES," "MOTIVES," "SUSPECTS," and "EVIDENCE." Then he drew a horizontal line across the middle of the board and wrote "QUESTIONS AND CONNECTIONS" at the top of the empty half.

"It's exciting!" Bea enthused with her mouth full. Bun blobs dangled from the corners of her mouth, threatening to escape. "Like a vision board for murder." She shoved the last bite of her sandwich into her mouth and rubbed her hands together.

Aseem wrote "body #1—tree plot guy," and "body #2—the professor" in the first column, under crimes.

"Don't forget the break-in at the ballroom," sighed Pat. "That goes under crimes." Bea gave Pat a reassuring pat on the back.

"It sure does," Bea said. "*Crimes,* not mistakes. And how 'bout this for the question box? Did whoever killed the professor get his secrets? And if they did, do they have enough info now to reproduce his technique? That's what matters most to me."

"Good question, Bea," Angela said as she walked into the room. She gave Aseem a big hug and a kiss, then grabbed a sandwich from the desk. She motioned to Bea and Pat to scoot over to make room for her on the bed.

Bea stood up and plopped back down and said, "Yeow!" She stood up again and rubbed her butt and looked at the bed to see what she'd sat on: the manila envelope Aseem's mother had left for him. She handed it over to him.

"There's something pointy in there," Bea said. "I was stabbed in a delicate area."

Aseem pinched the envelope in the middle, a curious frown on his face. "It doesn't feel that pointy. Besides, I don't think something pointy would be 'for my future.'"

"Sweetheart, you sure you don't want to open it and see?" Angela coaxed. Aseem grimaced without responding. "I think your mother wants to apologize. Are you sure you don't want to give her the chance?" She looked at him with a tilt of her head and tapped her hand lightly on her heart. Aseem sighed and grinned at her adoringly.

"Oh, brother. You two are so nauseating, you could star in one of my Betty books," Bea said. "There's an idea, you two could be the model for my next pair of unrealistically hesitant, otherwise perfect lovers. Nope, I'll have to think harder. You two are too sweet even for Treacle Town. You know, it would be *a lot* easier for us to make more money if you two moved in together. We're missing out on a lot of high-season revenue with you each having your own suite. If you cut down to one, I wouldn't have to write so fast," Bea said, bursting into ear-splitting laughter and slapping her knee.

Angela's face quickly turned red, which only made Bea laugh harder. "Maybe we should get back to the matter at hand," Angela said.

"There you go again, Angie," Bea snorted. "Just crack the whip on the old lady. For a person who's so nice she's practically perfect, you've taken to bossing me around like a duck to water. And to think all I'm asking you to do is live with your beloved." Bea paused for dramatic effect and leaned in Angela's direction with a lascivious look on her face. "You know you want to…."

"Bea! Don't you remember that talk we had about boundaries? The one we've had ten times, I mean?"

"C'mon, Angie. You know better than anyone that these suites are designed for sweet, suite romance. Get it?" Bea cackled. Angela's face got redder and Aseem just looked at the floor.

Bea made a show of shaking off her laughter with a heavy sigh. "OK, let's be serious, shall we? Of course, we must add the attack on Pat to the crime column," Bea said. "And whether the sweet-smelling stuff on the fabric is what knocked her out can go under questions—along with what the stuff is."

"Do you still have that cloth? I can look into it a bit more tomorrow," Aseem said. He looked particularly relieved about the change of subject. "And maybe even call my brother if need be." He smiled sweetly at Angela and she smiled back.

Bea rolled her eyes and made a gagging gesture. "Don't worry, I'm just kidding, you two. You do you. But hey, here's a thought, what if you two took one of the casitas—"

"What about the first attack—the one on the baby tree?" Pat interrupted. "And the whole S.O.S. connection, too."

Aseem added notes under "crimes" and "questions."

"Bea, if we moved into a casita, we'd give up even more revenue. Anyway, that subject is closed, OK?" Angela said. "Back to our case. Under suspects, I suppose we have to add Andy Mathers, even though it's not clear he has a motive."

"Motive is often revealed later," Pat said. "That's what all the famous detectives say. Means and opportunity first. We've got to look at the coincidences, to see who *could* have done it—"

"Yeah, and we ran into a big coincidence today," Bea said. "Technically, it started a few days before Thanksgiving, when Pat and I took our poker trip to Emeryville."

Bea explained how she and Pat had noticed that the apartment building across the street from the professor's building had an excellent view directly into the professor's loft, and shared their intuition that someone was taking advantage of it. Bea said she even thought she might have seen a telescope in the window.

"After we discovered the professor's body in his loft, we went across the street and snuck into that building. We found out the apartment with the big window had been rented by some company called 'GreenGene: a ThriveCore Company.' They'd moved out—but when we went back today to check for any clues left behind, guess who showed up?"

"Andy Mathers?" Angela squealed.

"Yeah, and he was trying to remove the only clue we saw, that door sign."

"Wow! I kept circling back to Andy in my interview, but I couldn't even get McGregor to consider him as a suspect. Andy must have had a persuasive alibi. Honestly, McGregor had me wondering if he'd already set his mind on a different suspect."

"Maybe McGregor was playing his cards close to his vest. It's possible he knows something we don't," Pat said. "Although that doesn't sound like him," she added, prompting a bark of laughter from Bea.

"Nailed that, Pat," Bea said. "If you're game, I say we go to the home store and talk to Andy tomorrow." Pat nodded.

"McGregor and McMahon asked me a couple times about the property on the other side of the foothill. They seemed focused on that newly beaten path we saw behind the trailer. I felt kind of stupid not knowing the answer. But how would I know what's over there? Property lines are my mother's department," Angela said. Maria had performed many amazing feats for Betty Snickerdoodle, Inc., over the years—including finding the inn property and negotiating a great price for it.

"Maybe we can find something online?" Aseem said. "Didn't Lexie find the inn's property lines on the internet somewhere?"

"Oh! That reminds me—Drew Faulkner sent me something connected to that. That's what I was trying to look at when I dropped my phone in the foot bath. I'll be right back," Angela said, racing out the door.

CHAPTER 17

Angela was back in moments with her spare phone. With a few taps, she connected it to her account and pulled up the text from Drew.

"Here it is!" she cried. "Oh. My. *Gosh*."

"Don't leave us in suspense, girlie!"

"Drew pinpointed the spot where the picture was uploaded to the *Bee*—the one supposedly sent by S.O.S., the one with the murdered tree. He says it was sent using a burner phone from the far side of the foothill. He even sent a diagram with property boundaries." Angela turned her phone's screen toward the others. "You can see whose property is right near the spot—and who might have been able to walk over the hill to our secret tree farm." Bea, Pat, and Aseem all leaned in to look, and Bea let out a cackle.

"Cal Banks!" Aseem said. "That's someone who might have an interest in our tree experiment. He could see it as a threat."

"Poor Cal. I tried to reassure him we'd still buy trees from him. I had a plan in the back of my mind to let him in on the experiment as soon as it was possible to reveal the secret. He was curious about the tree on the deck and the 'tree scientist,' but I can't imagine he'd have anything to do with—"

"Hot diggity, that reminds me of something," Bea said, reaching into her pocket. "I noticed these pine needles on the ground when we found the dead guy—"

"John Nixon. That's the dead guy's name—"

"Yeah, well I don't think that matters right now, 'cause we know it probably wasn't John Nixon who left those blue pine needles on the ground near his body. They're nothing like the needles of our experimental tree babies. But they might have come from—"

"Cal Banks's Christmas tree farm," Angela sighed.

"Does that mean Cal is our murderer?" Aseem said.

Bea's face took on a look of mischief and snark. "You know what they say: 'Never trust a ginger!'"

Angela groaned.

"What? In medieval times, everyone thought redheads were witches," Bea chortled.

"I like to think society has evolved since then," Angela said. She tilted her head down and put her face in her hands for barely a moment.

"Hey, wait," Angela cried. "Did you once tell me *you* were a redhead before you went gray?"

"It was just a dye job, girlie. I took a walk on the wild side to attract the boys."

"So you voluntarily turned yourself into an untrustworthy ginger?"

"It was *auburn*. Big difference. And back then, appearing untrustworthy could be an advantage."

"Hair color as poker strategy?" Pat laughed.

"I'd have done almost anything to win a few more hands," Bea chuckled.

Angela mouthed the word "hands" and looked at the palms of hers, remembering the gauze Cal had taped over his right one. "The needles don't prove it was Cal, though, do they?" she said, more quietly than before, pressing her thumb on her own palm as she spoke. "It's Christmas tree season. Anyone could pick up a few needles from a different kind of evergreen."

"Good point, Angie. You know, the more I think about it, the less I like Cal as a suspect. He doesn't seem like the criminal type to me, despite his leprechaun hair," Bea laughed. "OK, we've got some investigative work cut out for tomorrow, and it'll go faster if we divide it up. Pat and I will track down Andy. Aseem, will you keep working on this?" Bea handed him the scrap of fabric she picked up at the professor's loft.

Aseem nodded. "And I can look into GreenGene if you like. We've got all kinds of company databases for the incubator."

"Perf," Bea said. "What about you, Angie?"

"I've got a huge day tomorrow with the guests. There's the ornament design class in the morning and the essentials of tree selection and safety in the afternoon—oh, and guess who'll be there for that? Cal!"

"Excellent—so you can talk to the tree farmer/unlikely suspect," Bea said. "And remember, everybody, we're not just doing this for the fun of solving a murder before McGregor. We've still got a shot at keeping the professor's idea alive. So keep the big picture in mind! We've just got to get our mitts on those notes of his."

"Understood," Angela said with a heavy sigh, "even though it might be a longshot."

Pat stood up from the end of the bed. "Now that I've got my marching orders, I'll see you in the morning, Bea. I figure I'll head out to the trailer—"

"No need to tonight, Pat. McGregor told me Officer Babiak's going to be guarding the scene at least one more night, and maybe even until they make an arrest. You can stay with Bea," Angela said.

"OK under one condition," Bea said. "We're getting you a rollaway bed!"

Bea and Pat woke up early and got dressed for their outing, Bea in another of her favorite velour track suits (asparagus green), and Pat in selections from the collection of chinos and flannel shirts she kept stowed in the trunk of her car for stakeouts.

"If we leave now, we can get ourselves an iced coffee and an egg sandwich and still get to Andy's work right after the place opens," Bea said.

They pulled into the entrance of the gargantuan home and garden outlet store, and though it had been open less than half an hour, there was already a line for the parking garage. A huge Christmas tree lot had been set up in front of the garage. Employees were buzzing around, helping the early arrivals choose trees from all the varieties and colors of pines, spruces, and firs. At one end, home décor like wreaths, garlands, and fireplaces was on display.

"Look!" Bea pointed through the car window toward a young man helping a family tie a tree to their car. "Isn't that our Andy?"

"At least we don't have to find him in that huge store," Pat said.

"I agree. And I'm happy my lifetime streak of never entering a home improvement outlet will remain unbroken."

Pat eventually found a space on the third floor of the garage and she and Bea made their way back to the tree lot.

"That's an hour of life we'll never get back," Bea said. They watched as Andy helped another customer, waving to catch his attention and waiting their turn. He acknowledged them with a nod.

"I bet we'll lose another hour before we get to talk to him," Pat said. Her guess turned out to be right, but finally they got a few words with him between customers.

"Nice to see you, Miss Sickles. Thank you

again for the lovely Thanksgiving dinner at your inn."

"That's exactly what we'd like to talk to you about—Thanksgiving," Bea said. "Seems it worked out better for you than for John Nixon."

Andy gulped. "I heard something about that," he said, looking to his right and his left and lowering his voice. "Do you think we can talk about it during my break, in half an hour? We could meet in the paint department. It shouldn't be crowded today."

"So much for my streak," Bea said as she and Pat headed through the sliding doors into the store.

STILL IN HIS PAJAMAS, ASEEM LOOKED AT THE SCRAP of fabric Bea had left with him. He could see the Bos-Curae logo clearly. He decided to do some digging online before calling his brother.

Sanjay had been right: Bos-Curae was a veterinary products company for large animals, mainly livestock like cattle. It made him chuckle when he realized the origin of the name, and he looked forward to telling Angela about it later.

He sniffed the fabric: the residual aroma was now very faint, but he picked up a sweetish smell. He searched on the Bos-Curae website, and, sure enough, inhaled anesthetics were among their products.

Sanjay said he thought the company name sounded familiar from his days as an intern at a medical device company. Were Bos-Curae anesthetics used to test medical devices on animals?

He pulled out his cell and redialed his brother's number. The call went to voicemail after one ring.

On a hunch, he logged in to the research database he used at the incubator, where Gary Wheaton's whiz-kid analysts stored all their confidential reports on the companies they were monitoring. It was a trove of data on all kinds of new companies, new initiatives from big companies, virtually any kind of technical innovation that Gary might want to be a part of. He typed in "GreenGene" and found no results. Then he tried "ThriveCore."

Wow. I never knew corporations could do that!

Aseem took a shower and got dressed. He planned to find Angela, knowing she'd be busy with the slate of activities for the inn's first Christmas-season guests, but thinking he might intercept her during a free moment.

His cell rang.

Sanjay.

"I've got a few minutes before my next procedure, so I called you back. Glad to hear from you, little brother."

Aseem explained what he'd found and confirmed it with Sanjay. "This stuff—this livestock anesthetic—could it be used to put a person to sleep?"

"Sure. There are all kinds of safety precautions you're supposed to take while using it. If I remember correctly about that stuff, though, it's popular because it acts and wears off fast. Less risk of complications. I suppose if you're a human who's going to get knocked out by veterinary anesthesia, this is the kind you'd want."

"Comforting," Aseem said. "Thanks, big brother."

"Oh, no—you're not doing it again. I'm in a rush, too, but you're not hanging up without hearing my apology." Sanjay then explained that their parents' weird behavior at the dinner party had been his idea. "They told me again how they worry you're indecisive about your life—that you're not moving forward. It sounds monumentally stupid now. I should have just told them so. The truth is, when they told me again how anxious they are about you, I saw a chance to deflect the attention away from Preeti and me. You're not the only one they 'worry' about in that sometimes-overbearing way they have. That's why I came up with the idea for the 'test'—that's what we thought we were doing, a little charade, to test you. It was my idea. I convinced myself it was for your own good—"

"Even that ridiculous thing with Mira?" Aseem fumed.

"Oh, that part might have been Ma," Sanjay said sheepishly. "Anyway, at some point, the plan just took on a life of its own. We started having fun with it, the play-acting, and just… we just got carried away."

Aseem snorted. "Good to know my *life* is as much fun as a school play to you, brother!"

"We should have called it off during the dinner party, when it was clear it was a bad idea—"

"And why didn't you?"

"I guess—with Mira there, it just seemed too awkward to admit she'd been invited as part of a scheme. I think Ma also thinks very highly of Mira, and maybe she didn't fully realize how serious you are about Angela. I mean, she does now, of course. But in the moment, it didn't seem right to—you know, embarrass Mira. Like I said, monumentally stupid. And my fault."

Aseem exhaled but said nothing.

"Aseem, I'm so sorry. It's just, you know what it's like when they get obsessive in their fussing. It was because I was worried about Preeti, really—"

"What about Angela?" Aseem cried.

"You're one hundred percent right to be angry. But be angry at me. I know how protective Ma and Dad are of you. I saw a chance to take advantage of it. Please don't be angry at them—especially Ma. She's trying not to show it, but she's very upset."

Aseem took a moment to respond. "All right, then."

"It's not always easy, you know, being the first of the two of us to do everything. Did you look in the package? It'll help, I think."

Aseem pulled the unopened envelope out of his desk drawer. He pulled the tab to open it and found a box inside, wrapped in many layers of tissue. It was antique wood, with a design carved into the top. He unhooked the delicate metal latch.

"I don't get it. It's Ma's earring. What can I do with it?"

"Anything you want. I told you that it would

settle the debate over who the favorite son is." Sanjay laughed quietly, relaxing a little. "I am pretty sure Ma had an idea about how you could use it. For your—"

"Future."

"That's what she said. You should call her, Aseem. Please. I know she wants to apologize."

"I will. Oh, and Sanjay, before you hang up, I've got a completely unrelated question."

"Make it quick—I've got to scrub."

"Have you ever heard of a corporation sponsoring a university department's research?"

"Sure. I think it happens all the time. It's a way for companies to get access to R&D without setting up laboratories, and the universities like that it saves them millions of dollars. Win-win. Supposedly."

"AT LEAST WE'RE GETTING A LITTLE EXERCISE," PAT said as they wandered the wide aisles of the store.

Bea rolled her eyes. "I'd rather be dancing."

"Did you hear that sound? Like 'bizz-izz-izz'? It sounds like an electric drill. What say you—can we go check out the power tools? I could use a new drill. Shopping for one could kill that half hour."

"Lead the way, handy lady."

The power tools were in the back of the store —next to the paint department, where they'd agreed to meet Andy. They had to walk through the gardening aisle to get there.

"Look at this—Formort," Bea said. "It's the stuff the professor said was injected into the dead tree. The murdered tree in our plot, I mean."

"For precision killing of unwanted, invasive, or troublesome trees—leaves neighboring plants untouched," Pat read from the label. "It's like a sniper for trees."

"Or a neutron bomb," Bea chuckled. "Here's something else. The label says, 'Packed by Fruit & Flower: A ThriveCore Company'—GreenGene is in good company."

"I got my break a few minutes early," Andy said, rushing toward them, a little out of breath. "Can we head back to the paints?"

In the quiet end of the aisle, next to towering shelves of neatly arranged gallon cans, Andy explained in a soft, low voice that John Nixon was a newly hired coworker who had been asking everyone if he could take any shifts they didn't need. "The job was his side hustle to pay off student debt. He wanted some extra cash with the holidays coming. He'd already picked up shifts from a few other people who wanted time off for holiday shopping or whatever. He was persistent —he's got two kids, and money is tight. I know how hard it can be financially for my sister and her family, so I... I felt bad for him."

"Why did he think there'd be a shift to do on Thanksgiving?" Pat said. "Isn't the store closed?"

"It mostly is, but the tree lot is open for a few hours, and we have a big sale of artificial trees and decorations on the Friday after Thanksgiving that we have to prep for. All of us on the schedule had signed up last summer. It's a prime gig. We were getting paid double-time. I didn't want to give it up, but I still felt bad about John—"

"I guess you didn't feel bad about breaking your promise to keep the tree experiment a secret, though, right?" Bea said. "You could have let him take the double-time job and done the tree work yourself. Didn't care so much about hurting the professor, I guess?"

"Of course not!" Andy said, his face coloring. "I just thought... I thought I was lucky to be getting the double pay—I mean, I can use the money, too —and that if John took care of the saplings, then I could make it for the last part of Thanksgiving dinner at your inn. The saplings didn't need much done to them. I just… I see now it was selfish. But I didn't know it would be dangerous! And I hardly told him anything—I didn't even tell him the tree farm was connected to your inn, I just told him how to get there. I did tell him that he had to keep it secret—that the secrecy was really important, because I wasn't supposed to tell anyone about it. But I didn't tell him he had to guard the trees with his life or anything!"

"Did Sergeant McGregor ask you about this?"

"Not really. He just wanted to know if I was supposed to be there instead of John. I told him that John wanted work, and I wanted the time off. He said it sounded like a routine shift swap. Look… I feel terrible about this. I mean, the professor was always nervous about someone finding out, but I didn't tell John anything about the experiment. Really, I didn't. What did I even know about it? I dug holes and gave the trees the food the professor gave me. I knew that the professor was trying to grow trees fast, but I never knew what was in the serum." Andy's voice quavered. "It never occurred to me that someone might be killed for it."

"Or that two people could be killed, you mean," Bea said.

"Two people? But I thought—"

"Did McGregor ask you about where you were on Thanksgiving Day?" Bea said. "Earlier in the day, I mean."

"Or the night before," Pat piped up.

"Yes, he even called the store to confirm. They told him I was working that day and the night before."

Bea and Pat exchanged knowing glances.

"Why did you show up at that apartment across the street from the professor's loft?" Bea asked. "The one with the perfect view into his window. Were you using that apartment to spy on him? He told us he was worried people were after his secrets. Were you one of the people he was worried about?"

"Of course not! Dr. Woodward is my friend!" Andy's face grew paler and tense. "I'd never hurt him. I never even knew about that apartment until—"

"Then why were you removing the label from that door?" Pat said. "Seems like that label might be evidence."

"Yeah, and why were you doing it right after he was found dead?"

"The professor's... you mean, Dr. Woodward's... Dr. Woodward's *dead?!*" Andy cried. His mouth dropped open and he looked up at the ceiling. "The label—I did that for Brandon. I'd never seen the place before."

"Brandon?" Bea said.

Andy started to lose his balance and leaned back against the shelves, jiggling a few of the paint cans. "Dr. Woodward is—was—a dear friend. He was helping me switch careers. I was his graduate teaching assistant, but I realized that biomedical engineering wasn't for me. I was going to go into architecture—I mean, I still hope…."

Bea and Pat looked at each other uncomfortably as Andy started to cry. Bea patted him on the arm clumsily. "What were you saying about Brandon, Andy?"

"Brandon Kellan. You know, the professor's nephew."

Bea and Pat exchanged wide-eyed glances.

"Brandon was trying to change his life, too. We were… we weren't exactly friends, but we were friendly. We had something in common. All three of us did, really—Brandon, me, Dr. Woodward. We were all trying out new directions. Dr. Woodward wanted to work on his tree project. It was like a night job, but it was his passion. And he helped Brandon get a part-time job doing technology stuff at the university. That way,

Brandon could go take a few classes, try to finish his bachelor's degree. Dr. Woodward said he hardly had any family, and had cut ties with them, until he found he could help Brandon."

"Did Brandon say why he wanted you to remove the label?"

"Brandon said he'd been doing some part-time work for GreenGene, and that the company wasn't using the space anymore, and that he forgot to take the label off. Said he didn't want anyone to be confused, and that he wouldn't be back in Emeryville anytime soon to do it himself."

"Did he say what the work was?" Pat asked.

"No. We didn't talk about it. He just asked me if I'd do it in an email, and since it wasn't a big deal for me to go there, I said sure. I had to be at the Emeryville store yesterday, anyway. I just assumed it was something to do with the professor's tree experiment. GreenGene, and every other ThriveCore company—they make half the products here in the garden department. I didn't think to question it."

"Is Brandon still working for his uncle—I mean, had he been, until Thanksgiving?"

"I assume so. Since Dr. Woodward got fired, we don't all work together anymore. I just do what he asks when he calls me. I mean, I did—you know," Andy sniffed. He patted down his work shirt and adjusted his name tag absently. "I'm sorry, but I have to go. My break's over."

"One quick thing, Andy," Bea said. "Can you answer a question about this white paint?"

∽

"REMEMBER, ABOVE ALL, TO AVOID FIRES, KEEP your tree watered and away from heat sources like radiators, space heaters, and candles," Angela said cheerfully to the attentive guests who'd filled up the front half of the inn ballroom. A graphic reading "Essentials of Tree Selection and Safety" was projected on the huge video display on the stage behind her. "There you have it—all the basics of choosing your best tree and keeping it safe. Don't worry if you didn't take notes. There's an outline with all the information in the new Betty Snickerdoodle's Classic Christmas app."

She took a few audience questions, then pointed to three long tables in the back of the room. The tables were covered in red and green cloths, loaded with delectable treats, and invitingly placed near the fireplace, where a hearty fire crackled and whooshed. "Now please help yourself to the hot cocoa, cider, and Christmas cookies at the back of the room."

The audience applauded enthusiastically and made their way to the snacks. Aseem had come in near the end of Angela's presentation and was standing by the doors, still beaming and clapping loudly as the applause died down. A few attendees who'd been too shy to speak in front of the group lined up to ask Angela their questions individually. Finally, she made her way back to Aseem and greeted him with a warm hug.

"I thought Cal was presenting with you," Aseem said. "Where is he?"

"Good question," Angela frowned. "He never showed. I tried texting him a few minutes before the start of the session. He didn't answer."

"What do you think—should we drive by his place? Do you have time?"

"Yep. I'm done for the day. Let's do it."

They took the road that snaked the long way around the ranch and several neighboring properties, Aseem behind the wheel. Eventually they reached the entrance to the shared private road. Aseem drove down the narrow, empty road, past their tree experiment and the trailer. Angela noticed there no longer was a cop car on the roadside.

"I thought McGregor was keeping Babiak out here a while longer," Angela said. "At least until they arrested someone, he said."

"Maybe that's only at nighttime? Would they assume no one will tamper with anything in broad daylight?"

They climbed the grade up the foothill, then descended the other side toward a group of properties they'd never seen before. Angela pointed to the open field where whoever attacked Pat and then John Nixon might have walked onto the outer edge of Bea's ranch property, obscured by the trailer as they plotted their move.

"I wonder if Sergeant McGregor or Officer Babiak has taken pictures or looked for footprints already," she said. "I'm surprised that they haven't taped anything off over here."

Aseem continued to the intersection of the north side of the private road with the main, public one, then turned right to head to Cal's farm.

"The turnoff to Cal's farm is about a half mile from here on the right," Angela said. "You can make it out in the distance. See, there's a car pulling out—oh, wait—"

The car pulling out was a cruiser. Its lights

turned on, and it sped up slightly as it headed toward them and then sailed by.

"That was McGregor, wasn't it? And was that Babiak with him in the front?"

"Yep. But I'm more interested in who was in the back," Angela said.

CHAPTER 18

The next morning, Bea, Angela, Pat, and Aseem reconvened their mystery-solving meeting in Aseem's room. The three ladies were once more seated at the end of the bed, looking at the white board. Aseem was standing beside the board, pen at the ready. Bea kicked off the discussion with a question.

"McGregor arrested Cal Banks last night. I'd like a show of hands," Bea said. "How many of you think McGregor arrested the right suspect?"

Everyone looked around at each other and smiled, and not a single hand was raised.

"McGregor could be the blind acorn this time," Pat said. "You know—that poker thing you always say."

"Huh?" Bea said. It came out like the call of a deeply disgruntled Canada goose, earning winces from Angela and Aseem.

"I think she means the blind pig," Angela said. "You always say that even a blind pig finds an acorn once in a while."

Bea let out a cackle that was the perfect ear-splitting follow-up to her bird call. "Good thinking, Pat. But I don't think it's McGregor's turn to find an acorn again yet. Rumor has it he guessed something correctly back in 2011. More important, that conversation with Andy left us with too many questions to conclude Cal's the killer."

"Do you think Andy's a suspect?" Aseem said.

"Not really. But he is in the middle of this thing somehow."

"And Brandon, too," Pat piped up.

"Brandon?" Angela said. "Titus's assistant?"

"Andy told us that Brandon is the professor's nephew. Makes you wonder what Brandon's doing working for Titus, considering the professor seemed to find the guy so annoying," Pat said.

"I'm no expert on academia, but Brandon doesn't seem to have a whole lot of qualifications, either. Andy said Brandon was struggling to finish his bachelor's degree. Isn't a teaching assistant normally a grad student? And there's that conversation we overheard at the professor's loft, Pat," Bea said.

"Yeah, Titus was getting all fake-sentimental about how they used to be partners, but the professor seemed to think Titus got him fired."

"Remember what the professor said about his 'imbecilic relatives'?" Aseem said. "Maybe Brandon's one of them."

"Andy said that the professor was really trying to help Brandon," Pat said. "He said the three of them—Andy, Brandon, and the professor—were all trying a fresh start, that it was something they had in common."

"If Brandon's his nephew, then maybe Brandon's mother or father's an imbecilic relative," Bea said. "That could be why the professor wanted to help Brandon."

"Maybe mother—because of the different last name, I mean. Andy told us Brandon's last name is Kellan. Maybe his mother is the professor's sister," Pat said. "I can look into that."

"We should try to find out why the professor got fired, too—and whether Titus was behind it. You got university contacts through your incubator, handsome?"

"I'll see what I can dig up."

"By the way, speaking of your incubator, didn't anyone at that box of brains notice the professor wasn't even an expert on plants? Pat and I saw his diploma when we found his body. He was some kind of engineer—biomedical, if I remember right."

"We have a lot of university contacts, but the truth is, a lot of people in Silicon Valley don't even care about degrees. I doubt the incubator verifies anyone's academic record, much less a Ph.D.'s credentials."

"Wasn't there some billionaire who was paying kids to leave Ivy League schools without their degrees?" Angela said. "Like it was a test of entrepreneurial drive?"

Aseem nodded. "The Valley's not that great on background checks, either. Every few years, there's a big scandal over some high flyer lying on their resume."

"That's entertaining, but I have a better theory for why Gary's people didn't care in the professor's case. They didn't put up any of the dough! It's all *my* money in this venture. That's why we gotta find those documents of his."

"Bea… at least we didn't put up much money. And we'll get to keep the trees," Angela said quietly. "I mean… just in case we can't get the documents. I feel like we should prepare ourselves—"

"Girlie, I'm surprised at you. You can't give up now. Don't you still want to save the tree world?"

"I'm trying to be realistic. Someone stole those syringes from the tree plot. I'm just starting to think… if it turns out Cal's the murderer, he probably has those syringes. And if we assume he also has the documents from the professor's loft, that's a lot of pieces to the puzzle of the professor's technique. Cal's not a scientist, but he knows trees. Maybe he could even recreate the experiment himself. And whoever the murderer is, they could already have found a way to hide the documents, or pass them on to someone—"

"There was that agreement the professor signed, saying he'd give the secret to Bea in the event of his death," Aseem said, hopefully.

"He didn't tell me squat," Bea said. "And now that the event of his death has occurred, it's going to be hard to enforce the agreement."

"I suppose I could have worded that section a little better," Aseem said. "Sorry about that."

"Aw, honey, nobody expects to be murdered," Angela said. "But if the documents are found, even by someone else, does that agreement prove Bea is entitled to them?"

"We'd probably have to prove they were stolen. That's why I think we need to keep trying to find them. Then we can file for that patent ourselves—and do what you were saying all along, Angie," Bea said.

"Even if someone managed to steal the documents and samples of some of the serums, we've got the actual plants. They don't even have seeds. That means that right now, we're the only ones who can prove it works, which is essential for a patent," Aseem said.

"Maybe we'd better keep guarding those plants," Pat said.

"I think you're right. We noticed Officer Babiak's cruiser was no longer parked at our tree site," Angela said. "That was the first clue that McGregor had arrested someone."

Pat volunteered to head up to the trailer as soon as they ended the meeting, reassuring everyone that she'd be fine because she liked privacy and normally had a lot of time to herself, and that she could do her research just as easily from up there as at the inn. Aseem double-checked that the video feed was working again, both as a back-up and security for Pat, and suggested that they work out a schedule and trade off shifts at the trailer.

"I just got an idea," Angela said. "Lexie will probably be covering the murder for the *Bee*. Maybe she can help us figure out if Cal got the professor's documents—or if he's even the murderer. I'll call her in between guest events today."

"I just thought of something, too. Bea, you asked me to look into the professor's university experience. If he was actually a biomedical engineer, that could be connected to ThriveCore and Bos-Curae. I found out from my brother that Bos-Curae makes anesthetics for... for testing biomedical devices," Aseem said.

"What kind of testing?" Bea asked, an eyebrow cocked.

"Um... animal testing, my brother said." He exchanged a quick smile with Angela.

"What are you two smiling about?" Bea asked. "You aren't trying to pull something over on me about this 'Bossy-Curae,' are you?"

Angela's brow furrowed and Aseem changed the subject. "I also found out that ThriveCore has ties to Avalon. I'll try to find out more."

"I guess we all know what we need to do," Pat said, standing up from the bed. "Except... what are you gonna do, Bea? Do you want to come help me at the trailer?"

"Nope. I've given myself the most important job of all," Bea said. "But I'm not ready to tell you about it until I'm sure it will work. In the meantime, let's just say I'll be getting to know Betsy 2."

Angela laughed. "OK, Bea. You have fun with your new toy."

~

BEA DID INTEND TO HAVE FUN WITH HER "NEW" Selectric, but not the kind of fun Angela meant. She'd had a brainstorm about how the typewriter might help her recreate the professor's notes about his super-charged tree-growing method. She'd just needed some quiet time by herself with that beautiful machine to put her theory to the test, and now she finally had her chance.

She pulled a can of iced coffee from the small fridge in her suite and took a swig. Then, using all her might, she hoisted the heavy typewriter onto her desk.

"C'mon, Betsy 2, time to see what your memory's made of," Bea said aloud. She studied the machine for a moment and smiled. Whether or not her theory panned out, getting her hands on another Selectric was an unexpected pleasure. She intended to enjoy it to the fullest.

Bea opened the case, plugged the machine in, punched the sturdy "on" button, and enjoyed the typewriter's familiar hum. With a press of the tab key and a clunk, the carrier and the ribbon cartridge moved swiftly to the center.

"Looking good, ol' girl."

Bea turned the power off again, then lifted the top cover and peered in at the ribbon cartridge, spotting the little ejector arm on the right side. "Like riding a bike," she said, expertly popping the cartridge out of its holder. With her most delicate touch on the very edges of the ribbon, she slid it out of the thin clips that held it taut and moved it slowly past the type ball. Then she grabbed the plastic cartridge on its sides and extracted it from the inner workings of the typewriter.

"Just like that old game 'Operation,'" Bea chuckled to herself. "Now, little cartridge, it's time for you and your ribbon to have a thorough exam." Bea held the cartridge to her face and scrutinized it. "Let's see what you got." Bea gently pinched the top edge of the ribbon and tugged it a few centimeters out of the cartridge for a closer look.

Hot dog! Jackpot!

She looked at the ribbon closely, confirming it was the correctable film type. The last letters typed on it could easily be read. It was the type of ribbon that passed through just once, so everything typed on it was preserved. She couldn't believe her luck. The professor was so paranoid, she'd been afraid he'd have chosen a fabric ribbon —the preferred choice of banks and anyone else wanting to keep what they'd typed confidential.

Lucky for me, professor, you weren't a perfect conspiracy theorist after all. Or maybe you just didn't know all there is to know about these miraculous instruments.

Bea shut the cover and turned the typewriter off, then turned her attention to the ribbon she'd just pulled out of it.

It's gonna take a while to transcribe this, working letter by letter. Maybe a couple of days.

Bea remembered the piles and piles of pages she'd seen during her first visit to the professor's loft.

Scratch that. Maybe it will take a week or even longer, especially if I'm lucky and the instructions are all on this one cartridge.

She decided to replace the ribbon and then close

the machine back up in its hard case. Now that she had a replacement for her dearly departed Betsy, she intended to protect her new treasured companion from anything that might harm her, including dust. The box with the replacement ribbon was still in the deep pocket of the track suit jacket she'd worn to the professor's loft. The jacket was hanging over the plush chair in the corner of her suite, the plum color almost obscuring the charming vintage-Christmas design of the upholstery.

Bea slid the box out of the jacket pocket and put it on the desk next to Betsy 2, noticing that faint rattle again.

I hope it's not broken.

She carefully pulled open the tab at the end. As she grabbed the end of the cartridge and pulled it from the box, she found the cartridge had been altered. The ribbon had been removed, and a sort of cavity had been carved in the center with a knife. Wedged inside the little cavity was a cardboard container. It was a tiny matchbox, and as soon as Bea picked it up, she knew it was the source of the soft rattling sound that had come from the cartridge box.

Bea slid open the tiny box and laughed out loud. "Oh, professor, you really were a smartypants. I think I love you! Too bad you're not here to hear it."

A slip of paper the size of a fortune from a cookie was tucked inside the box. Bea pulled it out and read it:

Soak these seeds. (See ingredients to add to the water on reverse.) Refrigerate at least two weeks before planting.

Bea knew these must be the special seeds the professor had created—the first component of his rapid-growth process. She looked at the short list of ingredients on the back of the paper and wondered if any or even all of them were already here at the inn, given the many things they'd purchased for the tree experiment.

Angie will know.

Bea tucked the instructions back in the little box, hid the box in the pocket of one of the track suits hanging in her closet, and went to find Angela.

"Hi," Angela said, opening the door to her suite. "I just got off the phone with Lexie, and I've only got a few minutes before I need to start the next guest session."

"Don't worry, Angie. I'll be brief," Bea said.

"Let me tell you what Lexie said first." Angela explained that Lexie was, indeed, working on a story about the murders of John Nixon and the professor. Naturally, McMahon was not inclined to help her with the Emeryville part of the story, and, at least so far, he'd been unaffected by the saucy armaments in her battery of feminine wiles.

"Officer Babiak, though, is another story—he's single and Lexie's… you know, Lexie. So let's just say she's been working the wine country side of the story more aggressively. She's already even been in to see Cal—when McGregor was out, of course."

"That girl's creative and she's got moxie," Bea cackled. "And she moves fast. What has she learned?"

"Cal says that aside from overhearing that little bit from me that day in the ballroom, he only heard about the trees because he got an email message from—would you believe?—Andy Mathers. Cal's already admitted to killing our baby tree and sending that first message to the *Bee* claiming to be S.O.S. He said Andy asked him to do it, gave him specific instructions, and said it was the best way to save his business. Otherwise, Andy said, his Christmas tree farm faced 'certain doom.' Apparently, the emails were urgent and quite persuasive. Lexie even got copies of them from Cal's wife, and said she'd forward them over to us."

"Did you know Cal and Andy were friends?" Bea said.

"Lexie asked about that. Cal said they weren't —they just met each other back at our Halloween party—but that Andy emailed him from the form on his Christmas tree website."

"Has she already got her foxy FBI ex-boyfriend figuring out if the person Cal was emailing really was Andy?"

"Yep. I thought I'd check in with Drew, too. And if we get the emails, maybe Aseem can figure some of that out."

"So Cal's saying he killed a tree, but that's it. Does Lexie believe him?"

"She says it's probably too early to form an opinion, but if she had to bet, she'd wager that Cal was telling the truth. She did a little test, trying to trip him up with false information. She said, 'When were you last at the professor's loft in Vallejo?' He didn't blink, just said, 'I don't know any professor, and I haven't been in Vallejo in over a year.'"

"I like that—the old false location trick. I don't think Cal's sharp enough to bluff at that one on the spot. If we believe Cal was recruited just to scare us off—"

"By involving—or pretending to be—S.O.S., and generating the negative publicity, you mean?"

"Yep. If that's what Cal was up to, he probably doesn't have the professor's documents." Angela nodded, and Bea continued. "That means we've gotta keep doing McGregor's work for him. But I've got good news for you. We've got a back-up plan and we've still got a shot at getting that patent."

Bea explained what she'd found out about the typewriter ribbon—and the bonus good news of the tiny box of the professor's modified seeds.

"Whoa!" Angela squealed. "That transcription, though. It sounds like a lot of work. Maybe I can help?"

"You can, but first things first: we've got to get those seeds soaking ASAP. Do we have these items on hand?" Bea showed Angela the list of ingredients she'd jotted down from the back of the professor's message.

"Most of them—but I don't think I've seen this one or that one."

"That gives me an excuse to call Andy Mathers. Who knows, McGregor might get around to making him a suspect soon, too. I should quiz him about his 'friendship' with Cal before that happens."

"You know what else, Bea?" Angela said, looking serious. "We have to guard those baby trees with our lives. Because the professor put those seeds in that cartridge box for a reason. It was like a message to you and only you. Those must be the last of the seeds."

"I think so, too, girlie. And whoever's got the documents but no seeds is going to be desperate. They're going to try to steal cones to see if they can get their own seeds, or maybe even steal a whole tree."

"Aseem's right. We should rotate so that there's always someone up there," Angela said. Then her face brightened. "But we're so close now, Bea! If we get the technique down from that typewriter ribbon of yours, we can test it out with the seeds, then file our own patent—"

"Don'tcha just love it when a back-up plan comes together?" Bea said.

CHAPTER 19

For the next few days, Bea worked feverishly to transcribe the individual letters on the typewriter ribbon. It was slow going. The strings of letters needed to be sorted into words, and Bea had no way of knowing whether the professor was documenting his process in order or if she had jumped into the middle of it. To try to get her bearings, she compared the bits she'd figured out with the discarded pages she and Pat had found on the floor of the professor's loft, hoping to sort out the sequence the professor had in mind. But several days in, only a fraction of the transcribing was finished, and it was still too soon to make sense of what she was copying.

She and Angela were hardly losing hope,

however. On the contrary, they were energized by their task, and especially by the thrilling discovery of the seeds. Knowing they'd soon have both the instructions and the professor's doctored seeds, they felt optimistic that they'd be able to recreate the experiment—and beat whoever murdered the professor to the punch by patenting it. Those seeds felt like a miraculous gift from the professor from the hereafter, a special delivery to Bea via a Selectric cartridge.

They knew they had to get the seeds soaking right away. They had to follow the order precisely. Soaking had to be done before the seeds could be refrigerated, which in turn had to be done before the seeds could be planted. Bea called Andy about the missing ingredients they needed for the seeds' special soak, knowing she could kill several birds with one stone. She asked Andy to bring several gallons of that special paint she'd asked about in the store when he came by the inn to deliver the chemicals. When he arrived with the ingredients and the paint, she asked him to load the paint cans into the barn for safekeeping, since she planned to give them to Angela's mother next time she visited the inn. While Andy worked, Bea took the opportunity to quiz him about Cal.

"I only met Cal once, at your Halloween party.

I didn't tell him anything about the tree experiment—why would I? And I've never emailed him," Andy had said, visibly perplexed by Bea's questions. "And why would I say his Christmas tree business was doomed, anyway? The professor wasn't even interested in farming Christmas trees—I mean, he only saw conifers as a steppingstone to his real goals. I suppose there's the chance you all might go into the Christmas tree business here at the inn, and that might threaten Cal. But I would never have thought of that. I was focused on helping the professor. Why would I encourage Cal to hurt the professor's experiment?"

Bea thought Andy was telling the truth, and Angela did, too. But they kept that intuition—and Bea's entire conversation with Andy—to themselves. They didn't even tell Lexie. Angela felt a pang of guilt about that, since Lexie had helped them by sharing those emails between Cal and "Andy."

"Keep your eyes on the prize, Angie," Bea had said. "That's how we're gonna win this thing!"

Angela knew Bea was right. Keeping everything they knew about who might or might not have been involved in the murders under wraps was the best course. They didn't want to do anything that could cause whoever had the professor's documents to panic. Letting them think they were in control and getting away with it was smarter.

So they stuck to the task at hand and now the seeds had completed their nutritious soak and were hibernating in two separate refrigerators. Splitting the seeds into batches was Angela's idea. If anything went wrong with one batch, they'd still have the other. They placed half the soaked seeds in the little fridge in Bea's suite and tucked the remainder in the back of the walk-in cooler in the inn's kitchen. Because of the back-up generator, the walk-in would stay cold even if the inn lost power. And before they even began the soaking, Angela suggested they keep some dry seeds in reserve, just in case.

"If we don't get it right the first time, this way, we can try again."

"You think of everything, girlie," Bea said. "You're a natural-born leader."

Teamwork was boosting the gang's spirits, too. Everyone was excited—not just Bea and Angela, but Aseem and Pat, too—by the possibility of recreating the professor's experiment, though they knew it was still a longshot. And they were energized to work together to make it happen, which was a good thing, because their hours were long.

It was the first Christmas season that the inn had welcomed fans of Betty Snickerdoodle's *Treacle Town* books, and the place was abuzz with the guests' delight. That meant busy days and nights for Angela especially, as work on the tree project had to be balanced with the inn's first priority: catering to customers. Of course, Angela loved that work, too—in fact, there was almost nothing she loved more than mingling with the community of fans she'd brought together through her warm and ingenious marketing methods. Bea even got in the spirit, popping out of her suite every few days to give her readers the thrill of meeting Betty herself and getting their books autographed.

"Don't worry, Bea," Angela laughed whenever Bea protested that her fingers were cramped or she just wasn't in the mood. "I won't ask you to sign books every day. Scarcity helps keep the demand strong." On the occasions that Bea did her book signings, sales inevitably spiked. Happy superfans posting their autographed treasures to social media helped introduce many new readers to *Treacle Town*.

In the evenings, Angela would join Bea in her

suite to help with the transcribing. She'd bring along dinner—plates of whatever delicious holiday-themed treats the chefs had come up with for the guests—and after they ate, she'd type the letters into her laptop as Bea read them off the typewriter ribbon.

Eventually, after Bea had been at it for nearly two weeks, Aseem came up with a much more efficient solution. Bea could read the letters aloud and use her handy internet assistant, Rebecca, to record them. Then the recording could be uploaded onto Bea's computer and auto-magically transcribed by the word-processing program. From there, it was much easier for Bea to decipher the professor's words.

"You're awfully handsome to be so smart," Bea'd said.

"I only wish I'd thought of it sooner."

It wasn't surprising he hadn't. Aseem's job had been extra busy, too. The sheer number of year-end tasks he was responsible for at the incubator caught him completely off guard. He'd needed to spend more days in Silicon Valley, which meant nearly ten more hours a week for commuting alone. He'd been so busy, he hadn't yet gotten to the bottom of why the professor was fired. He hadn't analyzed the email threads Lexie had sent over, either. During the time he'd had available to work at the inn, it was all he could do to help Angela with the projects she'd planned for guests and take his turns staying out at the trailer, so that Pat could go to San Francisco for a few days at a time and take care of her own business obligations that were piling up at home.

"Don't worry, handsome. Just keep the farm safe. It's even more important, now that I've almost finished recreating the professor's documents, thanks to you and your brilliant solution. We're on the verge of a big startup score —I'm gonna be a tycoon, and your incubator's gonna have its first big winner!"

FINALLY, WITH CHRISTMAS APPROACHING, THE seeds were ready to plant. They decided that even though the seeds would start in pots, the planting still needed to be done at their little tree farm. The inn was chock-full of guests. The ballroom was needed for meals and activities, and there was nowhere else in the inn where they could plant the seeds and maintain the pots at outdoor temperature—much less keep the experiment a secret. Plus, the professor's notes specified robust, glazed ceramic pots—"to ensure nothing contaminates the soil." It would be easier to fill those heavy pots after transporting them than to move them when full.

They also decided that they shouldn't plant all the prepared seeds at once. Much to Angela's relief, they learned from the documents Bea had managed to recreate (with Rebecca's indispensable help) that the seeds could stay refrigerated for as long as eight weeks before planting.

"That gives us *three* tries, at least. The seeds we reserved, plus the two refrigerated batches," Angela beamed. "But, hopefully, we'll just need this one."

"May Mother Nature approve and bless our effort!" Bea said. "The sooner the better. Timing-wise, this is our best shot."

Pat had taken one of the UTVs with her to the tree plot. Aseem and Angela planned to bring all the supplies they needed out in the second, which was parked beside the barn, along with the little trailer. But before they started, Aseem and Pat wanted to share the progress of their investigations. Bea and Angela convened with Aseem in his room, and Pat joined virtually from the trailer, waving and smiling from the screen of the laptop on Aseem's desk.

"Since work at the incubator finally slowed down, I was able to look into the university's connections to ThriveCore. Pat mentioned that she'd also made some progress on Brandon, so we thought we'd have a quick debrief before moving on to the next phase of our experiment," Aseem said. He was standing beside the white board, marker in hand. "Pat, do you want to start?"

"Sure thing. First, Brandon indeed appears to be the professor's nephew. His mother's name is Polly Baker—formerly known as Polly Wiggins, Polly Conrad, Polly Kellan (when she was married to Brandon's father), and, you guessed it, Polly Woodward. She's not married to Baker anymore, either—just decided it was too much trouble to change her name again, I guess. She and Brandon moved last year into the next town over from Avalon University of California. She works as a waitress in a café right near the school—it's popular with faculty and students alike."

"That's a lotta exes and not much job. Sounds like she might have a financial motive to off the professor, if she thought she'd inherit," Bea said.

"Yep, and so might Brandon. I looked into the ex-husbands. They're mostly garden-variety hustlers and crooks. Kellan—Brandon's birth dad —has been in and out of prison, but he's a bit higher on the ne'er-do-well food chain. ATM skimming, identity theft. Those scams take brains."

"Do you think Polly hoped her brother would be a father figure for Brandon?" Angela said.

"Plausible," Pat replied. "I was able to trace hubby number three, Danny Wiggins, through one of my street contacts. He was around when the kid was in middle school, and says the boy had a real knack for computers. But the constant parade of wannabe dads, crappy apartments, and low-rent towns didn't exactly help the kid thrive academically."

"Did Polly move to be near her brother?" Angela said.

"She's gotta be in her mid or even late forties now. It's gotta be rough to wake up at that age and realize your only skill is waitressing. Maybe it dawned on her to help her boy build something for the future, and maybe she thought her brother could help."

"You're overlooking her talent for attracting high caliber dudes," Bea snorted.

"You know, she's still kind of a looker. I went by the café to snoop a little. She was doing a good job of working the nerdy professor types. You could tell she was making them feel special."

"Looking for bigger tips or an upgraded husband number five?"

"Maybe both. Anyway, what I learned about Brandon's computer talent fits with what Andy told us."

"Fits with something I found, too," Aseem said. "That email between Cal and Andy doesn't look like it was from Andy at all. It was sent from an Avalon University email address, but Andy said he doesn't have a login to university email any longer. What if Brandon held on to his access to the biomedical engineering department servers? He could have kept Andy's email active, or even reactivated it, and used it to email Cal."

"Looks like all your fine fingers are pointing at Brandon," Bea said, hopping up from the end of the bed and imitating a witchy display of crooked fingers and sinister facial expressions.

"There's one more thing," Aseem said. "ThriveCore. They're not just connected with the university—they sponsor botany research. The university does the work, but ThriveCore dictates the studies and owns the results. Got me thinking that maybe Brandon worked some kind of a deal with that company. What if ThriveCore found out the professor was his uncle, and hired him to try to steal the invention? Brandon might have thought it would be an easier way to get paid than to inherit a bunch of documents and then try to find a buyer.

"Plus, Titus's attempts to bring the professor's research into the university were going nowhere. Titus is the head of the botany department. What if Brandon found out the extent of ThriveCore's involvement from Titus? That might have given Brandon the idea of approaching them quietly, on his own. Given Avalon's left-leaning reputation, ThriveCore's influence over research is not something either side is publicizing. ThriveCore is secretive, and that makes many people think they're up to no good. They're mostly despised by environmentalists… and most botanists are environmentalists. But they've also got the deepest pockets around."

"Not bad. Let's call that a working theory," Bea said. "Helps explain Brandon's connection to the ThriveCore spy shack across the street from his uncle, too. There are still some pieces missing— no matter, though. Our job right now is to get those new trees started! We're in a race to prove this technique works."

"But what about the documents?" Angela said. "If we believe Brandon has them, isn't it just as important to stop him from selling them to

ThriveCore? Or should we at least tell McGregor what we know, so we can try to stop them from using the information?"

Aseem nodded. "Maybe ThriveCore was the reason the professor was afraid corporate bullies would find a way to steal his innovation. Remember that story he kept telling us about Robert Kearns and the windshield wipers, and how big companies had armies of lawyers who could steal his invention, even though he had the patent? ThriveCore's as big as General Motors—maybe bigger."

"First things first," Bea said. "We're close to growing our own trees. We can't afford to push McGregor into stirring up trouble. That might get those armies of ThriveCore's sniffing around here in a panic. Focus, people, focus!"

Angela sighed. "If worst comes to worst, maybe we have a few advantages that guy Robert Kearns didn't have. Like we know how to get publicity. The wrong kind of attention could make it harder for ThriveCore to get away with it."

"Yep, you could bring the wrath of social media down on them, Angie. But maybe we should tread a little carefully," Bea said. "Bad as the automakers were to Robert Kearns, I don't think he was up against murderers."

"I just thought of something we can and should do right now," Aseem said. "We can start working on that patent application. Then if the new seeds grow, we can file immediately."

"Good idea, handsome. I'll call my old friend Charlie Carter. He's the only lawyer I trust."

Aseem attached the trailer to the UTV and he, Angela, and Bea started loading it up with pots and soil and drip vials. They'd already filled the vials with the seedling serum, which they'd prepared in the barn the night before according to the professor's recreated documents. It was mid-morning and the sun was climbing in the bright blue sky, but the December air was brisk.

"We might need to make more than one trip," Angela said. "Since you're taking over for Pat in the trailer tonight, I'll shuttle her back here and pick up whatever doesn't fit."

"Sounds good. When you come back, you can grab my overnight bag from my suite, too—that'll save a little room."

Aseem started the UTV and Angela hopped aboard. "By the way, Bea, do you happen to know what those cans of paint in the barn are for? I don't recall ordering any."

"Oh, that's not for the inn. It's something I had Andy bring over for Maria."

"My mother? Is she coming here?"

"Maybe. Or I might have someone deliver them for her. Nothing for you to worry about, girlie."

Angela squinted at Bea but didn't say anything as she and Aseem rolled off toward the tree farm.

When they arrived at the plot, Pat was outside to greet them. Angela passed out gardening gloves and they got off to a fast start. They each took care of seven pots. Angela decided they'd work simultaneously on a section at a time. Before they started each step, she read that part of the instructions aloud.

"Twenty-one pots, twenty-one plants altogether," Aseem said. "I hope it's enough."

"Bea said that any gambler would tell you that twenty-one is one of the luckiest numbers."

"Mathematicians say seven is lucky—seven continents, seven days of the week," Aseem said. "And twenty-one is three times seven."

"Victory is assured!" Pat proclaimed.

They got the soil and seeds into the pots, then moved on to the next step: filling the drip ports. They got into a groove with their assembly line and were done in just minutes. Angela and Aseem had left five ports and assembly rigs behind at the inn, but they made short work of the first sixteen. There was room inside the enclosure for twelve of the completed pots. They placed the nine others, including the five pots that were still incomplete, along the outside of the fence.

"Who's hungry? I'm starved," Angela said. The noon sun was high in the sky. "How about I head back to the inn, drop you off, Pat, and come back with lunch and the last of the supplies? I'll grab your overnight bag, too, honey."

Angela dropped Pat off near her car. "See you in a few days," Pat said as she drove off for San Francisco.

Angela parked the UTV by the barn and loaded the last of the supplies into the little trailer. When she turned to head back into the inn to grab lunch and Aseem's gear, she was greeted by the delightful sight of five miniature dachshunds running down the trail toward the inn, Connie jogging behind them. The dachshunds were all dressed up in little Christmas sweaters.

"Oh, Connie, the pups are so big now! Well, still tiny, but almost as big as Bijou."

Bijou, the puppies' mother, was full-grown but still quite petite. She had an exquisite face and shiny copper coloring that she passed on to two of her pups. The others got their coloring from their father. Not yet ten months old, the pups were still full of bouncy puppy spirit.

Angela bent down to say hello to the adorable quintet. The dogs stood up on their hind legs to beg for attention, which Angela was happy to dish out in the form of energetic petting. "I haven't seen you five in ages!"

"I've been trying to keep them up at my place these last couple of weeks, since I knew the inn was busy. Hopefully absence has made the heart grow fonder, though, because I need to ask a favor," Connie said in her sweet, Southern way. "I've got an unexpected trip—our biggest deal yet is hitting the rocks." Connie had started a new division of her family business—one of the oldest, most admired whiskey producers in the country— selling barrels to California wineries. It was starting to take off and kept her on her toes. "Is there any chance you can take this little gang for a few days?"

"Of course! Always—oh, I mean," Angela caught herself and paused. "Is it OK if I take them for a little ride? There's... there's just something I have to do, away from the inn." Angela didn't want to leave the dogs alone while she was up at the tree farm, but also didn't want to reveal anything about the experiment to Connie.

Connie handed the five leashes she'd been carrying to Angela. "Why not? They love an adventure, and you already know they're fine in the car. Thank you!" Connie yelled, dashing off at a jog back up the trail. "See you in a few days!"

Angela snapped the leashes on the dogs' collars, pulled the tarp cover over the contents of the trailer, and went inside the inn to grab Aseem's overnight bag, the pups' car carrier, and the special lunch she'd asked the chef to pack, stopping in the ballroom on her way out. Jackson would be queuing up the afternoon's triple feature of Christmas movies, and Angela thought the pups would be sure to charm any guests who'd arrived early for the best seats.

She was surprised to see Finn and his mom, Helen, sitting right up front. Helen looked a little embarrassed. "I hope you don't mind that we came over to watch the movies. Jackson said it would be OK, even though we're not hotel guests. Two of them are Finn's favorites, and your screen is so big—"

"Of course!" Angela said. "Enjoy them, Finn." But Finn was too overjoyed at meeting the five small dogs to hear her. He was giggling uncontrollably as the puppies fought to crawl all over him. Angela laughed and asked Helen if she'd be willing to watch the dogs for a few minutes while she went to the kitchen.

By the time Angela came back with a water bowl for the dogs and lunch for her and Aseem, the triple feature was ready to start—which was a good thing, because Finn was so sad to see the puppies go, Helen was grateful the boy's favorite movie would distract him.

Angela buckled the sheepskin-lined carrier into the UTV and drove off with the dogs to the tree plot, extra slowly and cautiously to avoid jarring her four-legged friends.

"I see you brought company," Aseem smiled wryly.

"I didn't know how long we'd need to finish up the plants, and I thought we'd have a leisurely lunch. Plus, I can let the pups run around here without worrying about cars. You don't mind, do you?"

"Not really. It's just… I was hoping to persuade you to stay the night." He opened the overnight bag and revealed he'd packed the sweats and t-shirt Angela liked to sleep in. The antique wood box, which he'd re-wrapped in tissue, threatened to expose itself. Aseem quickly tucked it back in, under his clothes.

"Presumptuous," Angela laughed. "It might be fun to have a night out here, under the stars. But I didn't bring any food for these fur babies. Maybe tomorrow night?"

"OK, and how about you bring back champagne and something special to make for dinner? If everything goes according to plan, our baby super-trees will even have sprouted by then."

CHAPTER 20

"Rebecca, call Maria," Bea commanded the internet speaker. The speaker replied in its cool, soothing voice that it was dialing Angela's mother's number.

"Hi Bea. What can I do for you?"

"I called to tell you the paint is here. They say the stuff works wonders. Is everything else a go?"

"It's already going. I've hired some help, and they've already started. I can send you some pictures if you like. I think you'll be very happy with the result. My associate will pick up the paint soon."

"Wahoo! You move fast. I can see where your daughter gets her drive. When do you think the project will be done?"

"Depends on what you mean by done," Maria said. "We haven't really talked specifics, so we've just been working on the skeleton."

"Use your best judgment, but at the end of the work, I want the place move-in ready. And it should be nice—like something young people would like."

"You're looking to attract a higher-end tenant, right? A young couple, I guess?"

"Something like that," Bea said. "Or a single person. Just make it classy. You know better than I do what that means," Bea added with a mini cackle —sort of a cacklette.

"I hope you'll consider me for the listing," Maria said. "You know I also do rentals."

"I wouldn't list with anyone else. By the way— it needs to be furnished, too. Can you take care of that?"

"Sure. Sounds like fun. Maybe Angela would look at some catalogs with me."

"Now that's a great idea."

Rebecca disconnected the call and immediately announced that another one was coming through: Jackson, calling from the front desk.

"Miss Sickles, sorry to bother you, but there's a special delivery here. They say I can't sign for it— you need to sign it yourself."

"I'll be right there."

Bea accepted the manila envelope and sent the delivery man on his way. The afternoon sun coming through the large windows was waning but had warmed up the inn's reception area. Bea pinched the envelope from top to bottom and concluded it contained a small stack of paper. The return address on the front was from a lawyer's office in downtown San Francisco. She smiled, remembering the firm name from the business card she found in the professor's loft. Bea decided to sit in one of the chairs beside the beautiful, fragrant Christmas tree, and read beside its twinkling lights.

"Jackson, do you have any iced coffee back there?" Winter, spring, summer, or fall, Bea loved iced coffee most of all.

"No, but I can go get you a hot one from the kitchen—I'll be right back."

"Make it a cocoa."

Bea pulled the document from the envelope. It was about ten pages of minimal content on thick stock. Bea had skimmed most of it by the time Jackson returned with her drink. She had a big grin on her face as he handed her the cup with the sweet, steamy beverage. She took a huge gulp, painting a half-moon of chocolaty whipped cream that started on her upper lip and curved up on her cheeks.

"Have you seen Angela, Jackson?"

Ever the consummate professional—or perhaps simply inured from innumerable opportunities to practice a neutral expression—Jackson showed no sign of noticing Bea's edible makeup.

"I think she went back up to the—the—to wherever you all go with those UTVs."

"Hehe, nice sidestep, young man," Bea said, standing up to leave. "When she comes back, ask her to drop by my suite."

"Of course. Miss Sickles, would you like a tissue?"

"Nah. All good," Bea said.

ASEEM WAVED TO ANGELA AS SHE SLOWLY CROSSED the field in the UTV, the dogs in their carrier beside her, several sacks of provisions in the rear. He carried the bags into the trailer while she unleashed the pups, who happily trotted and nosed around in the ground nearby.

"Puppy food, check. Salad, check. Fresh pasta,

check. Mushrooms, check. Cream, butter, and cheese, check," Angela said as she unpacked the bags onto the trailer's small kitchen counter. She looked neat and pretty in dark jeans and a fleecy turtleneck sweater, her chestnut hair cascading from a thick, high ponytail. "Since you said we might be celebrating, I brought these, too." She held up a small box of handmade truffles. "The chef found a new source for chocolates and they're amazing."

"I see you brought the champagne, too. Check," Aseem said. He was trying but failing to suppress a grin of excitement, like a novice card player holding a royal flush.

"The sun's setting. Should we check the pots to see if they've sprouted? After all, that's what we're supposed to be celebrating, right?"

"I checked," Aseem said quietly. "Nothing yet. I was thinking… maybe we're overeager. Maybe… maybe we misinterpreted the instructions. We know the trees are supposed to grow extra fast, but a day and a half to sprout—that's just too miraculous, right? We could have misread the documents. Bea was trying to reproduce them from a typewriter ribbon, after all. I say we give it a bit more time—"

"But the plants are what we're supposed to be

celebrating," Angela said sadly. "And now we're going to have to tell Bea."

Aseem's face fell, like that same amateur card player realizing the ace in his hand was actually a four. "We don't have to tell her tonight, do we? Maybe the plants need one more night."

"We could review the instructions," Angela said seriously. She pulled the pages she and Bea had worked on from the cabinet, her face tightening. "We could double-check our work."

Aseem took the papers from her gently and put them back in the cabinet.

"Let's not. That can wait until tomorrow, right? Angel, for right now, it's not the most important thing—"

"Those trees could... they could change the world," Angela said. "How can you not see that they're the most important thing we're working on—maybe the most important thing we'll *ever* work on—" She was on the verge of tears.

"I'm sorry, Angel," Aseem said quickly. "I know how important the trees are. I do. But we've both been working harder than ever. Just for tonight... let's have a little fun—we'll make a nice dinner and enjoy the stars. The night sky is so beautiful here, you won't believe it. And it's so quiet, so peaceful. We have plenty to celebrate, even if the trees aren't cooperating—I mean, aren't cooperating *yet*."

He stepped down from the trailer door and held it open for her. "C'mon. Please? There are some other little souls around here who want to have fun, too, and I know you love them. I also know where we can find some world-class sticks."

Angela's expression softened into a smile and she followed Aseem out of the trailer. They found the sticks and began chucking them across the field, sending the dogs on a jubilant race to retrieve them. When it got too dark to continue the game, they went inside the trailer. While Angela fed and watered the dogs and tossed the salad, Aseem astonished her by whipping up a gourmet mushroom pasta.

"How did I not know about this talent of yours?" she beamed as he filled their plates.

"I'm glad you're learning," Aseem said with a laugh. "Some people say I'm a catch. Truth be told, though, I only know two or three dishes."

They finished the pasta and cleaned up the tiny kitchenette.

"Chocolate?" Angela said.

"How about chocolate and champagne? We could sit outside and look at the stars."

"But it's so cold."

"Don't worry. The trailer vendor thought of everything. You'll love it. Just give me a few minutes to set it up."

~

"Boop-boop-boop," chimed the internet speaker in the corner of Bea's suite, the ring around the top of the device flashing green. "Andy Mathers calling."

"Thanks for calling me back. I guess congratulations are in order," Bea said.

"For what?"

"Since you're calling me back, you must not be in jail!" Bea cracked. Andy didn't respond, creating an awkward silence. "OK, OK, that might have been a little inappropriate. But I'm glad you're still free to roam the streets."

After another pause, Andy asked if there was something he could help with.

"There is. I forgot to ask you if you knew why the university fired the professor."

"I'm not sure. I don't think anyone really knew except Dr. Woodward. The official statement was that he resigned, but Dr. Woodward told me and Brandon he was forced to."

"Any idea why?"

"Brandon told me it had something to do with expenses—that his uncle was accused of misappropriating funds from the biomedical engineering department for his tree project. But I always thought Dr. Woodward was exceptionally careful about that. He didn't even work on tree stuff in his department lab."

Bea nodded, remembering the lab table at the loft. "He did need a lot of money for the experiment, though."

"Exactly—he poured all his own money into the tree thing. If he'd been stealing from the university, why'd he go broke? Right from the start, he wanted it to be perfectly clear that it was not a university project."

"Did you know the professor thought that Titus got him fired?"

"Dr. Woodward didn't tell me that. Not in so many words. But I'm not surprised. They got along fine, but I don't think Dr. Woodward fully trusted Titus—er, Dr. Melville. Dr. Melville wanted to work with Dr. Woodward on his tree experiments. Dr. Melville was chair of botany, and —well, I always thought he was afraid he'd look bad if the biggest botany innovation didn't even happen in his department."

"Was Dr. Melville's research sponsored?" Bea

asked. She already knew the answer, but wondered if Andy did, too.

"Oh, yeah. ThriveCore sponsored research in both the botany and the biomedical engineering department, and a lot of other sciences, too. Well, in biomedical engineering, they were one of many sponsors. ThriveCore had the chance to own everything in botany, and they make so many gardening products—"

"Like Formort? The tree-killing stuff?"

"Yeah, ironic, huh? A lot of their products help plants thrive, but there are probably just as many that get rid of unwanted ones. Lots of specially created seeds, too. I probably don't need to tell you that a lot of people don't like that kind of stuff."

"Like S.O.S."

"Yep, hating ThriveCore's kinda what made them famous. That reminds me—Brandon said he thought Dr. Woodward made enemies at the university because he complained about ThriveCore. Dr. Woodward told me he'd started to regret some of the animal testing they were doing in biomedical engineering. He said it helped fuel his passion for his tree idea.

"Brandon said he heard people saying Dr. Woodward might have even tipped S.O.S. off, like giving them some new things to protest about and get attention. Brandon didn't believe the gossip, though—neither of us did. We thought it was just nasty rumors."

"Why would hating ThriveCore be a problem at Granola U?" Bea said. "I would have thought everybody at Avalon would hate ThriveCore. Come to think of it, how does the world-renowned hippie training camp get involved with the Evil Empire?"

"Dr. Woodward said that it's like a little dirty laundry. Lots of people at the university would never admit it, but they'd never be caught dead dissing ThriveCore. They have to walk a line because ThriveCore might be the only source of funding for their next project. That was truer for botany than biomedical, though. ThriveCore—Bos-Curae, their veterinary division—was only one of many sponsors Dr. Woodward worked with on biomedical research. And they didn't even put in cash funding. They sponsored the work with testing supplies, like anesthetics for—"

"Cows?"

"Right. How'd you know?"

"Bos-Curae—cow medicine. I might have used the phrase 'bossy cow' once or twice in my life, usually in a way that's unfair to actual cows," Bea said with a chuckle. "One more question. You said Brandon did tech stuff for the university—is that what he's doing now? With Titus, I mean?"

"He took care of the email accounts for several departments—biomedical engineering, botany, and a couple of the smaller science areas. And he worked on the inventory system for supplies. They didn't actually have a system before he came in to set one up. You know… now that I think about it, ThriveCore might have sponsored that. I think Brandon was setting up a system ThriveCore built. I guess it made sense because they were providing so many of the supplies."

"If someone left Avalon, was it Brandon's job to delete their email account?"

"I think he would just change the password, so that the employee could no longer access it, but all the old mail would be saved. That's what he told me would happen to mine, anyway. I wanted to be sure all my old messages were available to anyone who needed them."

Andy disconnected and Bea commanded Rebecca to call Angela's suite one more time. The internet speaker was a convenient suite-to-suite intercom, provided someone was in the other room to answer. But for the fourth time in as many hours, Bea had tried to reach Angela in her room and on her cell and had gotten no answer.

"Rebecca, this is just plain weird," Bea said.

"I'm sorry, I did not understand. Could you repeat the question?"

"Hehe, OK, time to go old school."

Bea had so much news to share with Angela. She didn't want to wait until morning. She could walk the halls of the inn to look for her, but she was already in her nightie. The prospect of changing back into her daywear made her grimace. Even she knew, though, that wandering the halls in her threadbare nightie was unwise, since every available room was filled with at least one visitor, and some of them even had impressionable children.

"Best not to scare the guests," she chortled to herself. "Not when our holiday business is off to such a good start."

She decided to put her purple track suit jacket on top of her nightie and pull on some stirrup pants underneath. The bottom of her nightie hung out of the top haphazardly, but when Bea looked in the mirror, she thought it looked like the filmy handkerchief hem of a ballet dancer's skirt.

"Rebecca, play 'The Dance of the Sugar Plum Fairy.'"

Standing in front of the mirror, Bea began her impression of a prima ballerina, lifting and pointing her fluffy slipper-clad toes in time with the delicate plucking of the strings.

"Who says I'm not dainty?"

As the delicate bell sounds of the celesta began, Bea pushed herself up and down on her toes. "Technically, you might say I'm on the balls of my feet, but I say close enough!"

The music gained momentum, with more instruments contributing to the stirring, swirling melody.

"Rebecca, louder!" Bea shouted.

Then she revved herself up and spun on the ball of her foot, completing nearly three-quarters of a wobbly revolution, which she celebrated with a hearty cackle.

"Oh, yeah, I still got it!"

The music sped up, and so did Bea.

"Time for the big finish!" she announced to the mirror. She inhaled deeply and launched an imitation of the Sugar Plum Fairy's iconic spinning chain of pirouettes, whirling erratically around the room like a disabled helicopter before finally crashing into her desk chair. She bounced off the chair onto her bed, face first.

"Whoa, Nelly, that wasn't so good," Bea

croaked, pushing herself up off the bed with a groan and heading for the door. "I should have started with the little girl Clara's dance. Sure glad you don't have video recording, Rebecca!"

"What was that? I did not understand the question."

"YOU WERE RIGHT. IT'S AMAZING." ANGELA AND Aseem were sitting near the portable firepit that he'd found stowed in the back of the trailer. The log burning inside the unusual apparatus was crackling and giving off warm flames, embers occasionally floating off into the inky night sky. The twinkling stars looked like a picture from a storybook. Angela fluffed the blanket that was covering her legs and reached over for Aseem's hand. "Thank you for a lovely night."

"You're welcome," Aseem said. "But there's one more thing."

Angela looked at him and her eyes had a starry twinkle of their own.

"No, not that," Aseem said, grinning. He stood up and leaned over to kiss her on the cheek. "Wait here a minute." He tossed the fleece from his lap onto his chair and rushed into the trailer. When he came back, he had the little box his mother had given him. He sat back down next to Angela, the box on his lap.

"What's that?"

"It's what was in that package my mother brought. And I want to show you—but first, I have to tell you what my brother said about my family's behavior at dinner."

"He apologized, right? That's all I need to know."

"Yes, he apologized. He said they all apologize. You see—it's not that easy to explain, but you already know that my parents have high expectations—"

Angela giggled. "I understand—you know I do. We talked about this. We have it in common, right?"

"Yes, you're right about that. But what Sanjay said was that he and my parents, they cooked up this scheme—sort of a way to nudge me to… to grow up, I suppose."

"Some nudge," Angela laughed.

"My brother admitted it was his idea. He said he wanted to deflect the pressure from him and Preeti to me. For some reason, he thinks that I'm Ma's favorite, but that's not true. Anyway, I just wanted you to know—this was an extreme example, but my family can be a little pushy."

"It's OK, honey. I could tell that something was up at that dinner—especially when I thought about it afterward. No lasting damage to me. Besides, it's you who has to deal with them."

Aseem tilted his head and stared at her a moment. "Maybe not now… I mean, that's what I'm trying to…. Here. Open this." He handed her the box.

"What a beautiful box," she said, running her finger over the intricate carving. "Must be an antique."

"It was my great-grandmother's. My mother's grandmother's."

Angela gently lifted the lid. What was inside the box made her gasp: a long, dangling earring with intricate filigree metalwork. As she carefully picked up the delicate ornament, its age and preciousness took her breath away. Centered near the bottom was an enormous gem, blood-red in color, with a slight pinkish cast.

"It's stunning. But I don't understand—"

"My great-grandmother gave one of her earrings to my mother and the other to my auntie when they were just little girls, still living in India.

The earrings were a gift to her from her own father. But they weren't meant to be worn. They were a form of security. He believed that the gems would protect them—financially, but in other ways, too."

"Is the stone a ruby?"

"It is. Rubies have long been treasured by cultures all over the world. My great-great-grandfather knew that royal families everywhere prized rubies. In India, they were called 'lord of the gemstones.' In France they were known as 'the gem of gems.' The ruby's preciousness is even described in the Bible. He knew that even in the direst financial upheaval, the stones would have value the girls could access. Rubies are thought to have protective powers, too. They are thought to give the bearer courage."

"Is that why your mother gave it to you?" Angela said. "To give you courage?"

"In a way, I think so." Aseem put his hand over Angela's. "She told me that her life with my father had worked out so well, that they've accumulated wealth and security, and that it was time for the stone to have a new meaning. She said that I could do with it what I wished, but that one possibility might be to… to put it into a ring."

Angela's mouth dropped open and tears filled

her eyes. "Are you saying what I think you're saying?"

"I am. And is your answer what I think it is?"

"It is—if you think I'm saying yes," Angela said, tears starting to fall.

Aseem got up from his chair and got down on one knee. "I want to do this right. We don't have a ring, but I still have a knee," he laughed, taking her left hand in his and kissing it gently. "You'll have to put up with my family. You can't say you weren't warned, Angel. So will you marry—"

Before he could finish, Angela jumped up from the chair and placed the box carefully on it. Then she threw her arms around Aseem's neck and kissed him. "I told you, I'm saying yes!"

CHAPTER 21

Bea was up before the sun the next day. She hadn't been able to track Angela down the night before. Since Pat was back home in San Francisco, Perry, her poker pal from back in the day, had agreed to give her a lift to the lawyer's office. With rush-hour traffic, they had to allow a couple of hours to be sure they'd arrive before nine, especially since, like all sensible people, Bea and Perry preferred to take the *most* scenic way. They'd go over the Golden Gate Bridge, rather than take the Bay Bridge to save a few minutes.

With the inn full of guests, the kitchen was already in full swing. Bea stopped in the breakfast room and helped herself to a strong cup of coffee and an egg sandwich. She didn't even have to make a special request. Most of the guests had heard about Betty Snickerdoodle's deep fondness for that particular breakfast through Angela's social media posts, and they were looking forward to enjoying it themselves. The chef responded by creating special, "elevated" versions.

"Not half bad. It's a little fancier than my favorite," Bea chortled to an early-rising guest in the breakfast room. She bit into the croissant and pastry flakes dropped down the front of her burnt-orange velour jacket. "Proves fancy's not always a negative. Caramelized onions and brie go pretty well with eggs."

She finished the sandwich and grabbed one to go for Perry. As she headed through the reception area to the main doors, she remembered that she still hadn't heard from Angela.

"Jackson, have you seen Angie this morning?"

"Not yet. Would you like me to try her room?"

If she hadn't easily figured out Angela's little secret, she might have been worried. Mainly, she just wished she'd been able to invite her to come along to the attorney's office, but with the inn fully booked, Angela probably couldn't have gotten away anyway.

"Nah, it's OK. When you see her, tell her

Perry's taking me to an appointment in the big city. Rebecca's saved her a message about it."

As Bea stepped out the main doors, the morning air was breezy and brisk. She saw Perry's car in the distance, moving down the hill toward the inn entrance. Then out of the corner of her eye, she saw the UTV making its cautious way toward her across the field. She stepped back inside the reception area and surreptitiously watched the little vehicle buzz down to the barn. Angela parked and rushed out of it with the dogs, who trotted by her feet as she hustled toward the inn entrance.

"Look who's doing the walk of shame!" Bea shouted to Angela.

"No shame, just walking," Angela chirped. Her expression was sunny, but Bea could see Angela's cheeks were getting pinker.

"You know we have guests, don't you? You could at least wear a fresh outfit and maybe brush your hair."

Angela reached up reflexively to smooth her hair. She found nothing out of place and gave Bea a sidelong glance. "I just... I had to rush over to check on something with Aseem this morning, so I brought the dogs with me. They love running around up... you know, up by our project."

"Nice try, girlie. It would be a lot easier if you two just shared a suite. And that would be way better than leaving *two* of them vacant overnight. That's a whole lotta negative ka-ching! You're not supposed to like that, madame president."

"Gee, Bea, it's hard to imagine why anyone might go looking for a little privacy around here. Besides—it's not what you think. I've got good news. But I've also got bad news about the seeds—at least, it seems bad—"

"Don't worry about the trees, Angie," Bea said as Perry pulled up to the curb. She pulled the passenger side door open and hopped inside. "It's gonna sort itself out. Listen to the message I left you with Rebecca. I was hoping you'd come with me to town, but I know somebody's got to mind the store. I'll see you later!" she called from the window as she and Perry drove off toward San Francisco.

The first half of the drive was predictably easy, until they passed through San Rafael in Marin County, where the commuter traffic slowed them down to half the speed limit.

"We've got about twenty more miles and forty-five more minutes to fill," Perry said. "I've caught you up on the unexciting details of my life, so how 'bout telling me a little about what you expect from this high-powered lawyer meeting?"

"I wouldn't call your life unexciting," Bea chuckled. "I thought your story about the wife coming into the cardroom and dragging her hubby out by the ear was pretty good."

"Listen, my dear, you may have the best poker face on the planet, but I can tell you're holding back something good—something much better than this week's version of 'poker rat busted by spouse.' Spit it out."

"I admit getting summoned to a snooty lawyer's office at a ritzy downtown address has me a little fired up, especially since I'm a mystery writer now. I'm expecting something straight out of an Agatha Christie book."

"Could it be one of those twists where the dead person isn't really dead?"

"I hope not," Bea cackled. "I'm supposed to inherit something, and I think it's gonna be big! Besides, I've actually seen his dead body."

"Now we're getting to the truth," Perry said, grinning. "Could be one of those video wills, though, like in 'Murder, She Wrote.'"

"That's more likely. The professor was the kind of person I could picture telling off everyone he loathed in a video. There's just one problem. He hated technology."

"Bummer. No video, then. Wonder what your big prize is."

"Oh, I know what it is. See, we've been doing this big Christmas tree farming experiment with the professor. He's been super-secretive about it… I mean, he was secretive… and so we were, too. He had the idea, but we had to put up the money, without really knowing how it worked—"

"Don't you mean *you* had to put up the money?"

"True. But Angela and Aseem put in the work. It was their idea. Problem was, the professor was so paranoid someone would steal his idea, he didn't even tell us how his process worked. He promised he'd tell me in the event of his death, but he didn't tell me anything before he kicked off, and we've been worrying that whoever killed him stole his papers and got the secret. But now that I know I'm in the will—"

"You're figuring he put the secret in it."

"Egg-zactly. What else could it be? I've only known the guy since Halloween. It's not like he's leaving me any personal mementos—except maybe his Selectric. But that's hardly worth an invitation to fancy-pants lawyer land. It's gotta be the secret. Putting it in the will would be the best way to give it to me in the event of his death, right?"

Perry pulled up to the curb near the skyscraper's revolving doors. "You sure you don't want me to come with you?"

"I don't think you'll be allowed in. Grab an overpriced coffee at the Ferry Building and enjoy the view. I'll tell you all about it over lunch when I'm done. S'posed to take a couple of hours."

Perry handed her a sticky note with his cell phone number written on it. "The front desk can call for you, right? Someday, you'll get your own phone. Then we won't have to go through this rigmarole."

"Never!" Bea cackled as she got out of the car.

"Good luck, my girl."

Bea arrived at the thirty-second floor and though she was a little early, she was surprised to be the only one waiting to see Philip Caravelle, esq. His assistant escorted Bea back to his large office. The far side was floor-to-ceiling windows, with a stunning view of San Francisco Bay and the Bay Bridge. One entire wall was filled with bookshelves and law books.

"Those are just for show," he said genially.

He appeared to be about the same age the

professor had been, but more robust and carefully groomed. His large, antique desk was made of burnished mahogany. The desktop was pristine, bare except for a single folder. A slip of paper was clipped to it that read "Woodward presentation." In front of the desk, in the corner by the window, there was a small conference table with several chairs upholstered in tufted cordovan leather. He pulled three chairs out from the table and placed them in front of his desk.

"Please, have a seat." The assistant came back with a tray full of coffee, bottled water, and miniature scones. "Refreshment?"

"No thanks," Bea said. "How'd ol' Gregory afford a lawyer like you?"

The attorney let loose a belly laugh of genuine surprise. "Let's cut right to the chase, then. He didn't. Gregory, that is Dr. Woodward, was my college roommate. He came to me for help because—well, you'll understand soon enough. I did the work pro bono. He promised to help save the trees, and since the dawn of the legal profession, we lawyers have killed a lot of them. I was happy to help. And like I said, he was an old friend."

Bea plopped into one of the shiny leather chairs, her feet barely reaching the floor, and stared out the window. "You do a lot of these will readings, counselor? Nice digs for it."

"Not at all. This was Gregory's special request." He got up and walked toward the door. "I'll just go check to see if the others have arrived."

No sooner had Caravelle exited the office than Bea scurried around the back of his desk to try to get a look at the professor's file. But in mere moments, she heard the attorney chatting with someone as he returned down the hall, and hustled back to her seat, muttering "Nuts!" under her breath.

The woman he brought with him looked to be in her mid-forties. Bea thought she had the look of someone accustomed to trading on her sex appeal but now facing the imminent end of her career. The woman wore an inexpensive pantsuit. Her heavily teased, bleached hair was pulled into a voluminous ponytail with a bouffant-like bump on the top of her head.

"You must be Polly of the many last names. Is it Wiggins? Conrad?" Bea said.

"Polly Baker. And you are?" Polly said sourly.

"Bea Sickles. I'm a recent friend of Dr. Woodward's."

Polly sat down to Bea's right and Bea noticed a ring on her left hand, a tiny diamond solitaire.

"What's with the chip on your finger?" Bea said. "Souvenir of one of your old husbands, or are you gearing up for marriage number… what would it be, unlucky thirteen? Twenty?"

Polly looked down at the ring with a slight smile and gently rubbed the skin underneath it, as if Bea had just reminded her the ring was there.

"I'll take that as evidence of another sucker recently snagged," Bea cackled, slapping her knee. "Hope wedded bliss doesn't elude you again."

Polly pouted. The attorney dropped his chin and eyed Bea over his glasses with what Bea interpreted as a mix of amusement and admonition.

"Ms. Baker, you believe that your son, Brandon Kellan, will not be joining the meeting, correct?" the attorney said.

"I don't believe Brandon can get here at this time. Let's go ahead."

"Dr. Woodward's will included a statement prepared by him that he instructed me to read," the attorney began.

"It's no secret to either of you that Dr. Woodward had no significant liquidatable assets. He invested all of his net worth into his rapid-growth tree experiment, including his proprietary seed modifications and his formulas, which he gave the placeholder names 'supersprout serums SUA37-1, SUA37-2, and SUA37-3.'

"As you both also know, Dr. Woodward—Gregory—was my friend. He confided in me what I'm sure you both already know: that he believed his discovery could benefit the environment tremendously, and that it would be irresistibly alluring to parties he feared would misuse it. This is why he asked me to help him with his will, and with the statement I'll present to you today. I will now read the statement of Dr. Gregory Woodward."

ANGELA LISTENED TO THE MESSAGE ON THE internet speaker with a mix of disbelief and delight.

She pulled her cell out of her pocket and called Aseem.

"Bea's in San Francisco right now. The professor's attorney summoned her there. Bea said it's because the professor has named her in his will. She thinks it must mean—"

"He passed the secret on to her before he died!" Aseem blurted.

"My thoughts exactly! Bea's, too."

"She's assuming, I guess, that we'll get the original documents—either because our contract with him will be reinforced by the will, or the will could say there's a complete set of documents somewhere else for Bea to inherit. Either's good, right?"

"I think so. I told her that the seeds hadn't sprouted. She said we shouldn't have to worry about that now."

"I think that's right. And Angel, I checked them again after you left, and I'm afraid it seems clear we did something wrong. But now even if someone came back to steal those pots, they wouldn't get what they want. They'd just get seeds that aren't going to sprout. We can stop for now and redo the experiment once we have the complete documents. You were so smart to reserve some of the seeds."

Angela smiled. "If we take the drip vials off the new pots, it won't even look like there's anything to steal. Just some pots with dirt. We could take the syringes off the mature trees, too—they've reached a good size for Christmas trees already, so we can let them grow normally. With no drips or syringes in place, we could make sure no serum was stolen, and we—I mean, you—wouldn't have to stay up there tonight."

"There's nothing saying I can't—we can't—though, right?" Aseem said. Angela's brow crinkled for a beat and she grinned. "It's nice here, isn't it? With the fire, and the stars…."

Angela giggled. She could almost hear a wink in Aseem's voice. "I suppose I could be talked into one more night of glamping. I haven't told Bea our news. I tried, but she was in such a rush, I didn't have a chance."

"Good. One more night to enjoy our secret ourselves, before telling anyone."

"Sounds perfect. One more night of privacy. Besides, the dogs love playing up there. I could bring them up as soon as I'm done with this morning's guest entertainment, and we could get started removing the serum drips."

"Oh, if it will make the dogs happy, it's settled," Aseem laughed.

CHAPTER 22

The attorney opened the folder, cleared his throat, and began reading Gregory Woodward's statement.

I'll begin by addressing Polly Baker, my dear sister—no, not so dear, not ever. The time for that pretense has long passed. Not that we were ever inclined to concoct white lies to keep the peace, were we? Often, there was no peace to keep.

How can we share so much DNA and yet be so unalike? It could be the greatest scientific mystery I've ever encountered. Perhaps I should have studied genetics instead of engineering;

then I could have searched for a satisfying explanation. Granted, we share only one parent—and anyone can see you've inherited his allergies to hard work and monogamy. Yet do you and I have even a single trait in common? I suppose the clever mind you somehow passed on to Brandon suggests a shared gene or two. The rest is baffling.

Oh sister, as I write this, I confess that the thought of dying before completing my experiments in rapid tree growth is most disappointing—and yet, as Philip can attest, I've felt more than a flicker of amusement at the thought of your current emotions. Because if I am gone, you must be imagining I've been caught unprepared. Do you think I wouldn't have understood my life might be at risk? Perhaps unprepared is how you feel right now. I do not believe in an afterlife, but if by chance I'm wrong, know I'll be wearing a smirk of utter satisfaction and exhilaration as I observe your unease from the Great Beyond.

Bea looked at Polly and her face become tense and drawn. Her eyes were wide, and her mouth had settled into a slight frown.

"Polly," the attorney asked, "would you like some water?" Polly didn't answer, but Bea took a bottle off the table and passed it to her. Polly accepted it silently. "May I proceed?" he asked. Polly nodded.

You assumed, I'm certain, that if I met a hasty dispatch from this earth before my discovery was proven, I wouldn't have yet bothered to make a will. As my nearest relative, you assumed you'd inherit everything. I'm delighted to disappoint you. Understand that everything contained in this document gave me exquisite pleasure in my dying moments, even if—as I have no doubt was the case—you personally sent me to my grave with the depravity and sloppiness that are the hallmarks of how you live your life.

Maybe my death will appear accidental. Even if that's how it appears, know that I know you were, in all likelihood, behind it. And now Philip knows, too—and so will the authorities. And let's face it: Are you intelligent enough to create the convincing appearance of a fatal accident? We both know the answer is no.

I may have died unwillingly, but in my final moment, I will have watched you kill me with schadenfreude, knowing that you will not prevail in your despicable plan.

It could only have been <u>you</u> who told Titus about my work and urged him to try to horn in on the discovery, though you'd have been happy to cast blame on your own son if it spared your neck. (Did you think I couldn't unravel your pathetic attempt to use Brandon's interest in technology to dupe me into giving my antique typewriters to you? You set a new standard for thick-headedness.)

Brandon has had barely a chance in this world to pursue his intellectual gifts, encumbered from birth with you as his mother. My desire to help him—our only descendant, the only possible force for good left in our family tree—is the only reason I nurtured any connection to you whatsoever. How dearly this sentimentality has cost me, and now I cannot even be there to see that modest wish to fruition.

Have you already pilfered my notes and instructions? Were you afraid that I'd manage to conceal them from you? Killing me—such a hasty, irrational act—was it, as I have deduced, all because you couldn't suppress your greed and impatience to plunder my life's work?

The attorney paused. Polly's eyes were filling with tears.

"He believed I would kill him? I don't deny I wanted to inherit his big discovery. Titus thought it would be worth millions. But… but I swear I'm not a murderer."

The attorney opened his desk drawer and pulled a pressed, monogrammed handkerchief from a stack and handed it to Polly.

"May I continue?" he said. "We're almost done."

"Go ahead," Polly sniffled.

But you didn't need to steal them. I'm delighted you've got them, and only hope you've already tried to parlay them. I spent countless hours typing—countless hours, Polly—just to be sure they perfectly reflected the vision in my head. And oh, how they did!

Are you confused? Are you thinking I mean the vision of how to grow trees with never-dreamed-of alacrity? No, Polly. That is not the vision I worked so hard to document.

I was realizing the vision of how best to punish my embarrassment of a sibling and her feeble pawn of a lover!

You picked another winner in Titus, Polly. A

born bureaucrat so deficient in scientific aptitude, he naturally rose to be top administrator of his department. I admit I'm impressed that your vile lizard instincts somehow led you to an ideal character to help you, a desperate pretender who would eagerly jettison his last shred of integrity for a chance to attach himself to someone else's priceless scientific discovery.

"Ol' Greg had a way with words," Bea said. "Even I have to admit it was a pretty mean way."

As she said it, Bea let out a sigh. It was beginning to sound to her like the professor's notes were just a trap for his conniving sister—and that all the hours she'd spent transcribing were a waste.

The attorney excused himself and stepped away from the office. He returned a moment later and resumed reading.

Polly, I have informed Philip that you had unimpeded access to my loft. You knew I left a key under the mat as a convenience for Brandon. You knew that, until I began my experiment with Bea Sickles and Angela Garcia, all of my trials were conducted in my loft—and all of my supplies were stored there, too. You knew that I was unwilling to patent my discovery to avoid enabling certain parties to steal it from me. And I have no doubt you were planning to sell my discovery to those very people at ThriveCore, with the help of your cretinous paramour, Titus. He's been ThriveCore's Avalon University lackey for years.

At the moment of my passing, at least I could revel in the knowledge that I'd thwarted you, Titus, and ThriveCore in one fell swoop.

I've known you most of your life. I fully believe that your parasitic character would allow you to contemplate murder. And now Philip and the authorities know that you also had the means and the motive. Little did you know, though, that your motive was a sham. I've gotten the last laugh, Pathetic Polly.

In the end, I was less afraid of dying than of enabling you and the greedy parties you aligned with to take advantage of my life's work. I'll take my secret to the grave to prevent you from profiting from it. Though I doubt you will listen, I beg you to cease contact with Brandon while serving your prison sentence. Give him a fighting chance to make something of his talents. You can finally make a positive contribution to the world in your preferred manner: without lifting a finger.

Bea sighed and smiled with resignation. In the moment, she couldn't help but find the professor's epic smackdown a little entertaining. Facing the evaporation of her investment was frustrating, though, and she was already wondering how she'd break the news to Angela. She was kicking herself for ignoring the details of the crimes and missing out on a chance to solve another case ahead of the cops. All this family intrigue could make a good Betty mystery, too—but what if she had overlooked the most interesting details? The prospect of getting nothing out of the entire adventure with the professor irritated her most of all.

Polly kept her head down, staring at the floor, her shoulders occasionally shaking.

The phone on his desk buzzed, and the attorney answered. "Yes, send them in."

A moment later, two San Francisco police officers appeared at the door, escorted by the receptionist. Polly gasped and covered her mouth with her hand.

"If you could give us just a few more moments, please," the attorney said. "The deceased asked that Ms. Baker hear his entire statement."

The officers nodded and stood at the wall beside the door.

Speaking of Brandon, I bequeath to him my collection of antique typewriters.

Brandon, I hope you value them and study them and not just sell them for quick cash, as your spendthrift mother would like. May the machines nurture your nascent appreciation for the progress of innovation over time, a worthy and fascinating pursuit. No one can ever know or comprehend all of history, not even for a narrow subject or passion. But the journey itself is invaluable. It will prime your mind for innovations of your own. The patience and persistence required will be rewarded, I promise you.

You have natural intelligence but will have to strive harder than other talented people. Key life lessons in tenacity, respect, and commitment that a young man should learn from his parents were never available to you. Instead, your primary example of adult behavior was a flighty woman whose only career aspiration was to perfect her skill as a chiseler. You will need to reeducate yourself, and resist and remediate bad habits of your own, to avoid following in her footsteps. I beg you to try. Don't let your gifts go to waste.

Polly lifted her head and spoke through tears. "I did the best I could for Brandon."

Bea looked at her with a soft expression of pity. Then a thought popped into her head. "Polly, was it you who rented the apartment across the street?"

Polly looked at Bea with confusion. "What apartment? Across what street?"

"Across the street from the loft—"

"Please—I'd like to continue," the attorney said. "We're almost done now." Polly continued to cry as she nodded.

Lastly, to Bea Sickles: I promised you my Selectric typewriter. It is yours. It pleases me that you appreciate the enduring brilliance of that invention as much as I do. There is a spare ribbon cartridge on the shelf in the loft, and it's important that you have that as well. They're hard to come by these days. I always keep one on hand.

Bea tilted her head slightly, one eyebrow and one side of her mouth raised in a curious expression.

For safety's sake, I have also secured the original owner's manual for the machine in a safe deposit box. It was a safe place to store our contract, so you'll find it there, too. Philip will provide you with the key and instructions to access it.

"Polly Baker," one of the officers said, "also known as Margaret Mary Woodward Baker, you have the right to remain silent."

"Did you say 'Margaret'?" Bea interrupted.

The cops nodded.

"That was you, then, 'Polly'—at the inn, looking for the professor?" Bea said, eyes wide.

"Yes, but not to hurt Gregory. None of us wanted to hurt him, we were just trying to persuade him. Titus was his friend—" Polly protested.

"Let's go," the cops said. He and his partner cuffed Polly and helped her out of the chair as they finished reciting her rights.

Moments after the officers walked Polly out of the office, Brandon hurried in, mouth agape, eyes darting from Bea and the attorney to the hallway where he'd just witnessed his mother under arrest. He was dressed like a twenty-something tech worker in jeans, sneakers, and a hoodie.

"What's going on?" he asked breathlessly. "I thought we weren't starting for another fifteen minutes. Where are they taking her?"

"You're a little late for the reading, kid, but you inherited some antique typewriters," Bea said. "Your uncle told me some relatives wanted to get their hands on them. Was that you and your mother?"

"Me mostly," Brandon said, craning his neck for a last look at the cops taking his mother away. "I thought they were really cool. My mother thought they'd be easy to sell."

"Did you ever go visit the typewriters when the professor wasn't home?"

"Why would I do that?"

"Just wondering if you're like me—when I like something, I get a little obsessive," Bea said.

The attorney interrupted them. "Brandon, you'll need to remove the typewriters from the Emeryville loft as soon as possible. The landlord is preparing to lease the unit and will discard anything left behind at the end of December. Your uncle stated you knew where he kept a key to his loft."

"He did? I do?" Brandon said. "Oh, right. I remember—under the mat. He told me it was there, but I've never used it."

"Why's that?" Bea said.

"He thought I might need to let myself in to see what supplies needed ordering, stuff like that. But whenever I did that work, he was there."

The attorney gathered some papers and opened his desk drawer to retrieve a small envelope. "Ms. Sickles, here is the key to the safe deposit box. The address of the bank branch and the instructions are written on this sheet. And I've made copies of Dr. Woodward's statement and official will for each of you."

Bea and Brandon walked together to the front desk.

"I'm sorry for your loss, kid."

"I miss him already," Brandon said, voice cracking. "I never really had anyone to talk to about… you know, academic stuff. I thought I was starting to get the hang of it."

"Read what your uncle wrote—the part he wrote to you. It might help. But maybe skip what he had to say to your mother. And good luck, Brandon."

Brandon stepped through the glass doors to the hall and pushed the down button on the elevator, looking lost. Bea turned to the receptionist and asked if she could help her reach Perry's number. The receptionist pointed to a phone by one of the waiting room chairs.

"Brandon, wait—" Bea called out as the elevator doors were closing. "One question. Why did you go to work for Titus after your uncle got fired? Wasn't he your uncle's enemy?"

Brandon stepped out of the elevator. "The job always included assisting Dr. Melville," he explained. "Uncle Greg didn't think much of him, but he thought the job was a good chance for me. The pay was good, and I could even take some credits toward my degree for free. And it was mostly computer stuff, which is fun—I helped Dr. Melville with the email accounts and set up the inventory system they got from ThriveCore. Dr.

Melville was in charge of tech for a few of the departments, not just botany, but some of the smaller ones, too, like Uncle Greg's. That's how Uncle Greg knew about the job. That was before Dr. Melville tried to convince Uncle Greg to partner with him on his tree project. It got kind of... awkward after that, and especially after Uncle Greg left the university."

Bea wished Brandon well and sat down in the waiting room and dialed Perry's number on the courtesy phone. "Wasn't what I expected at all. Lots to tell. Let's get our lunch, then you can come with me on a field trip to the bank."

THE EARLY AFTERNOON SUN WAS STARTING TO descend in the winter sky as Angela and Aseem hauled bags full of the syringes and vials they'd removed from the trees into the trailer. Angela carried the vials, which clinked against each other in the bag as she walked.

"Better to store them in here, right?" Angela said. "I mean, we don't expect any visitors, but—"

"Agreed. In the unlikely event someone tries anything, we've removed the temptation," Aseem said.

Angela giggled. "If they get past the motion-sensitive floodlight and the lock on the gate, they're in for a big disappointment once they see the farm's just rows of regular old evergreens and some pots full of dirt."

They tucked the vials in the cabinet where the vendor had so efficiently stored the portable firepit, which they left outside to light up again later. The other bag they put into the trailer's small shower.

They took their last opportunity to play with the dogs in the huge open field, tossing the sticks as far as they could, running across the grass with them, much to the dachshunds' delight. Soon all dogs and both humans were sufficiently tuckered out and the sky was dusky. Aseem and Angela went into the trailer, where they both checked their messages.

"I'm just about done," Aseem said half an hour later, typing a few rapid-fire sentences on the keyboard. "The quiet up here is the best productivity boost *ev*-ah. I've just about cleaned out my queue of pesky incubator tasks."

"Budgeting? Reviewing purchases? Email?" Angela laughed. "I know all about pesky management tasks." She was responding to emails and texts on her phone, refreshing her screen repeatedly. "Is it weird that we haven't heard from Bea yet?"

"Yes and no," Aseem said. "Yes, since she's been gone all day, and she knows you're dying to know what's going on with the professor's will. And no, because… *Bea.*"

Angela laughed. "We also have to keep in mind her complete resistance to cellular technology. Should I try Perry's cell? At least to find out if there's anything to worry about?"

She tapped out a short text to Perry and turned her attention to the trailer's tiny fridge. She'd stuffed a bag of ingredients for another special dinner into it. She pulled the bag out and spread the ingredients onto the kitchen counter.

"Tonight, we'll sample something from my limited repertoire. I hope you don't mind that it's another pasta dish—also with mushrooms," Angela said. "I'm adding spinach for a slight variation."

"I'm sure it will be delicious," Aseem said, walking up behind her and kissing her cheek. "It's not like we have much opportunity to learn new dishes or practice, living at the inn. But maybe we should take a class or something. Now that we're —you know—"

"The 'e' word?" Angela laughed.

"Yes—that one," Aseem said with a smile.

Angela's phone beeped and she stole a look at the screen. "Perry texted back. 'No news yet. On an errand related to will. Bea wants to play at Lucky Pines tonight. She says see you tomorrow.'"

"Angel, does it seem strange to you that the will would require an errand?"

"Kind of. But then, I've never been named in one before."

"Good point. Me neither."

OVER A LATE LUNCH OF CHEAP BURGERS ON sourdough at Red's Java House, a beloved culinary landmark on the San Francisco Embarcadero, Bea filled Perry in on the events of the day.

"It's been an up and down day. Started out running great, then hit a bad beat, now I think I've got at least a one-outer."

"You were running good when I left you—on your way to inherit the big secret."

"Correct. Then the speed bump," Bea said. She told Perry about the professor's statement, and how it revealed that the documents he'd been working on at the time of his death were decoys designed to trip up his enemies.

"Why's that matter?"

"Two reasons. First, I put in a lot of time figuring out what was in those notes from the ribbon of his old typewriter—"

"That's my clever Bea," Perry grinned.

"Too clever by half. It was all a waste of time. I was just transcribing his decoy."

"Bummer. And reason number two?"

"He said he'd rather take the secret to his grave than let his enemies have a crack at it."

"Ouch. Sounds like that means there's no copy of the real thing. But then, what's your one-outer?"

Bea pulled the small envelope out of her pocket and set it on the glass counter-top. "He left me the key to this safe deposit box. That's what our bank trip's about. He said he left a typewriter manual and a copy of our contract in the box. Who needs a typewriter manual? I think he might have left the secret in there, and the manual was another decoy. He just didn't want the others to know the secret didn't die with him."

"Sounds like long odds. You sure it's even a one-outer?"

"It's a longshot all right. He gave me one other clue, though. The statement said that I inherited a typewriter cartridge he left in his loft. It said the reason was because the cartridges are hard to come by, but I know that's not true. Plus, I already took the cartridge out of the loft, and I know what was in it: part of the secret."

"Fascinating," Perry said. "Never a dull moment with you, Bea. Ready to head to the bank?"

CHAPTER 23

Red's was right underneath the Bay Bridge, so when they got into Perry's car they drove right onto the ramp, escaping San Francisco just in time to miss the first wave of commuter traffic. They emerged from the bridge's shadowy, industrial underbelly and drove twenty minutes more to reach the professor's bank in Emeryville.

"Not far from Lucky Pines. We could play a few hands afterwards if you like."

"We'll see what happens at the bank," Bea said. "If I'm back to runnin' good, why not? That's as righteous a way as any to celebrate."

Perry sat in the lobby while the bank manager took Bea downstairs to the stuffy, musty vault. He used the bank's key, together with Bea's, to open the box, then placed it on the narrow table in the center of the vault.

"I'll leave you in privacy. If you need to reach me, use this intercom," he said.

Bea opened the box and sifted through its few contents. The professor had told the truth: the Selectric manual was there. It looked perfectly preserved.

"Maybe that machine will be a priceless collectible someday," Bea snickered to herself.

The professor's copy of their contract was there, too, folded in thirds. There was large kraft envelope labeled "Executed Avalon University Severance Agreement," which Bea set aside. And at the end of the box, a small envelope containing a note card. The writing on the outside said, "Bea Sickles."

The card was blank, but inside it was a handwritten message from the professor on a folded sheet of yellow legal paper.

If you're reading this note, Bea, I've run out of time. I meant to replace this note with documentation of my secret, to ensure my discovery might one day be fully realized. I truly did intend to. But I suppose I might also have run out of nerve.

It may have been wrong of me, I understand now, to keep the secret so hidden. Perhaps Angela was right: By opening it to the world, I might have helped the planet much more. I realize now that I could have trusted you and Angela. After what you've learned about my only sibling and my supposed friends and colleagues and their actions, however, you can surely see why I approach the world with a jaundiced eye.

Know that all is not completely lost. It's possible that expert botanists could replicate my method without my notes. You have most of the pieces they would need. One key to the puzzle is in the box with the typewriter cartridge. Hand it off to a university worthy of trust. Allow scientists experienced with our species of evergreen to examine our successful trees and take cuttings—or let them have entire trees. Qualified scientists—do I even need to say NOT TITUS?—could learn a lot from examining them carefully. The trees that flourished may also soon produce seeds—seeds that already have the right genetic makeup, that would just need the right nourishment. The records of supply orders could help. Ask Brandon for the early records, from before you began paying for materials. I'm sure it goes without saying that you should guard any remaining serum with your life, so that you can pass it to your trusted scientists.

Pursue a patent or whatever legal protections you see fit, futile though they may be, before taking these steps.

If, as is most likely, it all fails, tell Angela not to lose heart. This project has sparked dreams in her of leaving a positive mark on the world. Remind her that this was a single experiment. Even with our encouraging initial success, it was never certain we'd make the leap to more important tree species; the odds, in fact, were always long.

Above all, tell her not to worry about the Christmas trees around your inn. Despite my disdain for their frivolous purpose, it would be difficult to find a knowledgeable person who believes Christmas trees are a significant threat to the planet. On the contrary, many environmental scientists believe they're a net positive for the Earth. Even the extremists at

S.O.S. would say so. That's one reason I suspected my despicable sister was behind that obviously fake sabotage—though I must say that even though her plan wasn't very clever, it was rather clever for her.

Are you expecting an apology for losing your investment? Ha! Of course, you will not receive one! I'm aware that you are both very rich and a professional gambler. While I've learned you're quite good at wagering, even you must expect to lose occasionally. Surprised? Just because I reject modern technology doesn't mean I haven't done any research on you, Bea Sickles! I am, after all, The Professor.

Sincerely,

Gregory Woodward

Bea let out a cackle that reverberated through the vault. "Greg, you grumpy old blow-hard. I can't help it, I'm gonna miss you." She put all the contents of the box into the large kraft envelope, closed the lid, and headed back up the stairs.

"I'm ready to hit the cardroom," she said to Perry. "Nope, I'm not running good. The professor reminded me that I'm a professional gambler, though, and a darn good one at that. Maybe I'll make a dent in recovering my investment."

"Sounds like a plan. Angela just texted me—I'll let her know."

"Good. I'm not ready yet to tell her the news. Tell her I'll see her in the morning."

A line of cars had formed at the entrance to Lucky Pines.

"We're late. The after-work crowd is already arriving," Perry said.

"Excellent. I hope they brought their paychecks!" Bea said.

"Lot's full. I'll leave the car with the valet."

Perry handed the keys over to the attendant, an energetic young Filipino man in faded black slacks, a wrinkly white shirt, and a black tie. Bea hopped out of the car, still carrying the envelope from the deposit box.

"You sure you don't want to leave that?"

Bea looked at him with a furrowed brow and shook her head. She waited to explain until they'd walked through the gauntlet of smokers huddling outside the casino doors and were inside the cardroom.

"The professor left a copy of his severance

agreement in the box. I'm curious about why he got fired. I can read it if we have to wait for a game. Plus, not that I don't trust those valets, but these are the only copies of these papers." Bea was whispering, but it was hardly necessary. The sounds of the casino—the clacking of chips together, the constant announcements over the loudspeakers, and the chatter, laughter, and griping of the players—drowned out any single voice.

A new table opened up, and when the announcer called out "Perry" and "Mabel," they walked over to take their seats. Perry leaned over to whisper in Bea's ear, "I forget, what's Mabel's angle again?"

"Huh?" Bea honked in her most grating fashion. "You talkin' to me?" Then she purposely chose a seat on the opposite side of the table from Perry. He winked at her and she pretended not to notice.

"What game is this again?" she shouted loudly, as the dealer prepped fresh decks of cards and runners exchanged chips for players' cash. "War? Fish?"

"How 'bout Old Maid?" Perry jibed, playing along.

"That's not a nice thing to say to a sweet old lady," said a new arrival to the table. He was a skinny Asian twenty-something with a baseball cap and an intelligent shine in his eyes. "I'm J.C. And the game's Texas Holdem, ma'am."

Bea scrunched her face into an exaggerated expression of confusion. "I think I remember that one. What's the buy-in? I don't have much more than a thousand dollars on me. Maybe two."

The young man and the other grinders at the table looked simultaneously at Bea like hawks hovering over a lost rabbit.

"Here we go, boys," Perry said, as the dealer distributed the cards. "This oughta be fun."

"Huh?" honked Bea.

A few hours later, Bea and Perry brought eight full trays of chips between them to the cage to cash out. They decided to have a quick dinner in the cardroom's restaurant before heading back up to the wine country.

"Sure glad you had the day off today, Perry. That was fun. Too bad I didn't have my cane, though. Mabel's more effective when I can really ham it up. Nothing more fun than watching sore losers try to restrain themselves from smacking a frail old lady."

"I forgot how much I like playing with Mabel

the Clueless Wonder. Did you make back your investment in the professor's secret?"

"Not quite," Bea chortled. "Maybe ten percent of it."

"Maybe we can hit another game next week. You haven't brought out Bonnie the Bluffer in a while."

They ordered their food and Perry got up to use the restroom. Bea leaned back against the slippery vinyl of the booth and pulled the professor's severance agreement out of the envelope. When Perry returned to the table, Bea was standing beside it.

"We've got to go to the police. I just figured out who murdered the professor. I don't know what took me so long. They've arrested the wrong person."

"You sure you want to go now? It's awfully late."

"Yeah, but I'm not planning to come back to Emeryville any time soon."

∾

"TIRED?" ANGELA SAID. "READY TO TURN IN?"

"No. Not yet," Aseem replied, smiling and reaching for her hand.

They were enjoying their last quiet night under the stars. The arms of their lawn chairs were touching, their little fire was glowing and crackling, and their legs were snug under blankets.

"Do we start telling everyone our news tomorrow?"

"Why don't we wait for Christmas Eve?" Aseem said. "It's right around the corner, and Bea, Connie, and your mom will be at the inn with us."

"If you want, we could invite your parents, and Sanjay and Preeti, too."

"That's a great idea," Aseem said, standing up. "I suppose I should double-check the camera and the light one last time, just in case. Would you mind?"

Angela hopped up and moved around in the camera's field of view while Aseem tapped his phone and confirmed the camera was capturing her image. "All good." Then Aseem went into the trailer and turned the light's motion-sensor back on. When Angela moved, the spot lit up. "Works great." Then they let the light go out and she tested it again, this time starting behind the trailer, on the path that ran from the foothill that separated the inn property from Cal's farm, and ending her test at the edge of the road. "The repositioning worked, too," she said. "Cal couldn't slip by now if he wanted to."

"Especially since he's in jail," Aseem joked.

"Good point. I suppose he could be out on bail, though."

Aseem doused the fire and Angela checked with the dogs to see if any of them needed to go outside. The two liveliest puppies, Paprika and Dames, took her up on the offer and visited the sections of grass they'd claimed as their favorite spots. "All set, puppies?" Angela said, opening the trailer door to let them rejoin their little pack. Aseem stepped into the trailer behind them.

Angela paused to look up at the sky. "Good night, stars," she said, smiling a smile of utter contentment. "Thanks for the memories." Then she followed Aseem into the trailer and they silenced their phones and got ready for bed.

~

"WHAT IS IT WITH COPS AND LISTENING?" BEA complained. She and Perry had waited nearly two hours at the Emeryville police station for Detective McMahon to show up, and, when he did, she thought he seemed more interested in making his irritation known than considering what she had to say. "I thought McMahon was sharper than McGregor. Now I'm not so sure."

"He did say you woke him from a sound sleep," Perry said. "Nobody likes that."

"I handed him the solution to a murder! He hardly paid attention, let alone expressed any appreciation."

"I think he heard you. He just wasn't convinced it was enough to go make an arrest in the middle of the night. I think he wanted to get all his ducks in a row first. It sounded like he would go tomorrow."

"I know I'm right," Bea mumbled to herself, staring out the window as they crossed the bridge above the Carquinez Strait into Vallejo. "Polly's far from innocent, but she's not the murderer."

"But he's not dangerous, is he? You said that since Polly got arrested, he probably thinks he got away with it, and he knows the secret went to the grave with the professor. McMahon doesn't need to rush, does he? Better to make a solid case before arresting him, right?"

"Hmm. Polly might disagree."

Bea fell asleep as they drove along in the dark along the single-lane causeway that ran over the marshes, her head resting on the window. But when they finally reached the stop light that signaled the entrance to the wine country, she woke with a start.

"Perry—we've got to call Aseem. I hope he's not at that trailer tonight by himself! Where has my head been? I think that crook might try to steal something after all—and he's not going to go quietly if he gets caught. He already killed the last person who interrupted his thieving."

"I don't have his number—I can try Angela." He tapped Angela's number, and it went right to voicemail. Then he tried the inn—no answer at Aseem's suite.

"Do you remember the private road on the edge of the ranch property?" Bea said. Perry nodded. "Good, because we have to go there. Can this thing go any faster?"

They sped along the dark wine country roads. Luckily, Perry knew them well, and because it was late, they were empty and free of speed traps.

"What was I thinking?" Bea whined. "Why didn't I start paying attention to the murder sooner? I'm an amateur sleuth, not a venture capitalist!"

∼

ASEEM AND ANGELA WERE SOUND ASLEEP AND THE night was utterly silent when Bijou woke Angela with a low woof. Angela lifted her head off her pillow and heard the little dog's toes tapping on the laminate floor as she trotted toward the door.

"Girl, you don't really have to go out now, do you?" Angela said with a yawn. Bijou let out another woof—this one slightly more urgent. "OK. Let me get my shoes on."

Angela swung her feet out of bed, pulled her hoodie on over her pajamas, and slipped her feet into her sneakers. Bijou started to scratch at the door, and her puppies woke up and joined her. Bijou let out a bark.

"Shh, girl!" I'm coming.

Aseem woke up and rubbed his eyes. "What's going on?"

"Nothing. I'm just going to let Bijou out."

"Wait—" Aseem whispered. "Shh—I thought I heard something outside."

Angela picked up the dog to soothe her. "But who could be out there? The light didn't come on."

"Good point." Aseem quietly slid the trailer's window open and cocked his head toward it. "I don't hear anything. Must have been my imagination. Sorry!"

When Angela put Bijou down and opened the

door for her, she bolted out—then her puppies rushed behind her. "Bijou!" Angela hissed. But the dog was on a mission. As she raced into the path of the motion sensor, the grass between the trailer and the plot was bathed in light. Aseem and Angela watched as Bijou reached the gate and stood on her hind legs scratching at it, barking all the while. Her puppies came up behind her and joined in the clamor.

"Bijou, what are you up to? I can see from here the gate is locked!" Angela said, a little crossly. "I'll go get them," she told Aseem. "I've already got my shoes on."

"No—wait. I'll come with you. Just in case," he replied, rolling out of bed and grabbing his sweatshirt and shoes.

They walked across the grass to the gate, Angela clutching her arms against the cold and imploring the dogs to calm down. As they got there, the dogs briefly quieted, but Bijou still stood on her hind legs, pawing softly at the fence. Aseem put his finger to his lips and leaned an ear against the fence, his brow furrowed. He mouthed "stay here" to Angela and walked noiselessly toward the far side of the fence, peering around when he reached the corner. The floodlight's reach was mostly blocked by the fence around the tree plot. But with the stray light and the help of the partial moon, he saw something. He snapped his head and shoulders back behind the corner, then beckoned to Angela to approach him silently. They peered around the corner together and saw a tall aluminum ladder standing beside the fence.

Angela suppressed a gasp. Aseem touched his finger to his lips again and started to walk around the corner to investigate, but Paprika and Dames caught on and raced around the corner themselves. They found the ladder and started yipping and pawing at it. Angela leaned down and hissed at them, eventually luring them back to join their canine family.

Aseem quietly crept up the ladder. He reached the top and peered into the plot, but suddenly flew backward off the ladder. He groaned as he fell, then landed on his side with a roll, not far from ladder.

Angela watched in horror as he lay there, silent and motionless, and started to run to him. But then in shadow she saw the top of a man's head emerging from the enclosure. Someone was climbing another ladder from the inside! The dogs ran to Aseem, licking his face and gently pushing on his arms with their paws, but Aseem didn't move.

Angela fought back tears and panic as she watched the man's ascent. He had a pack on his back stuffed with large branches cut from the maturing trees in the enclosure. As his head fully emerged above the fence, Angela could make out who it was: Titus! She could see now that he was straining under the weight of both the pack and something in his hands: one of the heavy pots full of soil that she and Aseem had left in the plot.

She watched in desperation as Titus looked down to make sure Aseem wasn't moving. Then she saw Titus attempt to swing a leg over, encumbered by the unwieldy pack full of long, uneven branches and the heavy pot. Titus struggled to maintain balance as he attempted to move himself and his spoils between the two ladders.

Angela thought she saw Titus shaking as he girded himself to move from the ladder inside the enclosure to the one he'd left outside it. Under the awkward weight of Titus and all he was carrying, the light ladder jiggled on the uneven ground of the tree plot. As Angela watched him try again to heave his leg across, an idea burst into her head. She sprinted the few steps back to the gate and, hands shaking, managed to open the lock. Then she raced down the left side of the enclosure and dove for the bottom of the ladder, shaking it as hard as she could.

Titus cried out and hastily hurled his weight onto the outside ladder. It began to wobble violently, and Angela saw him lose his grip on the pot and fall sideways off the ladder. She ran out of the enclosure and saw Titus was face down with Aseem on top of him, twisting Titus's arm against the pack on his back. The ceramic pot had landed a few feet from the ladder. As Titus moaned, five miniature dachshunds stood guard in a semicircle around his face, barking with a ferocity that belied their tiny size.

Angela rushed to Aseem's side. "You're OK? You're really OK?"

"I'm fine," Aseem said, smiling as he gave Titus's arm a warning tug. "He caught me off guard when he shoved me with that heavy pot. Luckily, I know how to fall. I was just playing possum so I could shake the ladder on this side. You had the same idea—great minds think alike, Angel."

"My shoulder! My shoulder!" Titus cried. "I think it's dislocated."

"Tough break!" yelled Bea. She was leaning her head out of the window of Perry's car, which was racing up the private road toward the tree farm, its headlights gradually illuminating the scene. It squealed to a halt and Bea hopped out and hustled toward Titus. "Nice bag of boughs you got there, sleazeball botanist. Should have figured out sooner you'd be back for the samples you forgot when you murdered John Nixon. I guess it's hard to stay focused when you're killing an innocent man. I bet John would have been happy to settle for a dislocated shoulder."

"It wasn't murder!" Titus wailed. "The guy was crazy. He jumped me when I tried to grab the specimens! It was self-defense."

"You defended yourself by stabbing him in the neck with a syringe? I bet a jury will love that version," Angela said. "Yank his arm again, honey!"

"He tried to stab me with it first, I swear," Titus wailed. "I only intended to grab the branches and leave my S.O.S. message and go. I didn't kill your guard lady, did I?"

"Ha! What about your 'friend' Gregory Woodward?" Bea snarled. "Did you kill him in self-defense, too?"

"Sort of," Titus said pathetically. "Maybe not technically. Stupid Gregory couldn't see reason. He stumbled onto an agricultural miracle without a clue how to realize its potential and no desire to learn. What good would his discovery have been in his hands?"

"Thanks to you, his discovery may not be any good to anyone anymore," Bea said.

"What should we do now?" Aseem said. "Call an ambulance for Titus? Or the police?"

"We still get to have a little fun," Bea said. "Who wants to wake McGregor up?"

CHAPTER 24

Bea walked into the inn's kitchen and found Angela, Maria, and Connie already working together on several dishes for their Christmas Eve gathering later that night. Angela had closed the inn the night before and given the employees Christmas Eve and Christmas Day off. Maria was delighted to lead her convivial team of draftees, however limited their skills, through the preparation of her eclectic menu. The spiked cider they were sharing probably contributed to the palpable good cheer in the room.

"Whatever you've got cooking, Maria, it smells great!" Bea said.

"A whole bunch of things, Bea. Ready to help? I brought aprons for everyone." Maria and Connie were wearing red aprons with "Merry Christmas" stitched in beautiful white script.

"I want that one," Bea said, pointing at Angela. Hers said "Treacle Town *4-EVAH!*" in white on a green background.

"Don't worry," Angela said. "We'll be selling this one in the gift shop for sure. Thanks for the great idea, Mamá."

"I'm glad you like it," Maria said, pulling a rolled apron out of a bag on the floor. "What do you think of yours, Bea?"

Bea unrolled it and with a chuckle of approval, put it on. The design had a jingle bell hat at the top, curly-toed red and green shoes at the bottom, and bright red and green lettering that said, "I'm not short, I'm an elf!" in the middle.

"Not bad," Bea snickered. With her apron donned, Bea decided she should sample all the dishes bubbling on the stove and warming in the oven. She opened the lid of one pot and a spicy fragrance filled the kitchen. "What's this?"

"It's called 'vindaloo,'" Maria said. "One of the other real estate agents in my office is from an Indian family. She gave me the recipe."

"Thanks for doing something special for Aseem's parents," Angela said. She smiled faintly, her face taking on a faraway look, as if a beloved thought had popped into her head.

"You look awfully happy to be entertaining your boyfriend's parents," Bea said. "If I recall correctly, the last time you dined with his family didn't work out so great."

"Oh, that—that was just a misunderstanding. Everything's fine now. I'm looking forward to all of you meeting them."

"You seem to be taking everything in stride lately, Angie." Bea tilted her head sideways. Her lips formed a wry grin. "I think you've got some kind of happy secret you're not telling us. You even took the bad news about the tree experiment like a minor speed bump. I might have been more upset about it than you were," she added with a cackle.

"The professor's note made me feel a lot better. He was kind to think of me. And it turns out he was right: On balance, Christmas trees probably help the environment. They grow fast and clean the air. Besides, I'm sure we'll have many more opportunities to make our mark on the world. Aseem's learning about all kinds of new companies at his incubator. Who knows what kinds of startups we'll get the chance to invest in next? Maybe some kind of environmentally friendly artificial tree business—"

"Ha! While I'm glad you're embracing the faux firs, I'm done investing, girlie. In the future, all my gambling will be done at poker tables. What's the point of wagering if you don't have an edge? I'm making my mark right here, anyway—publishing great stories and helping the Keystone Kops of California solve mysteries."

"Speaking of which, are you going to give us your big reveal speech tonight?" Angela said. "We've all been waiting anxiously for it. We still don't know how you figured out it was Titus and not Polly in the end."

"What's the point, girlie? I don't deserve a command performance this time. I didn't solve the crime until it was almost too late. My eye was off the ball. Too dazzled by the possibility of fame and riches—"

"And saving the planet?" Angela said. "Admit it. I know you liked that part, too. At least a little."

"Maybe, but only because you did."

"I'd like to know how you solved the case," Maria said.

"Yeah, c'mon, Bea," Connie said. "We weren't along for the ride for this one."

"OK, it was like this," Bea began. She explained

how it dawned on her—once she stopped focusing on racing to replicate the professor's technique—that Titus filled in a lot of the missing links.

"For example, he's a botanist. The professor told me straight up in his note that a botanist might be able to recreate the technique by studying cuttings. Now, the professor thought Titus was too lame a scientist to do that. But what the professor didn't consider—and I didn't either, at first—is that Titus doesn't think of *himself* as a bad scientist.

"Also, Titus could have easily gotten into the professor's loft and murdered him. We already know that it's easy for anyone to get into the building, and Titus could have known about Brandon's hidden key. But even if he didn't, the professor would have let him in. Remember when Pat and I stopped by the professor's before Thanksgiving?"

"When you played that poker tournament in Emeryville?" Angela said.

"Exactly—when we got you that fancy spa prize. We saw Titus visiting the professor that day. Gregory obviously didn't like Titus much, but he wasn't afraid of him. He had clearly invited him in. Polly could have gotten in, too—either with the key, or the professor might have let her in. But it's hard to imagine her killing him with that typewriter. It was heavy. Titus, on the other hand, could easily have knocked the professor out fast with cow anesthetic—"

"Wait—you know about that?" Angela giggled. "Bos-Curae, I mean?"

"Yes, Angie, I know about 'Bos' being Latin for 'cow.' Where do you think all those Bossy cows got their names?"

"You didn't let on," Angela said, grinning. "And I know how you like to call certain detestable people 'cows.' Aseem just thought it was a little ironic."

"Yes, you two seemed to be enjoying the idea of me getting knocked out by cow juice a little too much. Sorry to burst you youngsters' bubble, but I knew all along," Bea snorted. "Anyway, I learned from Brandon that Titus was in charge of all the ThriveCore inventory—including Bos-Curae drugs for the animal testing in the professor's department. That meant Titus would have had access to the anesthetics.

"And then there were the comments about Titus in the professor's will—he called Titus a lackey for ThriveCore. Titus was in charge of Avalon University's relationship with ThriveCore. Getting his name on the professor's discovery might have boosted his standing with the company. Maybe he would even have gotten a stake in the invention. Anyway, surely there was some kind of reward involved. My theory is that he rented that ThriveCore apartment, too—but that'll be up to McGregor and McMahon to figure out."

"Did you know McGregor called to thank you? He seems really grateful."

"He even sent me a gift!" Bea roared. "A gift card to my favorite fast-food restaurant. I actually got a little choked up. I think he's just glad he got to one-up McMahon."

"What about Cal? And S.O.S.?"

"Oh, Cal," Bea said. "Should have thought about that one a little harder. We knew it was unlikely McGregor got the right guy, but I was so focused on our race to riches. Suffice to say that there were a bunch of reasons Cal was unlikely to have been the murderer—starting with how he'd even know who the professor was, never mind where he lived, like Lexie proved."

"What about the tree? He admitted to killing it, and to sending the picture to S.O.S."

"Lexie thought 'Andy's' messages were persuasive. Didn't you tell me that the tree business had been in Cal's family for several generations? Cal was probably petrified he'd be responsible for the tradition going down the drain. I could see Titus crafting a message that could scare him like that. Based on what real Andy said, his university account could still have been active—Titus could have used it, or even set up a fake one."

"Then did Titus cook up the S.O.S. scheme? And just tell Cal—I mean, as 'Andy'—what to do?"

"If you'd met Polly, you'd know in a minute she didn't pull that S.O.S. stuff off. I don't think the professor understood his dim sister at all. Sure, he was right that she wasn't too sharp and definitely not industrious. But I think she was in love with Titus. Her brother thought she was using those husbands of hers for crooked shortcuts, but I think all those marriages showed she was a true romantic. Titus had given Polly the tiniest little engagement ring, but I saw how she looked at it, all the hope in the world on her face. And I think Titus exploited her nature, knowing that her wish to believe their relationship was a great romance would give him more than one way to get his hands on Greg's innovation.

"The professor even said in his note that the S.O.S. fakery wasn't a very smart deception, but awfully smart for Polly. He was pointing the finger right at Titus without realizing it. Ol' Greg would've been a terrible poker player. It's a rookie mistake, assuming that because a player is weak in one aspect of the game that they don't have other skills to beat you. Titus climbed the ladder in that university. He had to be good at reading people. He understood what makes people tick. Heck, he managed to maintain a mostly cordial relationship with the professor, even though the professor suspected Titus got him fired. Poor ol' Greg didn't respect that kind of skill, but it's probably more useful than most science—"

"Comes in handy if you want to commit murder?" Angela laughed.

"Or wheedle your colleague into surrendering their big idea," Bea cackled. "Or spin a story that gets your colleague fired for using university resources for a personal project—that's what was in the professor's severance document. These are the kinds of stealth maneuvers that make big organizations go 'round. It's no wonder there's so many brainless snakes running things. They may not be good at hardly anything else, but if you're smart at this one thing, you can slither your way to the top."

"We're not going to have that kind of corporate politics around here, even when our media empire is big and strong," Angela asserted. She looked sunny and completely sure of herself.

"Angie, now I know you've got some big secret that's making you so jolly. You look like the cat who ate the canary—"

"If I did have a secret, wouldn't it be up to me to decide when to tell you?" Angela said with a sly smile. "C'mon, you and Connie can help me finish setting the tables in the ballroom."

Angela and Connie led the way out of the kitchen, and Bea hung back a moment.

"The job's all done, right?" Bea whispered to Maria. Maria nodded and handed her a key ring with a single key on it.

"Thank you," said Bea, tucking the key into her pocket. "Angie, wait up. You got any extra ribbon around here?"

A few hours later, Aseem, Pat, and Perry had joined the ladies in the ballroom. Angela, Maria, and Connie had taken a break from cooking to doll themselves up in Angela's suite. They came back wearing pretty slacks, festive earrings (Connie's looked like miniature Christmas bulbs), and velvet and satin shoes, and each wore a tasteful holiday-themed sweater from the gift shop. They brought the pups with them, too—all five of them wearing another matching set of adorable Christmas sweaters. Bea had gone to her own room to change into her elf outfit.

Now the dogs were happily wandering around the huge room, sniffing the presents under the big tree, vigilantly watching for birds and other potential intruders at the French doors, and trotting back to the fireplace when they needed to warm up. The roaring fire, mulled cider, and appetizers Maria had set out, combined with the piney scent of the Christmas tree, filled the room with a merry aroma. Christmas music was playing softly in the background, and the twinkling lights on the tree and all of Angela's other decorative touches helped create the perfect Christmas Eve mood.

"Sanjay just texted. They'll be here any minute," Aseem said quietly to Angela. "Should we get champagne ready?"

The punch bowl full of Maria's hot cider already occupied one end of the narrow drinks table that stood by the big windows. Aseem and Angela added crystal mugs for the punch and a dozen champagne flutes to the center of the table, and placed a bucket holding three bottles soaking in ice water at the other end. Aseem popped one of the corks and started filling flutes.

"We'll take care of that," said Pat, approaching

Angela and Aseem with Connie. She leaned in to quietly say to Aseem, "Connie tells me you might have an announcement for us."

Bea was standing halfway across the room with Maria, but somehow managed to hear Pat's remark. "I knew it! Something is up with you two. You've been way too jolly, and it's not just those overnight stays in the trailer!"

Maria's eyes grew huge and her jaw dropped. She made the sign of the cross and looked at her daughter.

Angela's face immediately started to pink.

"A *trailer?*" Maria croaked after an awkward pause.

"It's not *that* kind of trailer," Aseem piped up. "It's… it's fancy. It's an *elegant* trailer!"

Angela sighed and put her face in her hands. Then the dogs excitedly ran to the ballroom doors. Aseem's family had arrived. She looked at Aseem and they smiled, both of them grateful for the interruption.

"Don't worry," she said, kissing her mother on the cheek. "Trust me." Then she walked with Aseem to greet his family.

After everyone introduced themselves and got acquainted for a few moments, Aseem tapped a spoon on a champagne glass and asked the group to give him their attention for a moment.

"I'd love it if everyone could have a glass of champagne or punch, too," he said with a smile. "We might like to have a holiday toast."

Pat and Connie helped, Connie carrying empty glasses on a tray and Pat two bottles of champagne.

"None for me, thank you," Preeti said politely.

"Would you like cider instead?" Connie said.

"I would—I mean, if it doesn't have alcohol. It's just—I'm the designated driver." Sanjay had his arm around his wife and gave her a gentle squeeze.

"Of course," Maria said, flustered. "I should have thought that some people would like non-alcoholic drinks. I'll be right back. Would you prefer plain cider or ginger ale?"

A moment later, Maria returned with the cider in a pretty tumbler.

Angela looked at Aseem. "Ready?"

"I think some of you know what's coming," Aseem said, smiling at his mother and father. "And I know some of you have believed for a long time that I can be a little indecisive. You won't be saying that today. Because even though Angela and I haven't quite been together a year—"

"Not counting the years before that when you *should* have been together—" Bea interrupted.

"Bea!" Angela said, shaking her head and looking up at the ceiling.

Aseem laughed and continued. "The thing is, we may have been together just shy of a year, but I already know how lucky I am to have Angela by my side. I think you all know how lucky I am, too. That's why I've asked her to marry me. And I'm thrilled to say that she said yes!"

"I knew it!" Bea said, raising her glass. "That's why you've been so chipper, Angie. Congratulations."

Aseem's mother said, "I'm delighted, my dear son."

"You did give me a little push, Ma," Aseem said, laughing. "But it really wasn't necessary."

"You mean the earring?" she said coyly. "And will you do as I suggested?" She smiled at Angela, then looked conspicuously at her left hand. "I notice you don't have a ring yet, Angela."

"We're going to shop for one," Aseem said. "Angel prefers to find a simple diamond."

Angela immediately spotted the look of surprise and disappointment on her future mother-in-law's face.

"Of course, you must do as Angela prefers, my son. Happy wife, happy life and all that."

"Please—let me explain," Angela said. "The earring—that stunning ruby—it will be my honor to wear it. But I can't imagine separating the stone from its setting. It's not just a work of art, and it's not just a family heirloom. Aseem told me the history of it," she added, tears welling in her eyes. "That history is something that should be preserved."

Aseem beamed at her adoringly. "Ma, we decided to make the earring into a necklace instead. That way, Angela can wear it, but it won't have to be taken apart—we'll find a jeweler who can assure us of it."

"We'll want to tell our own children the incredible story behind it someday, won't we?" Angela said.

Aseem's mother put her hand to her breastbone and inhaled audibly. She smiled at Angela. And then Aseem's parents hugged Angela and Aseem, and Maria hugged Angela and Aseem, and Maria and Aseem's parents hugged each other.

"I'm glad you mentioned children," Aseem's mother said, her tone suddenly all business. "I hope you won't keep us waiting too long." She tilted her head in Sanjay and Preeti's direction with a look of mostly-faux disappointment.

Angela's eyes widened. "We haven't—we haven't even set a wedding date yet. I think it's safe to say—knowing us—we might want to take things a bit slowly."

"Now you know why we did that little trick—that unfortunate little trick at the dinner party," Sanjay said. "I'm still sorry about it, little brother. It was just that we… well, we were hoping to share some news of our own, but it was just too soon. And stress is not good—"

"—in the early stages of pregnancy," Preeti blurted. "But we can tell you now. Yes, Ma, you've got a grandchild on the way!" She opened the little velvet jacket she was wearing to reveal the beginning of a baby bump under her satin top.

"It took a little longer than we expected," Sanjay said. "We just wanted to be cautious about saying anything. Sorry, Ma and Dad. And sorry, Aseem—and you too, Angela."

"Oh, Preeti, that is amazing!" Angela said. "I hope we didn't steal your thunder with our news."

"Not at all! I'm thrilled to have a new sister in the family."

"I guess it's as good a time as any to give you two this," Bea said, dangling the key, which tinkled softly. Angela had provided a pretty red ribbon with a tiny jingle bell attached. Of course, she'd had no idea that the decoration was for her own present.

"What is it?" Angela said. "I mean, what does it open?"

"First of all," Bea said, "I'd like you to acknowledge that my detective skills are back on point. Because I guessed what you two were up to, Angie, when I caught you sneaking back from the trailer with that guilty look on your face."

"Bea!" Angela said, wincing and glancing at her mother. She relaxed when she saw her mother's mood was far too happy to be derailed.

"Then, of course, you two were discovered at the trailer again! That incident happily concluded with the apprehension of a murderer. I suppose that improves the optics considerably."

Aseem snorted and spit out his champagne.

"However, there is still the matter of you two wasting not one, but two—two!—of my perfectly excellent, in-demand suites—suites that could easily be rented to paying guests for plenty of cheddar. I even offered you a casita, and you still refused."

"I told you, that would make us less money," Angela said. "The casitas go for more than two suites combined. Whole families can stay in them. Besides, since when do you care about money so much? I remember when you lived in your tiny cottage and smoked cigarettes all day by yourself. As I recall, you were quite happy. You didn't even spend a fraction of your money."

A faraway look flashed briefly on Bea's face. "It's your fault, girlie. You changed my life. You started teaching me about business. You made me appreciate my fans. You made me rich… and most of all, you made me like it!" Bea then let out one of her signature cackles, causing Aseem's parents to wince and their jaws to drop. His mother's free hand shot up involuntarily to cover her ear.

"But speaking of my cottage, that's what this key is for. It's high time someone got use out of it. And don't you worry—your mother helped me get it all fixed up. Her crew repainted and everything —new plaster and special paint. No one would guess a smoker ever lived there."

Angela gasped and Aseem grinned from ear to ear.

"Is that why you were asking me about decorating the cottage?" Angela said to her mother. "I can't believe you kept this a secret!"

"I didn't know, either, *querida,*" Maria said. "I

only asked you because I thought you might know what younger renters would like."

"If you like, Aseem can move in now. He'll have an easier ride to the freeway for his incubator job. And you can wait to join him after you're married —you know, if you want to keep being old-fashioned," Bea said. "At least you have somewhere to go that isn't a trailer—"

"Oh, Bea," Angela said tearily, throwing her arms around her friend.

"Ugh. *Hugging,*" groaned Bea. "I give you a house, and this is how you thank me?"

CHAPTER 25

A few hours later, when delicious treats of every variety had been devoured and all were stuffed to the gills, the group pulled comfy chairs from the reception area and the guestrooms nearest the ballroom and sat together enjoying the fire.

"Bea, you like to say you're nothing like Betty Snickerdoodle," Angela said. "But I think your alter ego's rubbing off on you."

"Better be careful," Perry said, laughing. "I'd hate to see you go all soft and lose your laser-like poker instincts."

"Not a chance—" Bea started to say, but she was interrupted when the dogs all yipped and jumped at once and ran out the open ballroom doors toward the inn's front entrance.

"I'll go see what's got their attention," Connie said, jogging after them. The dogs came trotting back a moment later, Connie and Lexie walking behind them. In her tank top, leather jacket, skinny jeans, and boots, Lexie looked tired and decidedly unaware of the holiday.

"Well, if it isn't Hot Pants," Bea said. "It's a relief to see someone who's not all sweet and kind and pleasant. Merry Christmas!"

Lexie snorted. "Merry Christmas to you, too—I think."

"What are you doing out at this hour on Christmas Eve?" Angela said.

"Had to work late. Crime beat never sleeps. Luckily, I love it. I'm driving from Sacramento to my folks' place in Humboldt and I stopped to stretch my legs. I have news, too, about the Titus Melville story."

"Spill it, girl," Bea said.

"For a change of pace, I've had fantastic access to the cops this time around. McMahon and McGregor are desperate to one-up each other and be the hero of my story. Needless to say, I'm not mad about it," Lexie said with a smirk. "Of course, you're the hero, Bea. Thanks to you, they found everything they needed at Titus's home—evidence that he impersonated Andy and Brandon's email addresses on his computer, the typewriter that killed Dr. Woodward, even a listening app for a bug."

"Do you think he set up a bug here at Bea's property? I was wondering how he figured out that the farm was even here," Pat said.

"Me, too!" Angela said. "And what about that night with you in the ballroom, Pat? I was wondering how he could have known about the seedlings."

"My guess is that he bugged the professor's place," Lexie said.

"What if Titus managed to get a bug into the supplies we took from the professor's house to start the experiment? That would mean it's still here!"

Lexie laughed. "I don't think you have anything to worry about, Angela. The battery would have died weeks ago. Anyway, this story's so good, my editor's got me working on a series. Three parts, maybe four—the S.O.S. deception alone is fascinating stuff. Would you believe that the Michelle Healey you met was probably a fake —another ruse orchestrated by Titus?"

"I believe it," Bea said, winking at Angela. "That's what the professor thought."

"Wow!" Pat said. "Angela, remember how pleased we were to maneuver her and Titus and Brandon to avoid them seeing each other? I gotta tell you, it seemed a little too easy when I thought about it later."

Lexie said, "The S.O.S. bit's just the beginning. It's evolving into a huge story, and I thought you might want to be interviewed, Angela. Maybe on the day after Christmas, we can talk? You could air the Betty Snickerdoodle, Inc., side of the story—"

"Yes!" Angela said, nodding enthusiastically.

"The other thing is—Bea, you'll love this—I've been pulling threads related to ThriveCore and Avalon. The extent of ThriveCore's involvement with the university looks like it was a powder keg waiting to blow up. We've got ethical intrigue, sidestepped government regulations—all kinds of juicy white-collar stuff. I wouldn't even be surprised if another murder or two surfaces. What would you think about another true-crime book collaboration?"

"I love it. It'll help me earn back my investment in the tree farm," Bea said. "Sounds like we've got our New Year's resolution figured out. On an unrelated note, Lexie, does the *Bee* do engagement announcements?"

Angela looked down to avoid Lexie's gaze, which traveled from her to Aseem. "Not that I know of. We can put an announcement in the obituaries, though. 'The freedom of two otherwise healthy young people died today, the unfortunate result of self-inflicted wounds.'"

"Ha!" honked Bea. "Don't ever change, Saucepot. You're like a breath of fresh, snarky air."

"Right back at you. I'd better get going. Still five hours of driving ahead of me."

"Uh-oh. Hope you don't cross paths with Santa Claus," Bea said, standing up to say goodbye. "Never mind. You're obviously on the naughty list."

Maria pressed a little foil-wrapped package into Lexie's hand. "Empanadas and Christmas cookies, in case you get hungry on your drive. Nothing will be open tonight."

Lexie said her goodbyes and turned to leave, but one of the dogs let out another woof and the puppies charged off to the inn entrance again to investigate. Bijou picked her head up like she was thinking of joining them, but decided it was nicer to relax by the fire and let her little ones handle the latest urgent non-emergency.

A few seconds later, the dachshunds scampered back into the ballroom with a pint-sized companion running behind them, giggling ecstatically. He was wearing the elf hat Bea had given him at Thanksgiving and a tiny pair of shaded glasses.

"Finn! What are you doing here?" Angela said. But the boy ignored her and raced toward Bea. He yelled "elf!" and grabbed onto her leg and hugged it with all his might. His mother arrived at the door to the ballroom a moment later.

"I hope it's OK that we stopped by," Helen said. "Finn was all excited about the presents—those puzzles for color-blind kids, and especially the glasses." She started to get choked up as she spoke. "I'm sorry, I mean, I'm so grateful—those glasses work wonders with his type of color-blindness. But they're so expensive, and they're not covered by insurance—"

"I'm happy for ya, kid," Bea said, patting Finn awkwardly on the head. "But you don't have to squeeze my leg so hard. You training to be a treehugger? Besides, I don't know anything about any present."

"The box said it was from Betty Snickerdoodle," Helen said. "I just assumed—"

"Must have been Angela!" Bea blurted. "That's the kind of thing she'd do."

"The gift certificate for more glasses as Finn grows—I just don't even know how to thank you, Angela."

"It was *not* me," Angela laughed. "Nice try, Bea."

Bea looked down at Finn again, who was still clinging to her leg like a barnacle. "Tank you," he said, looking up at her.

"OK, kiddo, I admit it was me. But it was supposed to be our secret! Like I told you before, I've got a reputation to protect."

"C'mon, Finnie," Helen said. "Time to go home and go to bed. Otherwise, Santa can't come!"

The mention of Santa worked like a magical incantation. Finn released Bea's leg and ran to his mother's side.

"Before you go, how about some cookies for Santa? And if your mom says it's OK, you can have one now," Maria said.

Lexie, Helen, and Finn departed, and Angela turned to Bea and said, "I think we learned today that you are actually not the opposite of Betty Snickerdoodle, as you like to say. There's a heart of gold in there, Bea. And it's not the first time we've observed it, either."

Bea scowled at Angela then stuck her finger in

her mouth and made exaggerated gagging noises. "That tears it. Perry, get me to a cardroom and let's play some poker. I've gotta get the scent of all this niceness off me. If I don't act fast, I may go soft forever."

"You can't play poker tonight!" Angela cried. "It's Christmas Eve!"

"Sure is. Always some of the best action. That's when all the cranks who want to avoid good cheer head out to gamble. Most of them will have hit the eggnog and be in good shape to make bad decisions."

"Poker?" said Aseem's dad. "I've always wanted to learn to play—I mean, I know the rules, but I always seem to lose at the doctors' home game."

"I'd love to learn from a pro, too, Bea," Sanjay said.

"Me, too!" chimed in Preeti.

"I've got cards and chips in the trunk of my car. We could set up Bea's Poker School. Those two are surgeons, right?" Perry said, winking at Bea.

"Good point. How much cash you got on ya, docs? Never mind, your credit's good here."

"How much do you charge for poker school, Bea?" Sanjay said.

"Glad you asked, Sanjay," Bea said. "There's no

tuition, but you have to buy in with real money, because there are—"

"NO FREE LESSONS IN POKER!" Angela, Perry, Pat, Connie, and Aseem all said at once.

"That's right," Bea cackled. "No free lessons in poker—"

"Or investing," piped up Aseem.

"Or in life!" Bea said.

THE END

The Return of Betty Snickerdoodle (A Betty Snickerdoodle Mystery #1)

A Sleuth Is Born (A Betty Snickerdoodle Mystery #2)

Bake It Like Betty (A Betty Snickerdoodle Mystery #3)

Mixed to Death (A Betty Snickerdoodle Mystery #4)

Betty's Big Game (a Betty Snickerdoodle short)

Of Mice and Murder (A Betty Snickerdoodle Mystery #6)

READY FOR MORE BETTY?

Thank you for reading
Murder Takes a Bough

Be the first to know about upcoming releases in
the *Betty Snickerdoodle* series.
Sign up for Pepper's newsletter at
pepperfrostauthor.com/newsletter

Books 1- 6 are now available.

Sign up for the newsletter or follow Pepper on
Facebook to be among the first to know when
Book 6 is available in 2021.

Pepper's on Facebook!
Follow her at **www.facebook.com/
pepperfrostauthor**

To contact the author, email
pepper@pepperfrostauthor.com